the queen of attolia

the queen of attolia

by
megan whalen turner

greenwillow books
An Imprint of HarperCollins *Publishers*

The Queen of Attolia
Copyright © 2000 by Megan Whalen Turner
Printed in the United States of America. For information address
HarperCollins Children's Books, a division of HarperCollins Publishers,
1350 Avenue of the Americas, New York, NY 10019.
www.harperchildrens.com
The text of this book is set in Electra.

Library of Congress Cataloging-in-Publication Data
Turner, Megan Whalen.
       The Queen of Attolia / by Megan Whalen Turner.
          p.   cm.
       "Greenwillow Books."
       Summary: Forsaken by the gods and left to his own devices,
Eugenides, Royal Thief of Eddis, summons all his wit and wiles
in an attempt to conquer the rival Queen of Attolia.
ISBN 0-688-17423-X
[1. Fantasy.   2. Adventure and adventurers—Fiction.]
I. Title.   PZ7.T85565Qu   2000
[Fic]—dc21   99-26916   CIP
10 9 8 7 6 5 4 3 2 1
First Edition

For Susan Hirschman

the queen of attolia

*H*E WAS ASLEEP, but woke at the sound of the key turning in the lock. The storage room held winter linens, and no one should have been interested in it in the middle of summer, and certainly not in the middle of the night. By the time the door was open, he had slipped through a square hole in the stones of the wall and soundlessly closed the metal door that covered it. He was in the narrow tunnel that connected a stoking room to the hypocaust of a minor audience chamber down the corridor. The door he'd crawled through was intended to allow smoke into the storage room to fumigate the linens. Moving quietly, he inched down the tunnel to the open space of the hypocaust. Squat pillars held the stone floor above him. There wasn't room to sit up, so he lay on his back and listened to the thumping noises, like drumbeats, as people hurried across the floor of the audience chamber over his head. They could only be looking for him, but he wasn't particularly worried. He'd hidden before in the spaces under the floors of the palace. His ancestors had used the tunnels of the hypocausts to hide in since the invaders had built them to heat their new buildings hundreds of years earlier.

Noises traveled down the long, narrow tunnel from the stoking room: shuffling thumps and a crackle that he strained his ears to hear. A fire was being lit in the furnace chamber. Soon the warm air and, of more concern to him, the smoke would be fanned into the hypocaust to warm the audience room above and drive the quarry out. Silently, in the pitch-dark, he moved between the brick pillars to a wall and then along it to a flue in the wall with an opening slightly larger than the others. Even with the enlarged opening, it was not an easy task to fit himself into the narrow vent, and while he maneuvered, the warm, smoky air blew around him. He remembered how easily he had slipped into the flue the first time he'd tried it. His grandfather, who'd brought him to the palace, had grown too old and too big for most of the passages and had had to stay at an inn in the town while his grandson explored on his own, finding everything just as he'd heard it described.

Once inside the flue, he wedged his fingers into cracks and braced himself with his feet to climb until the space turned at an angle to join the chimney above the audience room. When he reached the chimney, he cursed silently, though what he found was no more than he should have expected. There was a fire in the hearth below. Fortunately they hadn't already had a roaring blaze going when they chased him out of the linen room. They must have just lighted the fire, but the air in the chimney was smoky and quickly growing hot. With no other choice, the thief climbed into the chimney and moved up it as quickly as he could, relying on the sound of the fire to cover the sounds his soft boots made on the ridged bricks of the walls. The chimney was much wider than the flue, and the ridged bricks were intended to be climbed easily by sweepers.

He went on until he reached an intersection where several chimneys came together into a much larger one that rose to the roof of the palace. The chimney was warm and filled with smoke, but instead of climbing it, he turned to another opening and climbed down. He guessed that the queen had soldiers posted on the roof of the palace to watch the openings of the chimneys.

He breathed shallowly and slowly, stifling a need to cough. Any sound might betray him. As he dropped lower in the chimney he'd chosen, the smoke grew thicker, his eyes watered, and he missed a handhold and slid down with a thump to a ledge below. He sucked in a lungful of smoke and then covered his mouth with both hands while his face turned red and the blood pounded in his ears. The breath trickled out between his fingers and he breathed in again more cautiously, but his throat burned and his head swam. His breath came and went in huffs of suppressed coughs.

He was on a ledge where the chimney divided into smaller flues that led down to several different rooms. He closed his eyes and listened for sounds, but there was no shouting, only the muted crackling of the fire somewhere below. He poked his head into one chimney after another, debating with himself before choosing one he hoped led to the stateroom of some foreign ambassador too prestigious to be disturbed in the middle of the night by soldiers wanting to light an unnecessary fire in his hearth.

The chimney he chose descended from the main one in a long, shallow slope. Once he was away from the main chimney, the air was free of smoke and he stopped to draw grateful breaths until his head cleared. When he reached the turn where the chimney dropped straight to the hearth below, he paused and settled himself to wait. There was no sign of a fire laid underneath him, so there was no immediate need to get down, and he thought it best to be sure there was no one waiting for him in the room below. After a long silence he heard the creak of a bed as if its occupant had shifted in his sleep.

Still cautious, the thief lowered himself down the chimney until he was just at the upper edge of the fireplace. Then he braced himself across the bricks and lowered his head to glance into the bedroom. It seemed to be empty of guardsmen, and he dropped soundlessly to the hearthstones. The figure he could see stretched out on the bed didn't move, and the room was otherwise unoccupied. He squatted there in the empty fireplace while he reviewed what he knew of the sleeping arrangements in the palace. He didn't think there were very many rooms nearby where the soldiers hadn't already lit fires. They probably hadn't disturbed the occupant of this room because they were waiting out in the hall for their quarry to open the door and walk into their arms.

He didn't intend to go through the door to the hall. The bedchamber was on an outside wall of the palace. The wall dropped straight down to a road that separated the palace from the city around it. He stepped past the bed and went to the window and pulled aside the curtains to look down at the perimeter road. He opened the window and glanced up to be sure that no guards on the roof were looking down. He saw no one leaning over the parapet and so swung himself across the windowsill and began to descend. The gaps between the marble facing stones of the palace were narrow, but wide enough for fingers and toes. He was halfway to the ground when there was a shout above him. He had been seen. The thief crabbed sideways along the wall, expecting a crossbow quarrel to bury itself in his shoulder at any moment, but none came. The queen's personal guard would have guns, he remembered, but no bullets came either. Maybe they didn't use the guns in the middle of the night, the thief thought. Maybe they didn't want to wake the queen. That didn't explain the absence of quarrels, but he had little attention to spare on the puzzle. He'd reached a window, and he swung inside.

He was in an office. Most of the floor where the queen's taxmen worked would be offices and storage rooms, many of them connected to one another. He'd eluded the guards on the floor above, and if he hurried, he could be gone before they'd reorganized the search. There was little point in trying to hide now that they'd come so close to catching him. He had to get out of the palace and safely into the town.

In the light of the lamps burning in the corridor, he got a good look at himself and winced. Though he was dressed in the household uniform of one of Attolia's servants, he was filthy, covered in soot and cobwebs, and much too dirty to pass as an innocent inmate of the palace awakened by all the noise. Not that there was any noise. It was a very quiet hunt moving through the corridors of the queen's palace in Attolia, with her guardsmen creeping quietly, hoping to surprise him, and him creeping even more quietly, hoping to evade them. It was an increasingly frantic game as he found soldiers at every turn. They were in every space he needed to move through until at last they were chasing him at a run, their boots crashing on the bare floors as he forced the lock on a door that led out onto a wall that enclosed one of the palace courtyards.

They were still behind him when he sprinted the length of the parapet, but they had slowed to a walk. There was a sheer drop of fatal length into the courtyard on one side and down to the perimeter road on the other. Another group of the queen's guardsmen was ahead of the thief, around the corner of the wall. Both groups were confident they would catch the thief between them. The thief could imagine too well what might happen to him if he were captured, and when he reached the corner, he didn't slow as the guards expected, and he didn't turn. He stepped onto the edge of the parapet and threw himself off it, into the black night air beyond.

Too late, the guardsmen raced to the edge of the parapet. They lay on their bellies on the wide stones to look down the sheer walls to the pavement of the road. Remembering their specific orders to capture the thief alive, they looked for the broken body in the interlocking shadows cast by the lanterns hung on the palace walls. The shadows made it difficult to see, and it took time to realize that there was no body below.

Finally one guardsman pointed to the rooftops on the far side of the boulevard that surrounded the palace. Stumbling, the thief had gotten to his feet and was crossing a rooftop as quickly as he was able. He dropped to a lower rooftop and was out of sight until they caught a glimpse of him as he dropped from that roof into the alley beyond. Someone in the group of guards swore, partly in frustration, partly in admiration.

"Did you see where he went?" a cold voice asked behind them, and the soldiers pulled themselves to attention as their lieutenant answered, "Into an alley, Your Majesty."

"Fire your crossbows into it. The guards on the ground should hear where the quarrels fall."

The queen turned and strode down the wall to a doorway leading back inside. She'd wanted to capture the thief in the palace. Four times in the last year she knew he had moved through one of her strongholds, once leaving a room only moments before she entered and once, she suspected, passing through her own bedchamber while she slept. He'd escaped only by a narrow margin on his last visit, and she knew he wouldn't escape again. Still, it galled her that he hadn't been captured within the walls of the palace.

In the alley the thief heard the quarrels clattering down behind him and heard a corresponding shout not far away. He gave up moving quietly and ran as fast as he could through the twisting streets. The drop from the palace wall had been a sickening one, and though he'd rolled, he'd been shaken by the force of the landing. His hands stung, and his shoulders ached. Before the hollow feeling in his chest faded, it was replaced by a stitch in his side as he ran on, sweating in the warm night.

There were so many turns and intersections to the narrow

streets that no pursuers could have kept him in sight, or heard his footsteps over the noise they themselves were making, but there seemed to be more soldiers at every corner, and no sooner had the thief dropped out of sight than he was found again. He was breathing heavily when he came to a straight street at last. He turned onto it and sprinted. He could hear dogs barking and thought they were not the city dogs that had been barking since the shouting started but the palace dogs brought out to hunt for him.

The road he ran on came to an abrupt dead end at the town wall. Like the palace, the town's walls were new, built shortly before the end of the invader's occupation. They were sheer, rising straight to the walks above, unlike the banked walls of older cities. He had no hope of scrambling up them, but at their base, where the narrow road canted into a ditch that drained heavy winter rains, there was a sewer that ran under the city walls. Halfway through the wall there should have been an iron grate, as there was in the other drainage sewers, but the grate in this one was broken loose. It had been repaired once, several years before, and the thief had spent three long nights filing through the new bars to reopen this private entrance to the city.

The drain was not large. Coming into the city, the evening before, the thief had moved slowly on his hands and the tips of his toes, taking great care not to get his clothes dirty. He'd washed his mucky hands at a public fountain, wiped the tops of his boots, and gone to buy his dinner.

With the palace dogs somewhere behind him, he raced at the walls without slowing and threw himself facedown at the entrance to the tunnel, sliding the first few feet into the sewer on the mud and slime inside. Behind him he could hear people running and dogs barking. When he reached the iron grate lying in the mud halfway along the tunnel, he crawled over it, then turned back to lift it upright. When he heard it scraping the walls, he yanked it harder, hoping that if the dogs pressed against it, their weight would force the grate further into place, not over into the mud again.

After crawling the rest of the way through the sewer, he dragged himself out from under the city wall at the edge of an olive orchard. Dawn was hours away, and with no moon to light the sky, he could barely make out his hand in front of his face, but he didn't need to see to know where he was. There were olive trees in front of him, planted in orderly rows. If he headed downhill between the rows, he'd reach the river at the bottom of the olive grove. Once in the river, he could pull himself out of the water into one of the trees along its bank. He'd lose the dogs and then could get farther from the city before the dawn revealed him.

The nearest gate through the wall was well away to his right. Pinpricks of light issuing from it were the lanterns of more pursuers. Trusting in his knowledge of the olive grove and the orderliness of the trees, the thief got to his feet and ran. The trees were shifting shadows against the black night as he headed downhill, moving faster and faster, placing his feet carefully in case he landed on a root. Thinking of the river, he had no warning when a shadow appeared directly in front of him and he ran face first into a wall. As he fell heavily to the ground, he was dimly aware that his feet hadn't hit anything, only his head.

The pain was overwhelming, and he lay on his back while he struggled to see past the lights flashing behind his eyes. He clutched at the sparse grass of the orchard, then rolled onto his stomach and pushed himself to his knees, trying not to be sick. He crawled to a nearby olive tree, following its roots through the hard dirt, and holding it, he got to his feet. The night, which had been dark before, had become impenetrably black. With one arm still around the tree, he waved a hand hesitantly through the darkness until he felt it strike something solid. It was a board, he realized slowly, stretching between the trees. He pushed on it. It was nailed in place. It was just at the height of his head, and a stone wall couldn't have been more effective.

He was wondering why it was there when he heard someone uphill shout. He managed only a few uneven steps away from the tree, not even certain of his direction, before the first of the dogs reached him. It jumped onto his back, and another dog hit him behind the knees. He was driven back down into the grass, feeling the dry, hard dirt underneath it. He curled into a ball and hoped the dogs' handlers arrived before the animals chewed him to pieces.

The queen of Attolia waited by the city wall, listening to the triumphant shouts of her men and the barking of the dogs. She was on horseback, and when they brought the thief to her, two guards half carrying him, he had to tilt his head back to look at her. The skin between his eyebrows was split, and a few drops of blood leaked from the tear. The blood from his nose flowed over his lips and down his chin to drop in heavy splashes that mixed with the mud on his house tunic.

"So good to see you again, Eugenides," said the queen.

"A pleasure to see you—always, Your Majesty," he said, but he turned his head slowly away and closed his eyes as if the light from the torches around her was too strong.

"Teleus," said Attolia to the captain of her personal guard, "see that our guest is locked up very carefully." She turned her horse and rode back to her gate and through the city to her palace. In her private chambers her attendants waited to undress her and comb out her long hair. When they were done, she dismissed them and sat for a moment before the hearth. It was summertime, and the fireplace was empty. Behind her, she heard a woman's voice.

"You have caught him."

"Oh, yes," said the queen without turning her head. "I have caught him."

"Be cautious," said the other. "Do not offend the gods."

Left by the guardsmen in a cell at the end of a hallway at the bottom of a narrow stair below the palace, surrounded by stone walls, the Thief dropped as gently as he could to all fours and immediately lifted a hand in disgust. The floor was wet. He turned his head to look across the cell. The dim light coming through a barred window in the door behind him reflected off the stone floor with little variation in its pattern. The floor was wet all over.

Turning his head had been a mistake. He crawled to a corner and retched until what was left of his dinner was gone. Then he crawled to the opposite corner of the cell and lay down on the damp stones. He prayed to the God of Thieves. There was no answer, and he slept.

chapter 2

*D*AYS PASSED BEFORE news of the arrest reached the valleys high in the Hephestial Mountains. A man from a wineshop raced the other talebearers and reached the palace of the queen of Eddis just as her court had gathered in the ceremonial hall for dinner. The queen stood talking with several of her ministers. Behind her was the elaborate ceremonial throne. In front of her the dishes were gold, and by her plate was the gold, figured cup the kings and queens of Eddis had drunk from for centuries.

As the queen took her place at the table and the members of the royal family, followed by the barons in residence at the palace and various ambassadors, did the same, one of Eddis's guardsmen crossed the hall to stand behind her chair. The court watched while he bent to speak to her quietly. The queen listened without moving, except to glance down the long table at her uncle, who was also her minister of war. The queen spoke to the guardsman and dismissed him, then turned back to the table.

"If my ministers will join me, I'm sure we will return shortly. Do please enjoy your dinner," she announced calmly. Then she stood and crossed the room with a decisive step that didn't match her finery. She moved toward a narrow doorway that led to a smaller throne room, the original megaron of her ancestors' stronghold. Her ministers collected around her, following as she led down the three shallow steps through the doorway and across the painted floor to the dais. The original throne room of Eddis was smaller, the original throne simpler than the ceremonial throne in the dining hall. Carved from stone and softened by embroidered cushions, the old throne was quite plain. Being a plain person, Eddis preferred it to the gilded glory of the new throne. She ruled her country from the smaller throne room, and saved the glories of the Greater Hall for banquets.

Pulling impatiently at her long skirts, she seated herself. "Eugenides has been arrested in Attolia," she said to her ministers. "A tradesman has come with the news from the capital city. I asked the guard to bring him here." She didn't look at her minister of war as she spoke. Her counselors exchanged worried glances but waited patiently without speaking.

Eddis's guard, as they escorted the Attolian in, watched him carefully in case he was less harmless than he appeared, but he only stood before the throne, nervously twisting the collar of his shirt. It was bad news that he'd brought, and he knew it. Having come so far to deliver it, hoping to be well paid, he was afraid of his reception.

"What do you know about the arrest of my Thief?" the queen asked, and the tradesman cleared his throat a few times before he spoke.

"They found him in the palace and drove him out through the town. He was outside the city walls before they caught him."

"They arrested him outside the city? Was he injured?"

"They used dogs, Your Majesty."

"I see," said the queen, and the tradesman shuffled his feet nervously. "And how do you know it was my Thief?"

"The members of the guard said so in the wineshop. We all saw him arrested, at least I and my wife did, but it was the middle of the night, and we didn't know who it might be, but the guards were talking the next day in the shop. They said it was the Thief of Eddis that the queen had caught and that . . ." The tradesman tapered off into embarrassed throat-clearing noises.

"Go on," said the queen, quietly, struggling to appear non-threatening when she wanted to shake him until his teeth rattled.

"They said she's going to make him pay for taunting her, leaving things in the palace so she knows he's been there."

The queen's eyes closed and opened slowly. It was Eugenides she wanted to shake until his teeth rattled.

She said, "You've come a long way in a short time."

"Yes, Your Majesty."

"Hoping no doubt to be paid for it."

The tradesman was silent. He'd ridden his horse to exhaustion and climbed a narrow mountain trail on foot, hurrying every step in order to be the first one to reach Eddis with the news.

"Give him a double weight in silver," the queen directed the lieutenant of her guard. "And feed him before he goes home. Give a silver griffin to anyone else who brings the news today," she added, "and I want to speak to anyone who brings fresh news."

When the tradesman was gone, she sat staring into space and frowning. Her ministers waited while she thought.

"I was wrong to send him," she said at last. The admission was as much concession as she could make to the horror she felt at her mistake. Eugenides had hinted that the risks would be greater if he returned to Attolia so soon after his last visit. She hadn't listened. She needed the information only he could get, and the Thief had so easily outwitted his opponents in the past, Eddis had assumed he would do so again. She had sent him, and he hadn't hesitated to go. She turned to her minister of war. It was his son who would die for her error in judgment.

"I am sorry," she said. "She won't take a ransom."

With a small shake of his head, Eugenides's father concurred.

Eddis continued. "He's too valuable to us and could be much too dangerous to her if she let him go. She won't be inclined to do anything in a hurry, and if he's been taunting her, and she's lost face in front of her court . . . whatever she eventually decides to do is going to be unpleasant. We will have to see," she said. "We will have to see what we can do."

Eugenides lay in his cell. When the pain in his head woke him, he opened his eyes briefly, then slept again. He should have tried to stay awake, but he hardly cared. Sometimes, in his deepest sleep, he thought he heard someone calling his name, and he struggled back to consciousness to find himself alone in the dark. He woke when food and water were pushed through a slot in the bottom of the door and sometimes crawled across the floor to drink the stale water. Other times the effort required was too great, and he left it.

Slowly the stones in the floor stopped heaving under him, and the blinding pain abated, leaving him with a headache marginally less fierce. More food and water were delivered from time to time. Finally the door of his cell was unlocked and opened. He felt sick again as he was hoisted to his feet but didn't know if it was from his headache or from fear. He leaned on the guards and tried to collect his ragged thoughts as they led him up from the cells to the queen's palace.

Surrounded by the splendor of her court, the queen of Attolia had listened to the veiled insults of the party of Eddisians sent from the mountain country to negotiate the Thief's release. Eddis had sent her best, and they had argued skillfully. Attolia had listened, appearing impassive and growing angrier and angrier. She'd sent no official notification to Eddis that Attolia held her Thief. She had only waited, deliberating on his fate, expecting Eddis to make some effort to retrieve him, not expecting the mission that arrived on her doorstep to toss threats in her face the way a man might bait a dog.

She had ascended her throne after the assassination of her father, and her country had never been fully at peace in her reign. Her army was well paid and therefore loyal, but her treasury was nearly empty. She awaited a good harvest to fill it again, and the ambassador from Eddis threatened that harvest. First, of course, he'd offered a ransom that he'd known she wouldn't accept. Then he'd politely insulted her several times over, and finally he'd told her that the gates of the Hamiathes Reservoir were closed and would remain so until the Thief of Eddis was returned home. The waters of the Hamiathes Reservoir flowed into the Aracthus River and from there into the irrigation channels that watered some of the most fertile land in her country. Without the water the crops would wither in the summer heat.

She'd sent for the Thief. Eugenides, when he was brought before her, blinked owlishly, like a nocturnal animal dragged out of its den into the daylight. The black-and-yellow-and-green bruise across his forehead showed through his hair. The split in the skin just above his eyebrows had scabbed over, but the dried blood was still on his face, and the black marks under his eyes were darker than the bruise above. The mud on his torn clothes was still damp.

"Your queen's ambassador has offered to ransom you, Thief, but I declined."

Eugenides was hardly surprised.

"You would only come sneaking back through my palaces, leaving notes beside my breakfast dishes. I told your queen's ambassador I wouldn't take a ransom of any size for you, and do you know what he said?"

Eugenides couldn't guess.

"He told me the water of the Aracthus won't flow until your queen has you back again. She's closed the gate from the reservoir in the mountains, and all my crops above the Seperchia will burn in the fields until you are sent home. What do you think of that?"

Eugenides thought it was a very good plan, but that it wasn't going to work.

The queen had lost face to Eugenides, and her court knew it. Moreover, she could hardly settle for a ransom she'd already refused. She had to consider that Eugenides, though he'd caused her no harm beyond stealing something she hadn't known she possessed, could become the measurable danger to her that he was to Sounis. Attolia ran her index finger lightly back and forth across her lower lip while she thought.

Attolia had seen the text of a message Eddis sent to Sounis the year before suggesting that no lock on window or door in his palace would save him if she had to send her Thief to call on him again. All Sounis's machinations to undermine the rule of Eddis had ceased.

Attolia suspected that more than a third of her own barons had accepted Sounis's money at one time or another to finance their revolts. She wished that she had such a tool as Eugenides to use against him, but only Eddis had the tradition of a Queen's Thief. Bitterly, Attolia admitted to herself that if there were an Attolian Thief, he'd be more threat to her than aid.

She knew that the walls of her own palace were as porous to Eugenides as the megaron of Sounis, and she didn't think that if she let him go, she could catch him a second time. There was no question of letting him go. She had heard that he had an aversion to killing people, but, like Sounis, she was reluctant to assume that a childish reluctance for bloodshed would prevent him from following the orders of his queen. He had already proven himself to be extremely loyal.

She stepped down from the dais to stand before Eugenides. He didn't look much worried about his possible fate. He seemed more interested in the pattern inlaid in gold on the marble tiles at his feet. She waited, and he slowly lifted his head. He wasn't unconcerned about his fate. He was frightened of dying and more frightened of what might come to him before he died, but the pain in his head made it hard for him to think what he might say to save himself.

He looked at her and tilted his head very slightly in wonder. He had forgotten, as he always forgot, how beautiful she was. Her hair was held away from her face by the ruby and gold headband that crossed her forehead just above her dark brows. Her skin was flawless and so fair as to be translucent. She dressed as always in imitation of Hephestia, but it was far easier to imagine the impersonal cruelty of the Great Goddess than to see cruelty in the face of the queen of Attolia. Looking at her, Eugenides smiled.

Attolia saw his smile, without any hint of self-effacement or flattery or opportunism, a smile wholly unlike that of any member of her court, and she hit him across the face with her open hand. His head rocked on his shoulders. He made no sound but dropped to his knees, fighting nausea.

"Your Majesty," said the Eddisian ambassador harshly, and the queen swung around to face him.

"Do not offend the gods," he warned her.

Attolia turned back to Eugenides and his guards. "Hang him," she said. "Take him out now and hang him. Send his body back to Eddis, and we'll see if the Aracthus flows." She stalked back to her throne and spoke from there to the Eddisians. "Remember that your gods are not mine. Nor will they be," she said.

She sat on the throne and watched as Eugenides was lifted to his feet by the guards. He had his hands cupped over his face, covered by his dark hair.

Beside her the ambassador from the Mede Empire shifted his weight and caught her attention.

"I don't know what Eddis thought she could accomplish," Attolia said. "She can hardly hold back a river forever."

"Long enough," suggested the Mede, "to insure her Thief a relatively easy death?"

Attolia turned to look at him, then back thoughtfully at Eugenides.

"This queen of Eddis is very clever," the Mede said softly, bending closer. "She knows how some of your other prisoners have died. You will let her Thief go so quickly?"

"Stop," she said, and the guards did as they were told. Eugenides hung from their arms. He was carefully placing his feet and straightening himself while the queen considered.

Whatever her neighboring monarchs thought, she very rarely made hasty decisions, and she didn't engage in violence gratuitously. If she executed traitors by hanging them off a city's walls upside down until they were dead, it was because she couldn't afford the luxury of beheading them in private, as Sounis did. Everything she did had to be calculated for its effect, and she had meant to think carefully before she chose a suitable punishment for Eugenides, something that would provide an example for unruly members of her aristocracy as well as satisfy her deep and abiding hatred of the queen of Eddis and her Thief. She resented being stampeded into a decision by Eddis and knew that the Mede was right; her anger had been exactly the object of the Eddisian ambassador's insults. He had indeed argued skillfully.

Attolia didn't particularly care for the new ambassador from Medea. His oily style of compliments and indirection didn't suit her, but that was the required form in the court he came from, and he was certainly insightful and in this case quite accurate.

The waters of the Aracthus would eventually overfill its reservoir and flood Eddis's capital city if the dam remained closed. For Attolia, the death of the Thief was worth the loss of a season's harvest, but his death was the least Attolia could accomplish and the best that Eddis could hope for. There was no reason to satisfy Eddis's hopes, and she had every desire to confound them.

"Bring him here," she said, and the guards obediently brought Eugenides back to the base of the throne. Attolia leaned forward in her chair to look at him. He swallowed convulsively but met her eyes without flinching even as she cupped her hand under his chin.

"That was hasty of me," she said. She continued to stare into Eugenides's face but spoke to the guards. "Take him back to his cell and let him wait. I believe," she said slowly, "I will think a little more before I decide what's best to do with you."

Eugenides looked at her without expression. He turned his head to go on looking at her over his shoulder as he was led away. She wondered if he guessed what punishment she had in mind. Let the Eddisian babble about offending the gods, Attolia thought, sitting back in her throne. They were not her gods, and she would not worship them.

"A pity about the ransom," she said.

"Not a significant sum, surely?" the Mede beside her replied.

"Not to your emperor, perhaps," said Attolia. "Here on this coast of the middle sea, where we are less wealthy, I could put a sum like that to good use."

"Then take it please, as a gift from my emperor," said the Mede, as Attolia had hoped he would.

"You jest?" she asked the Mede.

"Not at all," he answered. "Nothing would please my master the emperor more than to be of assistance to so lovely a ruler as yourself." He made an elaborate bow, and Attolia smiled, very pleased.

chapter 3

EUGENIDES STOOD IN his cell with his shoulders against the damp wall. Resting the back of his head against the stones made the front hurt worse, so he dropped his head toward his chest. He didn't want to go back to sleep. He imagined his grandfather waiting for him at the gates of the afterworld, and he didn't want to have to tell him that he'd spent the last few hours allotted to him napping. The old man would not be impressed by false nonchalance.

All the tools of his trade were still tucked into their pockets in his clothes, but none of them was of any use. No part of the locking mechanism on the door was accessible. Eugenides had checked.

Pulling himself away from the wall, he staggered along it. His balance was off, and he kept his right hand on the wall to steady himself, feeling the cool stones with his fingertips. There was a gouge in the heel of the hand. The pain from that wound distracted him from the worse one in his head, and from the innumerable tears where the dogs had caught him with their teeth.

He circled the cell. There was no window with bars to be filed through. The only light came through the narrow opening in the door. There were no loose stones or miraculous tunnels, and the door remained unshakably closed.

Silently he called on the God of Thieves but didn't even

know what to pray for. Should he pray to die quickly? It seemed too much to ask to escape Attolia entirely. In the end he prayed for help, any help, and left it to the god to decide what was best.

Someone slid a tray of food through the slot in the bottom of the cell door. He staggered to the upper part of the door and looked out at the prison keeper.

"I heard she was going to hang you but she changed her mind," said the keeper. "Don't worry, lad, she never changes it for the better." He laughed and banged the bars of the window with his truncheon. Eugenides snatched his fingers away. "Enjoy the meal. It might be the last," the man advised as he moved away.

Eugenides sat down to drink the watery soup but left the hard chunk of bread beside the bowl. He didn't enjoy his meal, but sick as he was, he probably appreciated it more than any of the other prisoners in the queen's cells. Once sitting, he didn't have the strength to stand. His head hurt abominably. He could neither rest it on the wall behind him nor lean it on his knees, pulled up in front of him. Finally, reluctantly, he lay down and pillowed it on his arms, and darkness closed over him again. His grandfather would heap scorn on him like coals.

He was still asleep when the keeper returned much later.

"Look lively!" he yelled into the cell. "She's made up her mind."

While the keeper turned the key in the lock and pulled the door open, Eugenides struggled to his feet and was standing, though unsteady, when the prison guards came in to take his arms.

He walked between guards down underground passageways to an open doorway. The room stank of blood. He could smell it from outside, and he hesitated, but one of the guards nudged him forward. He took a shaky breath and stepped across the threshold. There was fire burning inside on a circular hearth surrounded by a low stone wall. Long-handled iron tools that looked like blacksmithing tools but weren't rested on the wall, their tips in the fire to heat. The fire smoked, and the room was unbearably hot.

There was a huge wooden framework threaded with ropes and pulleys, oddments hanging on hooks on the walls that Eugenides didn't want to see. And dragged out to the middle of the room, sitting cockeyed to the fire, covered with dust as if it had been stuck in an unused corner for a long, long time, was a chair with overlong arms and leather straps to keep a person in it.

Near the chair, dressed for dinner in a cool green gown the color of sage leaves, was the queen of Attolia. Embroidered around the neck of the dress was a ring of flowers, white petals on the green ground, with delicate leaves a shade darker than the dress.

The Thief stopped in the doorway. He looked from her to the chair beside her. He was puzzled only for a moment. He looked back at her but cried out to the patron God of Thieves, "God, no," and threw himself backward. The guards caught at him. He sank through their arms, then stood again to drive the heel of his hand up under one guard's nose. The guard dropped as if he'd been hit with an ax, but it was all the strength the Thief had in him. He grabbed for the doorway, but they pulled his fingers free one by one and carried him thrashing to the chair.

The guards swore, but the Thief made no sound that she could hear, except that one plea to his god. She had thought believers were as rare in Eddis as they were in Attolia. The Thief, though, had seemed to cry out in earnest, not merely from habit. Faith did return in extremis, Attolia observed. She had seen that happen before.

Finally the guards forced him into the chair and, as they did so, banged his head against the back of it. The little fight remaining in him went out in a breath. His eyes rolled white in his head, and his head dropped to his chest. After a time his eyes opened, and he lifted his head again. The leather straps fixed him to the chair, and he couldn't move.

"Your Majesty." He turned to her and said desperately, "Let me serve you. Let me be your Thief."

Attolia shook her head. "I offered you a position in my service once before. You refused me for a mistress you said was more kind."

"I could serve you now," Eugenides whispered.

"Could you?" Attolia asked.

"Yes," the Thief swore. She could see the tendons in his neck as he strained against the straps.

With plausible seriousness, the queen asked, "What could you steal for me, Thief?"

"Anything," he assured her. "I can steal anything."

"And why would I trust you?"

"I would give you my word."

"Your word?" The queen was amused. "What good is that?"

No good at all.

Attolia smiled. "And what about your queen? She would rather see you serve me than see you suffer? Did she tell you so before you left Eddis?"

She had.

"Of course," said Attolia. "And Eddis has nothing I want, so you are no threat to her. What a wonderful tool you are, one that cannot be turned against your mistress."

She bent over him, reaching for him with both hands. He shuddered at her touch, but she only cupped his face in her hands and looked into his eyes. "Your queen thinks she is safe sending you to me because I cannot use you against her. I think I can. And what I want is not what Eddis chooses to give me.

"Your ambassador says your queen has accepted my right to have you hanged," said Attolia. "But not to have you flogged to death, nor to have you hung upside down from my palace walls, nor to have you starve to death in a cage in the court-yard. He says I mustn't exceed the restraints of law and tradi-tion. He says I might offend the gods, though he didn't say which ones. I care very little for the opinion of any god, but I still think tradition might hold the best solution to my prob-lems with you."

She released him and stepped back. A burly jailer unracked a curving sword from its place on the wall. Eugenides had been frightened before, so frightened that he'd felt as if his heart had turned to stone in his chest. Seeing the sword in the jailer's hand, he looked again at the queen and felt the whole world turned to stone. The air around him was solid, and he was suffocating. He threw himself against the leather straps of the chair, against the solid air all around him, against the ob-duracy of the queen of Attolia.

He begged, "Please, please," as if his heart were breaking.

The man beside him lifted the sword. It caught the firelight on its edge a moment before it swept down, biting deep into the wooden arm of the chair. His right hand disappeared be-hind the blade.

Attolia saw his body jerk against the straps. She had ex-pected him to cry out, but he made no sound. He turned away from the sight of his right arm, and she saw his face grow white as the blood under his skin drained away. His eyes were squeezed closed, his mouth twisted in pain.

He struggled for breath as his thoughts circled like birds

that couldn't find a perch, searching for a way to change the truth, to change the queen of Attolia, but her decision was final, the action irrevocable.

"Eugenides"—he heard her cool voice through the agony—"have I exceeded the restraints of tradition? Have I offended the gods?" and he heard someone whisper with his voice, "No, Your Majesty."

"Cauterize the wound," the queen said briskly. "And have a doctor check it. I don't want it infected." The cauterizing iron was ready, and she stayed to see if he would scream when it was applied. He jerked again against the straps but still made no sound, only breathed in sharply and didn't let the breath go. Attolia watched as his lips flushed blue, and then he fainted, his head dropping forward to his chest, his dark hair covering his face. She leaned close to be sure he breathed again, then repeated her instructions to have a doctor check the wound for infection and left.

As she climbed the narrow staircases to the upper part of her palace, she thrust aside her feelings of unease and concentrated instead on where to temporarily relocate the court. She thought she might move inland. It was time to look into the affairs of the barons there. She would give the necessary orders to begin packing.

Three days later she stood in the doorway of the Thief's cell. She could hear him before she could see him, and she listened to his labored breathing as her eyes adjusted to the dark.

He lay on his side in a corner of the cell with his injured arm cradled against his chest and a knee pulled up to protect it. He sweated in the damp cold of the cell and didn't move until Attolia prodded him with one slippered foot. He opened his eyes and looked up at her without expression. The lamp that someone held behind her shone down on his face, and she could see the scar on his cheek. His skin was so pale that the scar showed dark against it.

His eyes were bright, and she bent down to look into them, expecting the hatred she often saw in the faces in her prison, but in Eugenides's eyes there was only fever and pain and an emotion she couldn't put a name to.

"Please," he whispered. His voice was low but clear. "Don't hurt me anymore."

Attolia recoiled. Once, as a child, she'd thrown her slipper in a rage and had knocked an amphora of oil from its pedestal. The amphora had been a favorite of hers. It had smashed, and the scent of the hair oil inside had lingered for days. She remembered the scent still, though she didn't know what in the stinking cell had brought it to mind.

She bent over Eugenides again, needing to be sure her punishment had been effective.

"Eugenides," she said, "what can you steal with only one hand?"

"Nothing," he answered hopelessly.

Attolia nodded. Eddis would think twice before risking a favorite in Attolia's power. He was very young, she realized. She hadn't considered his age before and reminded herself that his age didn't matter. All that mattered was the threat he posed. Still, seeing him huddled on the floor, she felt a little surprised that Eddis would endanger someone so young. But Eddis was not much older, Attolia thought. Not many years ahead of Eddis herself, Attolia was a far more experienced queen. She turned to the jailer.

"I said I wanted a doctor to check him."

"He did, Your Majesty."

"The bites on his leg are infected." She pointed with one finger at the swollen red skin that showed through the torn cloth.

The prison keeper looked suddenly wary. "He checked the burns, as you ordered, Your Majesty."

"Only the burns?"

"I suppose, Your Majesty. Those were your orders, Your Majesty."

Attolia sighed in irritation. A familiar, not uncomfortable emotion. "If I didn't want him dead of one infection, why would I want him dead from another?"

"I'm sorry, Your Majesty."

"You'll be sorrier." She turned to the captain of her guard, who had accompanied her. "Get him back to Eddis before he dies." She left the cell and made her way up the many stairs of the palace to her private anteroom. She passed through it and into her bedchamber, where she sent away her various attendants and sat for a long time in a chair looking out over the sea as the last sunlight faded from the sky. She dismissed thoughts of the Thief lying on the floor of his cell, but found herself thinking instead of her favorite amphora, broken, and the oil spilled.

chapter 4

THE QUEEN OF Eddis stood in the courtyard to meet her Thief when they brought him up the mountain. With her stood those of the court she couldn't order to be elsewhere. She remembered Eugenides asking once why so many of the events around her looked like a circus and why he always had the part of the dancing bear. When she saw the litter they carried him in, it looked like nothing so much as a cage, though it was closed off by curtains and not bars.

Eddisian soldiers carried the litter. They'd taken it from the Attolians at the base of the mountain and carefully lifted it up the winding road that followed the old watercourse of the Aracthus River. The Attolians walked beside it, and her ambassador and his party walked behind. Meeting her gaze as they entered the courtyard, the ambassador shook his head slightly, warning her to expect the worst. He'd sent her word already of events in Attolia.

When his messenger had delivered the ambassador's news, Eddis had ordered the room emptied and had stayed to sit by herself on the throne. When the daylight falling in the skylights had faded, a servant had come with a taper for the lamps, but Eddis had sent him away. There was no formal dinner that night. The court dined in its private rooms, and finally the most senior of her attendants had come to coax the queen to bed.

"There's nothing you can do, my darling, sitting here in the dark. Come to bed," Xanthe had said.

"I can think, Xanthe. And I need to think a little more. I'll be up soon, I promise." And Xanthe had gone upstairs to the queen's chambers to wait patiently as the night passed.

In the morning Eddis had spoken privately with her ministers and then waited, knowing Attolia would send Eugenides home when she was done with him and not before.

The litter was a fine one, used no doubt to carry an Attolian noble through the narrow streets of Attolia's older cities. It had doors that slid closed and locked to keep the ornamentations and fabric of the interior safe when the litter was not in use. They had also served to keep the Thief locked in until he reached Eddis. This had hardly been necessary, but the Attolian guards sent with the litter had been ordered to take no chances and to hurry.

They'd turned the litter over to the Eddisians and followed it up the mountain to see its contents delivered. Once the litter had been lowered to the ground, the ranking officer among the Attolians stepped forward to slide back the curtain that screened the interior. "He'll need a hand getting out," he said, and another of the Attolians choked on a laugh. The officer reached in and, grasping Eugenides by the back of the neck, slid his unconscious body off the cushions and onto the sun-warmed stones of the forecourt.

"Our queen said to tell you this is how we treat thieves in Attolia, and she awaits the water of the Aracthus," said the Attolian, but the sly expression on his face faded as the queen stared at him impassively. From where she stood she couldn't know if the Thief was alive or dead, and she didn't look as if she cared. The Attolian lifted one hand to rub the back of his neck where his hair was prickling, realizing he may have been sent on this errand because his guard captain didn't care if all that returned was his head.

"Galen," said the queen, but the palace physician was already stepping forward with his assistants.

"He's alive still," said Galen, after checking for a heartbeat. He started to pick the boy up, but the minister of war tapped his shoulder and stooped himself to gather Eugenides in his arms and carry him inside. The crowd parted to allow him to pass, onlookers catching a single glimpse of Eugenides's face and then swiveling to eye the Attolians.

The Attolians shifted from foot to foot and drew themselves together. Eddis summoned her steward. "These men will want to eat before they start down to Attolia," she said quietly. "See that they are fed and paid for the service they have rendered us in returning our Thief."

The Attolians exchanged nervous glances, concerned that their payment might be fatal, but beheading them was something Attolia might do, not Eddis. They would each receive a silver griffin and a good meal before being escorted to the border.

To the senior Attolian, the queen said, "Tell Attolia I have freed the waters of the Aracthus. They will flow by sundown." The message was for formality's sake. News of the water flow would reach Attolia long before the messengers did. Eddis turned, and the crowd, which hadn't regrouped entirely after the passage of the minister of war, parted again for her and then trailed silently after her into the palace.

Eddis seated herself on her throne. "Where's the messenger?" she said, and one of the soldiers charged for that day with the duty of carrying the queen's messages stepped forward.

She noted that he was one of her first cousins, which suited her.

"Crodes," she said, "carry me a message to the engineer at the reservoir telling him to release the waters of the Aracthus this evening as we agreed. Then go on to the officer in charge of the bridge at the pass."

The country of Eddis lay in the mountains between the two

countries of Sounis and Attolia. Through the Hephestial Mountains there was one pass to carry trade between the two lowland countries. It had been carved by the Seperchia River as it cut through the softer limestone of the coastal mountains on its way from Attolia to Sounis and the middle sea. All traffic between Attolia and Sounis climbed the mountain pass, crossing several bridges in the process, the most important being the Main Bridge, which spanned the chasm of the Seperchia near the top of the pass. On one bank there was no traversable path to Attolia, and on the far bank there was none to Sounis. All traffic bottlenecked at the bridge, and Eddis controlled it.

"To the officer at the bridge," said Eddis. "My compliments to him for his well-performed duties, and he will detain the next ten Attolian traders and their trade caravans. He is to confiscate everything but the clothes on their backs and turn them loose. If they protest, tell them they may apply to their queen for compensation."

"Yes, Your Majesty."

"Your Majesty." People in the room turned to look at the Attolian ambassador. "It is my obligation to assure you that news of this will not be well received by my queen."

"I expect not," said Eddis, and turned back to her messenger. "Crodes," she said, "tell him the next ten large caravans."

Politically the loss of Eugenides's service was severe. Sounis was still eager to expand his borders, and only his fear of assassination kept him in check. But Attolia hadn't had merely a political loss in mind. If she'd wanted Eddis to be without the Thief's services, she could have executed him. She meant to hurt Eddis at every level, and she had succeeded. A hundred caravans of merchandise couldn't repair the damage. Sighing inwardly, Eddis excused herself and went upstairs to see her Thief.

The library was empty, but the connecting door to Eugenides's study and bedchamber was open. Eugenides lay on his bed, and Galen, the palace physician, bent over him. He straightened as the queen entered.

"He's unconscious?" Eddis asked, standing by the bed.

"He's drugged," said the physician. "We got some lethium drops into him." He was glad she hadn't come earlier. Eugenides was feverish and hadn't recognized anyone when he'd wakened. They'd had to hold him down and force the lethium into his mouth. There'd been no way to measure what had gone in and what he'd spat out again.

"How is his arm?" the queen asked.

The physician shook his head and gestured to the filthy bandages. "I haven't gotten to his arm. I assume it was well cauterized or it would stink more." The physician pushed the hair off Eugenides's forehead. "His head isn't broken, although clearly it might have been. You can see the bruising on his forehead, but if he'd cracked his skull, he'd probably be dead already. I'm more worried about his right eye, which is infected. See the grit on his eyelashes." The physician pointed it out, sweeping his finger above the lashes, careful not to brush them.

"If it's prison glower," the physician explained, "he'll lose the sight in that eye, and if the infection spreads, he'll be blind in both." He shrugged helplessly.

Two servants bearing ewers of warm water slipped into the room behind the queen.

"You can't treat it?"

"I'm not an oculist. I've sent for one in town, but as far as I know, there isn't a treatment. There's a man in Attolia who says he has an ointment that will keep the infection from spreading, but whether he does and whether he'd come here . . ." He held up his hands.

"He'll come if I say he will," said Eddis.

"He's Attolian, Your Majesty."

"He'll still come," she said.

The physician looked up. The queen gave him a brief hard smile. She wasn't joking. She'd have the Attolian abducted and dragged up the mountain if need be.

"Your Majesty, it may not be glower. The oculist from town should be here soon."

"How soon?"

"An hour or two. Until then, Your Majesty, I do have work to do."

Eddis nodded. "I leave you to it then. I want to know what the oculist says."

When Eddis was gone, the physician looked down at Eugenides and saw the glint of his eyes through his lashes. He looked closer. "You'll need more lethium," he said.

"I won't," Eugenides whispered.

The physician looked at the bandages that still needed to be changed.

"You will," he said, and went to mix several drops of the medicine with water in a tiny horn cup. When he came back, Eugenides's eyes were open, and he was watching the physician carefully. When he raised the cup, Eugenides turned his head away.

"No more trouble, please, young man."

"Galen," he whispered, "do you think that if people are crippled in this life, they are crippled in the afterlife as well?"

The physician lowered the cup. "You would know that better than I," he said.

"No," said Eugenides. "I don't know."

Galen raised the cup again, but Eugenides continued to turn his face away. "Galen, I don't want to be blind when I die."

Galen sat silently with the cup held in his hands and his hands resting in his lap. His assistants slipped away.

"You aren't going to die for a long time."

"I don't want to be blind when I die, if I live to be a hundred."

"Do you imagine I am going to pour a cup of lethium down your throat and let you go?" Galen asked finally.

"I'd appreciate it," Eugenides said.

"I took an oath to heal people."

Eugenides didn't argue. He only turned to look at the physician, with his eyes underlined by black bruises and bright with fever. The scar on his cheek showed against the yellowed skin around it.

Galen sighed. "It might not be glower, and there's no need to talk about breaking oaths yet." He raised the cup in his hand. "Drink this for now."

When Eugenides woke, it was dark and the oculist had come. The room was lit by candles that reflected in the many panes of the glass windows and shone on the two men sitting by the bed. Galen had awakened him with a gentle touch on his arm, but even that gentle touch had worsened a hundred different pains, and the dull ache in his head, and the burning in his eye. Both of his eyes felt as if full of hot sand, and the rest of his body hurt so badly he couldn't be sure where the pain came from.

The oculist examined him as gently as possible, holding a lighted candle close to his face, then moving it away again.

"When did you notice the infection?"

Eugenides could only shake his head and then regret it. He didn't know what day it was or how long he'd been in the queen's prison cell. He tried to think, but his thoughts teetered on the edge of a black pit filled with memories that threatened to drown him.

"Before she cut off my hand," he said finally.

The oculist looked at the physician.

"Say a week ago," he said. "Maybe ten days."

The oculist lifted his candle again. Eugenides flinched but didn't complain. "Sticky-eye," said the oculist finally. "If it were glower, the eye would be more red by now and much more sensitive to the light. Keep it clean; try to get some decent food into him." He looked down at Eugenides and said firmly, "Hundreds of little children survive this every year with their eyesight intact. You have nothing to worry about on that count."

On that count, Eugenides thought, and when Galen offered him another dose of lethium, he drank it and slept.

In Attolia, the queen sat at dinner. The hall was lit with the finest candles, the food was excellent. The queen ate very little.

"Your thoughts seem elsewhere tonight, Your Majesty," said the man seated to her right in the place of honor.

"Not at all, Nahuseresh," Attolia assured her Mede ambassador. "Not at all."

Eugenides's fever grew worse. He slipped into the pit of his memories, and Galen repeatedly dosed him with the lethium to give him some rest. No longer recognizing Galen or his assistants, he fought every dose as he'd fought the first. He had to be held down, and Galen, with most of his weight on Eugenides's chest, tipped the lethium into his mouth as Eugenides screamed. To keep the lethium from spilling out again, Galen covered the boy's mouth with his hand, and covered his nose as well. Eugenides couldn't breathe until the lethium was swallowed, and he fought with all his strength, struggling to turn his head away. Galen could feel his body arching underneath him as he tried to throw the weight off his chest. Not until he was exhausted and nearly unconscious would he swallow.

Eddis sat, white-faced, in the library.

"He won't thank you for listening to this," said her minister of war, sitting down beside her. He, too, had come to the library to check on his son.

"Have you ever . . . ?"

"Heard him make a noise like that? No."

Eddis couldn't remember a time herself. His screams sounded as if they were dragged out of him with a hook. "Is he getting worse?"

Eugenides's father shook his head. "The same, I think." He settled into his chair. "If he fights this much when they try to get the lethium into him, I suppose he's got some strength in him yet."

"Is it like this every time?"

Her minister of war nodded. The queen left her chair abruptly and went to stand in the doorway of the bedchamber.

"Eugenides!" she snapped.

Galen looked up, meaning to send her away, but the struggling figure on the bed had frozen. Eugenides opened his eyes, blinking them in bewilderment. The people around the bed relaxed.

"Stop making an ass of yourself and swallow the lethium," she told him.

Eugenides swallowed and shuddered as the bitter draft went down. Galen took his hand away. "My Queen?" Eugenides whispered, still confused.

"Go to sleep," ordered Eddis.

Eugenides, obedient to his queen and the lethium, closed his eyes.

"Effective," said the minister as she returned to sit next to him in the library.

"We'll see what Galen says," the queen said, embarrassed, but she waited instead of returning to her meeting with her minister of trade. To her surprise, the physician, when he appeared, was pleased with the results of her interruption.

"He recognized you. He hasn't recognized anyone else. Come back when you can."

In the morning Eddis sat by Eugenides's bedside, waiting for him to wake. She asked Galen about the bruises under his eyes, and he said that the black marks were old blood that had been trapped under the skin. She'd known that much, but she wondered why his nose hadn't been broken then, if the bruising around his eyes was so dark. Galen explained that the blood was from the blow to his forehead, and it had drained into his eye sockets. He said it might take several weeks to fade. In the meantime the bruises made his face seem even thinner and his skin more pale.

She sat and watched him sleep, remembering many other times she'd seen him with bruises. He'd often had them after fights with his cousins. They'd teased him because of his name and teased him more as his grandfather's interest in him grew. Eugenides had a tongue that sometimes moved faster than his thoughts, and he responded with taunts of his own, usually more cutting, sometimes so effective that the cousins' attentions were diverted to his victim and Eugenides escaped. More often the teasing ended in blows and in bruises.

When his mother had died, Eugenides hadn't waited to tell his father his intentions to be the next Thief of Eddis. His father, the loss of his wife still fresh, had been enraged. Eugenides and his father had fought, both of them exercising their grief in anger with each other, in front of the entire court. The cousins, who idolized the minister of war, increased their attacks on Eugenides, and bad feelings grew until Eddis had moved him out of the boys' dormitory and into the only free room that she could think of, an anteroom to the rarely used palace library.

He'd cleaned the dust off the shelves and honed rudimentary reading skills into a taste for scholarship not uncommon among the Thieves of Eddis, and when he had fought his periodic, disastrous losing battles with his cousins, he had retreated to the library and his study-bedchamber to nurse his bruises. Eddis had visited him often in times of internal exile.

She hadn't taken his side. It was too obvious to everyone involved that he had brought trouble on himself and was anything but a helpless victim. His cousins had begun to lose
cherished objects and find them again on the temple altar
dedicated forever to the God of Thieves. Eddis hadn't supported his cousins either when they had come to her with
their complaints. They were her cousins as well, and she'd
fought with them herself until her two older brothers had died
of fever within the space of a few days and she had become
the heir to Eddis. Within a few months she had become
queen, and after that no one fought with her except in formal,
polite, tedious ways—no one except Eugenides, who continued to abuse her about her taste in clothes and relatives, as if
the existence of the cousins were her fault.

"Exile them all," he'd suggested.

"You know I can't. Someday they're going to be officers in
my army and my ministers of trade and the exchequer."

"You can make me an officer instead."

"You tore up your enrollment papers during the last fight
with your father."

"I'll be your minister—"

"Of the exchequer? You'd rob me blind."

"I would never steal from you," he'd said hotly.

"Oh? Where is my tourmaline necklace? Where are my
missing earrings?"

"That necklace was hideous. It was the only way to keep
you from wearing it."

"My earrings?"

"What earrings?"

"Eugenides!" She had laughed. "If Cleon beats you, it's because you deserve it!"

She never worried about his complaints. She worried only
when he was quiet. Either he was plotting something so outra-

geous it would bring her entire court to her throne howling for his blood, or he'd been fighting with his father, or on very rare occasions it meant he'd been seriously hurt. One of his cousins had broken several of his ribs once in a beating, and once he'd slipped while making his way across an icy wall and had fallen to the ground with his leg twisted underneath him. It was a hazard of thieves, to fall, often to their deaths, as his mother had done.

When hurt, he'd been white faced and quiet, staying in his rooms until he started to heal, and then, when he was feeling better, he'd complained constantly. He didn't, however, tell her who had broken his ribs or how he'd sprained his knee. Numerous eager tattletales told her about Titus, and the other bit of news she dragged out of the palace physician who'd dragged it from Eugenides while working on the leg. Galen was also used to seeing Eugenides's bruises and listening with no visible sympathy to his complaints.

Eddis leaned forward to brush the hair away from Eugenides's damp forehead. Galen had cut off most of the Thief's long hair, and he looked very different without it. She wouldn't have guessed that his hair, cut short, would form small curls at his temple and behind his ears. She brushed one of them back into place.

"My Queen," he said quietly, opening his eyes.

"My Thief," she said sadly.

"She knew I was in the palace," he said in a low voice, sounding very tired. "She knew where I was hiding, she knew how I'd get out of the city. She knew everything. I'm sorry."

"I shouldn't have sent you."

He shook his head. "No. I made mistakes. I don't know what they were. I've been trying to think. I just don't know. I failed you, My Queen," he said, his voice getting weaker. "I'm sorry," he said. "I'm sorry."

"Sorry," said Eddis bitterly, and Eugenides's eyes opened

again. "I'll tell you she will be sorry when she's the one hanging head down from her palace walls." She was crumpling the fine fabric of her dress in her fists. She smoothed it out and then stood up to pace.

"Galen will throw me out if I upset you," she said, sitting down again.

"You're not upsetting me. It's good to see you storming around. She doesn't storm," he said, looking away into empty space. "When she's angry, she sits, and when she's sad, she sits. If she was ever happy, she'd just sit, I think." It was more than he had said for days, and when he was done, he closed his eyes. Eddis thought he was sleeping. She stood and walked to the window. It was set high in the wall. The sill was at her eye level, and the glass panes reached nearly to the ceiling. By standing on her toes, she could look down into the front courtyard. It was empty.

"She was within her rights," Eugenides said behind her.

Eddis spun around. "She was *not*."

"It was a common punishment for thieves."

"Don't be stupid," snapped Eddis. "They haven't cut the hand off a thief in Attolia in a hundred years. And anyway, you're not a common thief. You are *my* Thief. You're a member of the royal family. She attacked all of Eddis through you, and you know it."

"Eddis had no business in her palace." Eugenides was whispering. Eddis knew he was tired.

"Attolia has no business treating with the Medes," she said, her voice raised.

Galen opened the door and gave her a warning look.

"Go away!" she snapped.

He shook his head but stepped back, leaving the door open.

"It was the act of a barbarian!" Eddis turned back to Eugenides. His eyes were closed. "And she's going to be sorry," she said as she left.

*   *   *

Out in the library Galen bowed very formally, excusing himself before he stepped past her. After he'd seen Eugenides and dosed him again with narcotics, he found Eddis waiting in the library. She was in one of the armchairs with her knees up and her feet pulled in under her skirts.

"Both of you in tears now," he said.

Eddis sniffed. "I'm angry."

"He's not strong enough for you to be angry." He looked helpless for a moment.

"Oh, I know," said the queen, sighing. "He's too weak to listen to me yelling, and if he dies, it's my fault, and it's already my fault that he's lost his hand, and I've only the gods to thank he isn't blind as well." She pulled back her skirt a little way to reveal an underskirt, which she used to wipe her eyes. She sniffed and then stood up.

Galen watched with amusement. She smiled at him. "Go on with your lecture."

"Which is?" Galen asked.

Eddis held one hand to her chest and orated. "If you choose that, after a lifetime of service to your family, my advice is to be ignored and I am to leave my post, then that is your prerogative, but so long as I am Physician of the Palace, I will insist that my prescriptions for the well-being of my patients will be observed. . . . Am I getting this right?" she asked.

"Yes."

"I think I can guess the rest as well," said the queen.

"Thank you, Your Majesty," said Galen. "I am grateful not to have to say it myself."

So the queen of Eddis visited Eugenides while he slept. The fever passed but left him terribly thin and unable to do much more than sleep most of the day and night. Galen said it might be some time before he regained his strength.

On the rare occasions when Eugenides was awake, Eddis talked to him about the harvest, which was good, and about the weather, which was good, and not about her meetings with her ministers, the directors of her mines, the master of the royal forge, or the commanders of her small army, nor about the many diplomatic messages arriving from Sounis and Attolia. When he was in less pain, and awake more often, she told him what gossip she could from the court and apologized for coming to see him infrequently.

"If you had more time, Galen wouldn't let you in anyway."

"True." The queen agreed. "And he listens to make sure I don't upset you. I'll bet his ear is flat against the door even as we speak," she whispered, and got a rare smile in response.

She leaned back in her chair and pulled the thin gold circlet from her head in order to run her fingers through her short hair. "I'm going to pull it all out before I'm thirty," she said. "I swear there's someone asking me one thing or another from the moment I wake up until the time I close my eyes at night. When Xanthe wakes me in the morning, she asks me if I'd like my breakfast. I wish she'd just put it in front of me. It would be one less decision to make."

He didn't ask what decisions kept her preoccupied. She didn't tell him. "I'll see you in a few days, if I can." She leaned over the bed to kiss him on the forehead. "Eat something," she said, and left.

In Attolia the queen listened carefully to a report sent by her ambassador in Eddis.

"The fever didn't kill him," she observed.

"It seems not, Your Majesty."

"Very well," she said.

chapter 5

*T*HE EARLY FALL in the mountains had already come when Eugenides decided he'd looked long enough at his ceiling and dragged himself out of bed to look out the window. There was frost on the ground in the front courtyard. An army messenger was riding in on a mountain pony shaggy with its winter coat. Eugenides turned away and went to sit in the chair by the fire that was waiting for him. He was wrapped in a warm robe and had slippers on his feet. The stump of his arm was bound in a clean white bandage. The bandage was unnecessary; the wound was healed, but Eugenides didn't want to look at it, and keeping it bandaged seemed the easiest solution.

His left hand, taking over the tasks of his right, seemed clumsy and uncoordinated, though Eugenides's grandfather had always insisted that both hands be trained to serve interchangeably. Eugenides supposed they worked equally well with the thieves' tools, and buttons were no difficulty, but buckling a belt was tedious, and his grandfather had never insisted he practice sweeping his hair out of his face and hooking it behind his right ear with his left hand. An oversight on his grandfather's part, now revealed. Eugenides looked into the flames for a while, then ran his fingers through his hair, which had grown enough to fall down over his eyes, and looked around the room. There was a bookcase to the left of the fireplace and his desk to the right. Pushed to the back of the desk was an awkward pile of papers. In the center of the pile, he supposed, was the scroll he'd been recopying before he'd gone to Attolia. If it was there, it was hidden by the bowls and bandages and phials of different concoctions left by Galen and his assistants. The desk chair was missing. It had been moved to the library when they'd brought in an armchair to sit between the foot of his bed and the fireplace.

He stood up to poke at the papers at the back of the desk, but the medical detritus took up too much space for there to be any room for sorting. At some point ink had spilled across the text he'd been copying, obscuring the left half of a long paragraph. Eugenides sighed. He would probably remember most of the words, but they would still need to be checked carefully against another reliable copy. He rolled the scroll up and tossed it back into the pile of papers, then sighed again. There were few reliable copies of Thales's original thoughts on the basic elements of the universe. That's why his scroll was valuable and why he had been copying it. If it was left at the back of the desk much longer, it was likely to be completely ruined. It should have been returned to its case and reshelved in the library.

He made himself go look for the case and found most of his books, scrolls, and other materials shifted into piles on one of the library tables. He searched through the piles until he found the case labeled with Thales's name and the title of the work. He slid the scroll into it and slid the case back into its slot on the library's shelves. Then he went back to his chair by the fire. He was dozing there when Galen came by. He had a small amphora of lethium, and he carefully refilled the phial on Eugenides's desk.

"The library's a mess," Eugenides said.

"I had noticed that," said Galen. "I went looking for the Aldmenedian drawings of the human body last week, and I couldn't find them."

"So why hasn't anyone cleaned it up?"

"It's your library."

"It isn't. It's the queen's library. I just live here."

"Whoever's library it is, I would say you're the only one who's going to set it to rights." He started to leave.

"Galen," Eugenides said.

"Yes?"

"Get your trash off my desk. I want to use it."

Galen snorted. "I'll see if I can find someone who's not too busy."

Despite Galen's unsympathetic words, one of his assistants showed up in the afternoon to collect the medicines, bowls, and the unused bandages. Eugenides looked at the remaining clutter but didn't move to sort it. He turned away and stared into the fire for the rest of the afternoon. The desk sat untouched.

In the morning he picked up the pen nibs that had been spilled. He dropped them one by one into their case, where they landed with tiny ticking sounds. When the case was full, he stirred them with one finger before he fitted the lid into place and went back to sitting in front of the fire.

Every morning, when the sunlight forced its way around the edges of the window curtains, trimming them in light, he dragged himself out of bed and went to the desk to clear something away before he sat down in the armchair. He wasn't used to being awake in the morning. He was used to being awake late in the night, when the rest of the palace was sleeping. He sat in front of the fire until early afternoon, then went back to bed until evening. Galen came to check on him every few days. Eddis and his father alternated in their weekly visits. Except for the servants who delivered trays of food, he was alone. He stayed in the quiet of his study, and no one bothered him.

When the desk was clear of all but a small phial of lethium, a few drops of which he took every night in order to sleep, he moved on to the library. One day that, too, was tidy, and he had to think of a new reason to get out of bed in the morning. Finally he got up to collect a few scraps of paper and one of his pens and sat down to see what writing with his left hand was going to be like.

He had to open the ink bottle with his teeth. The paper slid on the desk and needed to be held in place. If he used his stump, the bandages didn't give him any purchase unless he pressed down quite firmly. The stump was tender, and it hurt. If he used his forearm, he not only covered up most of the paper he was trying to write on, he covered the top part of it—meaning that as he wrote, he would smear what he'd written. Sighing, he got back up and went into the library and over to the chest that held maps in wide, flat drawers. There was a deeper drawer at the top to hold map weights, but it was almost empty. Only two mismatched weights were left. There was a third he almost overlooked at the back. Eugenides put them in the pocket of his robe and carried them to his desk. They held the paper in place. He dipped the pen into the ink and began trying to write.

He practiced his writing a little every day and was working on it one afternoon when someone crossed the library to knock on the frame of his open door. He looked up to find his father's secretary standing with another man just behind him.

"Yes?" said Eugenides.

"I've brought a tailor," said the secretary. "Your father mentioned that you might need your dinner clothes refitted or a new set altogether before you can come down for dinner."

"Am I coming down for dinner?" Eugenides asked. He hadn't thought about it. Now that it had been brought to mind, he longed for a permanent excuse to miss the formal dinners with the queen and her court.

The secretary looked at him without speaking. The tailor waited patiently.

"I guess I'll have to, eventually," said Eugenides, and rinsed his pen. "I don't know why the old suit won't fit, though."

The tailor helped him dress, doing up the buttons on the undershirt when Eugenides fumbled with them. Dressed, Eugenides bunched in his hand the extra fabric of what had been a fitted overshirt.

"I'm thinner," he said, surprised.

"Probably because you don't eat," muttered the tailor through the pins in his mouth, and looked up in time to catch a warning glance from the minister of war's secretary. He looked back down at the cloth he was pinning, but he didn't forget the rumors he'd heard. Having seen the queen's Thief with his own eyes, he thought that they were probably true: that the Thief sent his food back to the palace kitchen without touching it, that he kept to his room, seeing no one, that he'd probably die soon, and the whole city grieving as if he were already gone and that vicious bitch of Attolia to blame. The tailor shrugged and paid close attention to his work.

"The undershirt will have to be recut," he said. "I might need a few days to get it done."

"Take your time," said Eugenides.

The gibbous moon, slightly more than half full, shone from a clear sky on the queen's palace in Attolia. In the summertime, when the palace windows were open, she could lie in the darkness of her bedchamber and listen to the wheels of the heavy carts rumbling in the streets as farmers dragged their produce into the city for the morning market. It was winter. The windows were closed, and when she woke and looked into the darkness around her, the room was silent. She flicked the covers off with an angry sigh and stood up. From the doorway to an anteroom, an attendant appeared. She collected a robe and gracefully slid it over the outstretched arms, settling it on her mistress's shoulders.

"Does Your Majesty require something?" she asked.

"Solitude," said the queen of Attolia. "Leave me." The attendant dutifully left her post and went to stand in the hallway outside the queen's chambers. The queen moved to a window and pulled aside the heavy curtains to look at the moon while passing a sleepless night, one of many.

When Eugenides paused in the entranceway to the lesser throne room, those closest to him halted their conversations, puzzled to see a stranger in the doorway, then shocked when they recognized him. He looked older, and unfamiliar after his absence. He'd had the barber clip his hair short again, and his right arm was hidden in a sling. As the court looked him over, silence spread away from the bottom of the stair into the throne room like a wave through a small pond, and he stood immobilized by the stares.

"Eugenides," said the queen.

He turned to find her in the crowd. She held out a hand, and he stepped down the stairs and across the throne room to take it and bow over it.

"My Queen," he said.

"My Thief," she answered.

He lifted his head. She squeezed his hand, and he forbore to argue with her.

"Dinner, I think," said the queen, and the court moved into the Ceremonial Hall, where dinner would be served at the queen's pleasure and a little earlier than the kitchen had planned. Cursing under his breath, the chef rose to the occasion.

Eugenides sat between a baroness and a duchess, the queen's younger sister. The loudest sounds in the room were the footsteps of servers bringing the food. People tended to look in sequence at Eugenides, then at the queen, and then at the plates in front of them. Someone coughed or cleared his throat. Someone at the far end of the table mentioned the harvest, which had been good, and the duchess to his right picked up the thread of the conversation. She chatted about the weather, which was cold. It was winter, so that wasn't surprising. When the food came, Eugenides ate the vegetables. He left the meat, because he couldn't cut it, and ate a small piece of bread without spreading cheese on it, because he couldn't do that either.

Wine was served with dinner, and when he finished his first serving, his cup was refilled. It was a ceramic cup with a tall, narrow stem and a flared top. Eugenides admired the design painted around the inner rim as he drank from it. Centaurs chased each other in a circle, their bows drawn and arrows notched. Two hands, Eugenides thought to himself, and put the cup down empty.

When dinner was over and the queen stood, Eugenides stood with the rest of the court. Three fingers splayed unobtrusively on the table, with the knuckles turning white, kept him from swaying. He stayed at his place while his dinner partners excused themselves and drifted off. His father came to slide a hand under Eugenides's good arm, and Eugenides thankfully shifted his balance to lean against him.

"Did they not water the wine tonight?" he asked.

"Same mix as usual, I think. Two parts water." That was only civilized.

When the room was empty, his father helped Eugenides away from the table and then upstairs to his room.

"I won't need the lethium tonight anyway," Eugenides said as they reached the door. "Wine's a pleasant substitute." He felt his father stiffen. "I was joking," he said, not sure that he had been.

The second dinner was much the same. Eugenides's food arrived in front of him cut into bite-sized pieces, and every diner had a small bowl of olive oil to dip the bread into instead of cheese. Except that he had to reach across his plate to get the bread into the olive oil, everything went well. The conversation was the same. The harvest and the weather. The rest of the table spoke in hushed tones, difficult to overhear. Eugenides drank less and stared at his plate, unwilling to watch the queen carefully not watching him.

The third night he didn't appear. His place sat empty at the table. When dinner was over and his father went upstairs to look for him, Eugenides was waiting, dressed in his formal clothes, sitting on his bed. He was leaning against the headboard and had his boots up on the spread. The fabric for his sling lay in a limp bundle across his lap. He looked up at his father, his face bleak.

"I couldn't face it again," he said.

He dropped his gaze to the toes of his boots. "I already know the harvest was good, and the weather's still cold. I could try again in the spring."

"Tomorrow," said his father, and left.

Eugenides tilted over until his face was buried in a pillow.

When he fell asleep, he dreamed the queen of Attolia was dancing in her garden in a green dress with white flowers embroidered around the collar. It started to snow, dogs hunted him through the darkness, and the sword, red in the firelight, was above him, and falling. The queen stopped dancing to watch. He woke with his throat raw from screaming, still in his clothes, lying on top of the bedcovers.

He stumbled into the library and sat there in front of the empty fireplace. The room was cold. If it had been a month before, one of Galen's assistants would have been sleeping in the library, ready with the lethium when Eugenides opened his eyes, and Eugenides would have been unconscious again before the visions of his nightmares had had time to clear from behind his eyelids.

He sat in the cold library for several hours without stirring the coals of the banked fire. Only at dawn did he move back into the warmer room, where he stretched out on the bed, still dressed, and slept again.

"And the Thief?"

"The Thief, Your Majesty?"

Attolia drummed her fingers on the armrest of her chair. She was in a small receiving room to interview the man who collected information for her from various sources. His official title was Secretary of the Archives.

"The Thief, Relius. Is he recovering?"

"Our ambassador in Eddis can provide only limited information these days, but he says Eugenides seems to be recovering slowly. He attends the court dinners about once a week. He seems very little interested in the political situation. It is not discussed on the nights he attends dinner. He doesn't otherwise leave his rooms."

"Does he see the queen?"

"Not often. She is very busy, of course."

"Does he see anyone else?"

"I understand that his father visits from time to time, but he does not invite other company. They say he suffers from nightmares," he added.

"I'm sure he does." The queen snorted delicately.

Relius was looking pointedly over her shoulder. Attolia turned to see the ambassador from Medea, who'd entered the room behind her without being announced.

"Nahuseresh," she said, twisting in her chair to hold out both of her hands, which he took and bowed over. He was a remarkably attractive man, she thought, or he would be were it not for his beard, which he dyed crimson and divided in the middle and greased into two neatly oiled points. He might, if he remained in Attolia, give up the Medean style of dressing his beard, but he'd been at her court for some time and showed no signs of acclimating. "I didn't realize that you'd joined us," she said.

"I have committed a great transgression by sneaking in behind you," said the Mede. "I beg Your Majesty will condescend to forgive me." He bowed again and kissed her hands.

"Of course." The queen smiled. "But give me back my fingers. It is awkward to sit like this."

The Mede laughed and relinquished her hands.

"You seem very interested in the welfare of this Eddisian, Your Majesty," said the ambassador. "Surely he's no threat. What can he do with one hand?"

"I met his grandfather once, many years ago. He told me a thief's greatest asset, like a queen's, was his mind."

"He sounds overly familiar," said Nahuseresh with disapproval.

"He was, I suppose. But I wasn't queen then. I wasn't even a princess of any particular importance."

"You could have killed this thief."

"I could have," Attolia agreed. "This has been as effective and more . . . satisfying." She was lying. She already wished that she'd killed Eugenides and been done with him. She turned back to the secretary.

"Does the queen still call him her Thief?"

"She has done so before the court, several times," said Relius.

"You must forgive me, Your Majesty," the Mede said. "Your rituals are arcane, and there remain many with which I am not entirely familiar. Am I right that he was her Thief by virtue of stealing some heirloom and then surrendering it to her?"

"Yes."

"Your heirloom?" the Mede persisted.

"From a temple in my country."

"Which was then dropped into the lava of their Sacred Mountain."

"Heavens, Nahuseresh, you are well versed. What is it you don't understand?" The queen laughed.

"How could she replace him?" he asked.

"It was a hereditary title for many years," Attolia answered thoughtfully. "It could go to the child of one of his sisters." She turned back to her secretary. "What does the court call him?"

"Eugenides," said the secretary.

The queen nodded. "Of course," she said.

"I don't understand," said the Mede plaintively.

"The Thieves often take the name of their god, so it is like a title as well as a name."

"I see," said the Mede.

"I think that will be all for now, Relius," Attolia said, and dismissed her secretary with a flick of her fingers. When he reached the door, she called him back. "There is one other thing."

"Yes, Your Majesty." He knew what it was.

"You'll take care of it?"

"Immediately, Your Majesty."

The master of Her Majesty's spies bowed carefully before slipping out the door to put his not inconsiderable energies into discovering how the Medean ambassador came to interrupt the queen and to do so without being announced.

Nahuseresh excused himself not long after and returned to the rooms allotted to him and his ambassadorial party. His own secretary waited for him there.

"The messenger from the Three Cities brought a message to you from the emperor," the secretary warned him. "It is with your papers."

Nahuseresh found it there, folded and sealed. However, the seal was broken. Nahuseresh examined the folding carefully in order to open the papers without tearing them. Each of the folds was crisp and complete. It had not been opened and refolded. He glanced over at his secretary, who smiled.

"I didn't recognize the pattern," the secretary admitted, "so I left it."

"I'll teach it to you someday soon, Kamet," Nahuseresh promised while glancing over the message. "The emperor catalogs the gold we have given the barbarian queen and asks if we have struck a bargain together and received a receipt for our purchases."

"He is early in pressing for success, isn't he?" the secretary asked.

"He doesn't press as much as he urges us to make haste," Nahuseresh corrected him, eyes still on the paper he held.

"Haste hasn't made his empire," Kamet pointed out.

"It is unlike him," Nahuseresh agreed. "But no doubt he has his reasons." He refolded the message and dropped it onto his desk. "Try working out the folds yourself. Let me know if you need help. We will send a message to the emperor this evening saying we hope the queen will remain preoccupied with her Eddisian Thief while we work. You have spoken with the servants in Baron Erondites's household?"

"I've spoken with them. Not ingratiated myself. They're a little reserved yet, not sure where I fit in their hierarchy."

"I see."

"They don't have many slaves here," Kamet observed.

Nahuseresh shook his head. "No. They have a relatively small population and not a great deal of wealth."

"I could run away and make myself a free man," joked Kamet.

"Oh, I'd find you." Nahuseresh smiled. The slave's almond-shaped eyes and red-brown complexion would set him apart from the residents of Attolia. "What do you think of Baron Erondites so far?"

"He's a likely one, very sleek. Thinks well of himself. What do you think of the Attolian queen?"

"She's quite beautiful," Nahuseresh said.

"Yes?" prompted Kamet.

"And she has the most appealing of feminine virtues, especially in a queen. She's easily led," said Nahuseresh, smiling.

"She's held the throne for some time," the secretary said cautiously.

"She secured her throne with brilliant tactics early on that were no doubt those of an advisor, probably the Baron Oronus, or Erondites's father. Whichever of them it was, they are both dead now. She has been shrewd or perhaps lucky in advisors so far. She has to choose another if she hopes to work her way out of her present difficulties."

"The one with the most gold?" Kamet asked.

"One hopes so," said Nahuseresh.

When Attolia was dressed for bed and her hair was carefully combed and braided, she sent away her attendants and wandered slowly through her chambers. She ran her hand across the covers of the bed, turned back invitingly, but didn't get in. She gathered her robes around herself and sat in a chair by the window, looking out at the night sky. After a while she relaxed enough to drum her fingers on the arm of the chair.

"I should have hanged him," she said out loud.

She said nothing else, and the room was silent as the moon sailed slowly over the roofs of the palace and eventually dropped its light through the window to the carpet by her feet. Exhausted, she finally went to bed and slept without dreaming.

chapter 6

As the winter passed, he forced himself to get up in the morning, even if it was only to sit in the chair at the foot of his bed to watch the fire in the fireplace. Some days he practiced his handwriting. In the night, when the palace was quiet, he woke and lay in bed for hours, staring at the shadows the fire cast on his ceiling. It was a thief's time, the middle of the night. Old habits died hard, and he couldn't sleep. He counted himself lucky if he didn't wake screaming and was glad that when he did have nightmares, there was no other apartment near the library where people might hear him.

In the late winter he was still working on his handwriting and studying the books and scrolls from the library. He was reading a text on a system for categorizing plants and animals when someone knocked at his door. He looked up to find a man standing in his doorway. Beside him, as if he'd just put it down, was a square leather box with a handle on top.

"Can I help you?" Eugenides asked, puzzled.

"They sent me up to show you some things," the man said awkwardly.

Eugenides had no trouble fitting a number of people into the category "they." "What things?" he asked.

The man pushed his box a little closer to where Eugenides sat. He unlatched and lifted the top to display the contents. Held in place by leather straps was an assortment of prosthetics: false hands and hooks. The hands were carved from wood, some of them fists, some partly open. The hooks were set in shiny brass or silver cups, inlaid or plain.

"Get out," said Eugenides.

"Young sir," the man protested.

"Get out!"

"When you've looked." The man stood his ground.

Eugenides got up from his chair and, after the briefest of looks into the box, fled. He strode across the library and slammed its door behind him.

Eugenides went down the hallway past several startled servants and was running up stairs two at a time before he realized that he didn't want to go to the roof. On a fine day in late winter it would be peopled with ladies walking the lookouts, tired of being shut in by the cold. He racked his brains to think of a refuge, but the library was his refuge, and he'd been driven out. After a moment he turned and went back down the stairs and along the hall to another flight of steps, hurrying past people without speaking, thankful that he was dressed in clothes and not in his robe, as he often was in the morning, until he remembered that he was dressed only because his father's valet had stopped in that morning to prod him, no doubt in anticipation of his visitor. The thought made him savage, and the valet was lucky to be far away.

He left the palace by way of a tiny courtyard that had a door in its stone wall that let him out onto a grass-covered slope.

There was a paved path of white stones that led uphill from the gate to intersect the wider pavement of the Sacred Way. The Sacred Way swept back and forth across the hillside working up to the great temple of Hephestia, which overlooked the palace.

There were still patches of snow in the shade, and the wind blew through his thin shirt. The hill was steep, and he was quickly out of breath, but he climbed on until he reached the empty porch of the temple. He turned to look down at the palace, but there was no one climbing the Sacred Way behind him. He went through the main doors, twenty feet high and open to the cold air, into the pronaos of the temple. The smaller set of doors that led into the naos was also open.

As he passed from the pronaos into the naos, his footsteps were quiet from habit. The altar was deserted. The incense burned in braziers unattended by a priest, and there was no sign of supplicants, or of a recent sacrifice. The great gilded statue of Hephestia looked down on no one but Eugenides. He walked to the alcove just before the great altar, where there was a smaller altar dedicated to Eugenides, God of Thieves. A curtain provided privacy to supplicants. Eugenides pulled it closed and sat on one of the marble benches that ran along either side of the alcove. He lifted his feet up onto the bench, out of sight of any casual glance under the curtain, and wrapped his arms around his knees.

He'd left his room without his sling. He wondered if anyone had had time to stare when he was hurrying past. He tilted his head back against the marble walls behind him and closed his eyes. He didn't look at the altar, decorated with an assortment of objects stolen by his ancestors and himself. He hadn't come to pray. He'd come to hide.

The stars were out when Eugenides picked his way carefully down the road from the temple. He shivered as he slipped through the doorway into the courtyard and nodded to a guard as he entered the palace. The hallways were empty, and he passed no one else on the way back to his rooms.

The library doors were open, and the light from the fireplace inside flickered in the dark hall. He paused at the doorway to look in and saw his father and the queen sitting in silence in his armchairs, waiting for him.

"You shouldn't be here," he said.

They both stood. Eugenides looked at his father. "I was in the temple," he said.

"We knew that," the queen replied. "You could hardly be dragged home from there without risking a rain of thunderbolts, and now that you've been safe from being disturbed all day, you're blue with cold. Sit at the fire."

Eugenides didn't sit by the fire; he lay down on the hearth in front of it, close enough to be burned by stray sparks, and pillowed his head on his arms, shuddering from the cold.

"Cowardice has its own rewards," his father observed, looking down at him.

"More than you guess." Eugenides spoke into his arms. "Moira came. She brought me a message from the gods."

The queen and his father were silent. Eugenides rolled over on his back to warm his other side. He stared at the ceiling. He knew that after the destruction of Hamiathes's Gift the year before, what had seemed an indelible belief in the goddess-given authority of the Gift had slowly faded from most people's minds, until the gods were once again a vague possibility instead of a nerve-racking reality—even for his father. He counted on Eddis, who had held the Gift, to believe still in the immortals. She looked suitably wary, whereas his father looked only politely interested.

"Stop whining," Eugenides said.

"What?" Eddis's expression shifted from wary to puzzled.

"That was the message. For me, alone among mortals, the gods send their messenger to tell me to stop whining. That'll teach me to go hide in a temple. "

"Eugenides—" said Eddis.

"And I thought that I was doing fairly well," he said bitterly.

"You've been locked in your room all winter practicing your handwriting," Eddis said.

"Yes," said Eugenides.

"And what did you plan to do when your handwriting was perfect?" his father asked.

Eugenides sat up and shifted to lean against the heated stones beside the fireplace, with his legs stretched out in front of the fire to warm. "I thought I might go to one of the universities on the Peninsula," he said at last. "I thought that if I went away to study, I could come back in a few years and be . . . useful."

He pulled his knees up. "I'm sorry." He shrugged. "I thought it was a good plan."

Eddis looked at him helplessly and then at his father. The minister of war bent forward to put a hand under his son's armpit and lift him to his feet. "Bedtime, I think," he said. "We can discuss messages from the gods when we've had some sleep. Things," he said, looking at the queen, "are sometimes not as they appear."

The queen left, and the minister helped his son to bed with a minimum of words. He pulled the overshirt and undershirt over Eugenides's head with a sharp tug, then directed him to the bed.

"Sit," he said.

Eugenides sat, and his father pulled off the rest of his clothes and dropped a nightshirt over his head. Then he pushed his son down onto the bed and pulled the covers over him.

"You can wash in the morning," he said.

Eugenides lay with his head on his pillows, looking up at the ceiling.

"Do you need to eat?" his father asked.

"I ate the ceremonial bread in the temple."

His father shook his head in wonder. "No lightning bolts?" he asked.

"Not one," said Eugenides.

"How fortunate." He went to the door and stopped. "That business of going to the Peninsula to study . . ."

"What about it?"

"It was a reasonable idea."

Was? Eugenides wondered as he fell asleep.

chapter 7

*I*N THE MORNING Eugenides slept late. When he woke, his room was full of light, and the magus of Sounis sat in the chair at the foot of his bed.

"What are you doing here?" Eugenides asked, not pleased.

"I didn't think I'd get a chance to visit again soon, so I came up. You know I like Eddis."

"The country or the queen?"

"I prefer my country," the magus admitted.

"And my queen," said Eugenides. "Well, you can't have her."

The magus smiled. He had done his best to maneuver the unwilling queen of Eddis into a political marriage with his king and failed, largely because of Eugenides. In spite of the difference in their ages and their goals, they had a great respect for each other.

The magus was privy to the reports of his king's ambassador in Eddis and had read them carefully throughout the fall and winter, his personal desires in conflict with his political ones. His king had been delighted at the outcome in Attolia. The magus had grieved, but he'd gone on with the plans he'd thought in the best interest of his country. He was cautious, though, and he'd come to see Eugenides for himself before he encouraged his king toward open conflict with Eddis.

"What's keeping you busy in Sounis that you think you won't be back soon to ogle my queen?" Eugenides asked.

The magus had been prepared for apathy but not for ignorance.

"Sounis will declare war on Eddis by summer," he said.

Eugenides stared.

"Maybe you also don't know that your country has been at war with Attolia since the fall?"

"That's not possible," said Eugenides flatly. "Why would we go to war with Attolia?"

The magus pointed one finger at Eugenides's right arm.

"Don't be ridiculous," Eugenides snapped, and got out of bed. He pulled his robe from his wardrobe and threw it around his shoulders. "If this is your idea of a joke, I will kill you," he snarled.

"You were returned to Eddis with the understanding that the waters of the Aracthus would be restored. Did you know that?" the magus asked calmly.

Eugenides sighed and dragged his desk chair around to sit facing the magus. "Yes," he said, and waited for the magus to continue.

"Your queen agreed to open the sluice gates on the reservoir above the Aracthus. She simultaneously ordered confiscated the property of the next ten Attolian caravans through the pass. Attolia protested. Eddis described them as reparations. Attolia called it an act of war and demanded the contents of the caravans be returned. Eddis suggested arbitration by the Court of the Ten Nations, but Attolia refused. She sent an ultimatum that Eddis return the caravans or consider herself at war."

Eugenides waited.

The magus sat back in his chair and crossed his arms. "Your queen's entire two-word answer: 'War, then.' She ordered the

Attolian ambassador and his retinue confined to their rooms and opened the main gates of the Hamiathes Reservoir. The floodwaters of the Aracthus swept through the unprepared Attolian irrigation system and destroyed most of it. Eddis sent a raiding party out from the base of the mountain to move through the farmland on the far side of the Seperchia. More than twenty-five percent of Attolia's crops were burned in the field. Eddis lost the raiding party." The magus looked at him closely. "This is news to you?"

"Go on."

The magus did. "By the time Sounis heard of the attack, and before Attolia could enter the market and drive the prices up, Eddis had bought most of the local grain surplus. Checking the records, I found that she'd bought most of it even before the ultimatum from Attolia. Did you really not know?" he asked again, finding it hard to believe.

Eugenides stood up again to pace, shaking his head. The magus was reminded of a bear, chained in a pit, albeit a small bear.

"Eddis's council voted unanimously for war," the magus said. "The minister of war abstained."

"Why?" Eugenides wailed, wondering about the actions of the council, not those of his father.

"I think they like you," the magus said.

"They never did before," he said bitterly.

The magus said, "I think if you took the time to look, you might see that over the space of a year you turned into the greatest folk hero Eddis has ever known."

Eugenides dropped into his chair and covered his face with his hand. The magus saw that he'd raised both arms at first, then tucked the arm with the hand missing back into his lap.

"I don't want to know this," Eugenides said.

"I did hear," the magus went on, "that you were rarely out

of your rooms this winter. Did you have your head buried under your covers?" He stood and walked to Eugenides's desk in order to flip through its contents.

Eugenides sighed, tilting his head back in the chair, keeping his eyes closed. "You could go away now," he said.

"You're studying biological classification?" the magus said, holding up a book. "And human anatomy, I see, and Euclid's *Geometry*, or are you just recopying the text?" He looked at the scraps of paper covered in Eugenides's labored handwriting. There were more in a pile on the floor next to the desk. He picked up the pile and shuffled through it. "You'll have to pardon me," the magus said. "But with your country at war, I can't see how any of it really matters."

Standing up, Eugenides pulled the papers out of the magus's hands. "It matters, because I can't do anything, anymore, for this country, and it matters," he yelled as he threw the papers back to his desk, "because I only have one hand and it isn't even the right one!" Turning, he picked an inkpot off the desk and threw it to shatter on the door of his wardrobe, spraying black ink across the pale wood and onto the wall. Black drops like rain stained the sheets of his bed.

In the silent aftermath of his fury, they heard the queen behind them.

"Magus," she said from the doorway. "I'd heard that you had come."

Eugenides swung to look at her. "You started a war in my name without telling me?" he asked.

"You will have to excuse me," said the queen to the magus as if she hadn't heard. "I overslept, or I would have greeted you earlier."

"Are we at war with Attolia?" Eugenides demanded.

"Yes," said his queen.

"And Sounis?" asked Eugenides.

"Nearly," said Eddis.

"How could you come once a week to talk about the weather and not mention a war?"

Eddis sighed. "Will you sit down and stop shouting?" she asked.

"I'll stop shouting. I won't sit down. I might need to throw more inkpots. Did Galen stop you from telling me?"

"At first," the queen admitted. "But after that you didn't want to know, Eugenides. You're not blind, you had to see the things happening around you, but you never asked."

He thought about what he'd heard and seen without being curious: the military messengers on their horses riding in and out of the front courtyard, familiar faces disappearing from the court dinners. All the maps were missing, along with the map weights, from the library. His queen had been too busy to visit more than once a week, and he'd never wondered why.

"Who—" He choked on the word and started again. "Who was in the raiding party?"

"Stepsis." Eugenides winced, and she went on. "Chlorus, Sosias"—all cousins of Eugenides and the queen—"the commander Creon and his soldiers."

"Well"—he stumbled over the words—"this explains all those nights without conversation at dinner. What else have I missed that I should have been told but didn't want to hear?" he asked.

"Not too much. Hostilities between us and Attolia were suspended for the winter. It was an early one, remember. Everyone's told you about *that*. Magus?" said the queen politely. "Would you excuse us?"

The magus bowed his head and left without a word. When he was gone, the queen sat herself in the armchair he'd lately occupied. She rubbed her face and said, "I'm hungry. I left Xanthe standing in the middle of my room this morning with the breakfast tray, and I didn't eat anything last night at dinner. I was worrying about you," she said reproachfully, "sitting in an unheated temple, sulking."

"I thought I was whining."

"Sulking, whining, keening piteously."

"I have not," Eugenides insisted angrily.

"No," she admitted, "you haven't. But you've been in a wallow of self-absorption and despair all winter, and no one could blame you. We could only wait and hope you'd recover. Then you tell me that you want to leave Eddis and go to a university on the Peninsula. I need you here, Eugenides."

"What possible use could you have for a one-handed former Queen's Thief?"

"You're not a former queen's Thief; you're *my* Thief. So far I'm still queen."

"You know what I meant."

"It's a lifelong title. You'd be Queen's Thief if you were bedridden, and you know it."

"All right, what do you want a useless one-handed Thief for?"

"I want you not to be useless."

"I can't steal things without two hands," Eugenides said bitterly. "That's why she cut one off."

The queen of Attolia was only ever "she." The name Attolia rarely passed his lips, as if Eugenides couldn't bear the taste of the word in his mouth.

"There are a lot of things that a person with two hands couldn't steal," Eddis said.

"So?"

"Surely if it's impossible to steal them with two hands, it's no more impossible to steal them with one. Steal peace, Eugenides. Steal me some time."

She sat back in the chair. "Sounis has pushed Attolia to the brink of a chaotic civil war. No one could claim that she's been anything but brilliant, holding her throne for this long. Her people support her, but her barons hate her, ostensibly because she rules in her own right and has refused to take one of them for a king. What they really hate is the success she has had at centralizing the power of her throne and preventing them from running their estates as their own private king-doms. But she has reached the end of her resources. She in-vited the Mede to a treaty. You know that's why I sent you to Attolia. If she takes help from the Mede, if they land on this coast, they will eat us alive: Attolia, Sounis, and Eddis. I sent you because I needed to know how close her contacts with the Mede had become, because Sounis *will not* stop his attempts to unseat Attolia."

"Go to war with Sounis."

"I can't. Sounis is too strong. Eddis and Attolia together might beat him, but Attolia won't have anything to do with Eddis. She hates me too much, and she's too much concerned trying to keep a grip on her own country.

"She came to my coronation, you know," Eddis explained. "She took me aside and gave me a lot of advice on how to hold on to the throne: raise taxes so that I'd have the money to put down insurrection, increase the size of my army, and purge my council regularly. Trust no one, and execute any threats, no matter how insignificant, immediately."

Eugenides stared, and the queen shrugged. "She'd only been on her throne a few years. If Eddis had been anything like Attolia, it would have been good advice. She's hated me for not taking her advice and for having a country where I didn't need to. And she's hated me because I have you, Eu-genides, to keep Sounis and his corruption out of my court."

She stood and stuffed her hands in the pockets of her trousers and paced the room, pausing to rise on tiptoe to look out the window. Eugenides wondered when she'd started wearing trousers again. Thinking about it, he couldn't recall seeing her in a dress except at the formal dinners.

"You'd never threatened her directly, but you were a threat to Sounis," said Eddis. "If Sounis had someone else to harass, he'd have less time to devote to Attolia. He's been barking up our tree from the moment she cut your hand off." She turned back to Eugenides.

"Sounis could be entangled for years trying to secure power for himself here in Eddis. He'd find us easy to bite off but not easy to swallow." She smiled thinly. "Attolia could have had the same result by killing you, but she wanted something that would hurt you and me more." She looked at him. "You know all this," she said.

"Most of it," Eugenides admitted. "I didn't know why Attolia hated you."

"Get dressed," said his queen, "while I order breakfast, and I'll tell you some more."

"Without you to deter Sounis, he was ready to begin a campaign to weaken Eddis. I think my court is too loyal to be bought with his money, but his real power is trade. We depend on imports. Sooner or later he was going to stop those. And if Attolia was trading with the Mede, we wouldn't get any supplies from her."

"I know this," said Eugenides.

"Of course. What you don't know was that I'd been thinking for some time about deposing the queen of Attolia."

Eugenides blinked.

"It is a measure of complete desperation to unseat a neighboring monarch, and there isn't a successor that's much more palatable, but Attolia has been growing more and more unstable as she tries to counter Sounis, and with the Mede hanging over us like vultures, instability is more dangerous than anything else," said Eddis, pacing the library. "Then she cut off your hand, and I stopped caring if she ended hanging from her own palace walls. Every single person in Eddis agreed with me. Your father and I thought that if Sounis had an opportunity to install a puppet government in Attolia, and if it could be done too quickly for the Mede to interfere, Sounis would leave Eddis alone."

The queen shrugged and admitted, "In that sense, we are no better than Attolia. To save Eddis, I'd throw her country to that dog Sounis without hesitation."

"And?"

"The magus, of all people, stopped us in our tracks. He told Sounis that Attolia would treat with the Mede if Eddis and Sounis both attacked her. He may be right, but I believe she's treating with the Mede anyway. I hoped that if they had to deal with an internal war and an external one, the country would close ranks against the Mede and against the queen as well. They would accept a puppet king from Sounis, at least for a few years, and we would be rid of her. The Mede emperor cannot interfere without an invitation from the acting government of the country without breaking his treaty with the Greater Powers of the Continent. The Greater Powers don't want the Mede on this coast any more than we do, and they are also ready to interfere at the first excuse, but the *last* thing we need is to have the conflict fought out on our ground."

"So what's happening now?"

"Sounis wants Eddis and Attolia both. I offered him a chance to help me, but he's choosing instead to join Attolia, although he hasn't committed himself yet. She's going to try to bring an army up the pass when the weather breaks. It will be slow, and most of the losses will be hers; there's no room for her to maneuver. Should she get to the main fortifications, Sounis will bring his army up the other side of the pass. He wants to know that the defenses on his side of the Seperchia won't be reinforced before he attacks. We've evacuated the people from the coastal mountains and moved the livestock over the bridge to this part of the country. We're up to our eyeballs in sheep right now. If we don't start slaughtering them soon, they'll have grazed out the pastures. The silver mines have been packed with explosives that can be detonated if we're going to lose them.

"Trade has been suspended through the pass. I did that," said Eddis. "I thought that I might as well do it before one of the lowlanders did. Goods are being moved by ship through the coastal islands. There has been an unsurprising increase in piracy," she said dryly.

"Can we stop the Attolian army?" Eugenides asked.

"No," said Eddis bleakly. She ran one hand through her hair. "Not without throwing our entire army down the pass. We'd stop her, but we'd be defenseless on every other front, and that's what Sounis is waiting for."

"When do you expect the army?"

"Attolia's army is loyal and competent, but she has to supply it somehow, and that's slowing her down. That and a long winter. The snows still have the main pass closed, and after the thaw the tributaries down to the Seperchia will keep the roads impassable. We usually spend weeks or more on springtime repairs before the pass is opened. Obviously we won't be doing repairs this year."

"When?"

"The middle of our spring, if we're lucky."

"And what are your plans?"

Eddis looked grim. "To abandon the country west of the Seperchia: the coastal mountains and the silver mines. We can hold the entrance to these interior valleys. We have enough grain to get us through next winter."

"And then?"

"We hope that Sounis and Attolia bring each other enough grief to reduce their interest in Eddis. Please gods, they can't maintain an alliance long, and one of them may be willing to break off and ally with us before we starve."

"And if they remain allied with each other?"

"Then we surrender, Eugenides, and I am the queen that gets deposed. Attolia would probably take the coastal mountains and silver mines. Sounis would have the Hephestial Valley and the iron mines, unless he tries to grab the whole. At any rate, you could be a former queen's Thief yet. Now I have to go speak to Xenophon. He's been waiting for me."

"Yes," said Eugenides. "Go talk to Xenophon, by all means." He went back into his bedroom and shut the door.

That night, after a day of staring into the flames of his fire, Eugenides left his room and wandered the deserted hallways of the palace. He was thinking. Absentmindedly he passed familiar things: a panel that opened into a passage behind the queen's chambers, a storeroom with a tiny window from which he could reach the equally tiny window of his cousin Phrinidias's dressing room, a useful hiding place behind a twisting staircase.

The palace slept at this time of the night, and he'd always felt these hours belonged to him alone, so he was surprised, when he turned into a passageway that led to a staircase up to the roof, to find a guard at the end of it. He forced himself to continue down the passageway. There was no reason to turn back just because he'd been seen. He reached the doorway to the staircase, and the guard shifted his weight in order to stand squarely in the middle of it.

"I'm going to the roof," Eugenides explained, puzzled.

"No, sir," said the guard.

"What do you mean, 'no, sir'?" said Eugenides. "Why not?"

"I have my orders, sir."

"What, that no one is allowed on the roof?"

"No, sir."

"No, sir, no one is allowed on the roof, or no, those aren't your orders?"

"No, those aren't my orders, sir."

"Well, then, what are your orders, and stop calling me sir." No one had ever called him sir before he'd stolen Hamiathes's Gift, but since then it had been cropping up quite often. He didn't like it.

"My orders are not to allow you onto the roof, sir."

The Thief stared, dumbfounded.

"Eugenides."

He turned. The queen stood at the end of the passageway, flanked by two more soldiers and a third man.

"What do you mean, I'm not allowed on the roof?" said Eugenides, outraged.

The queen walked toward him. The third man, Eugenides saw, was one of Galen's assistants. He glanced from the assistant back to his queen.

"You have someone watching my door," he accused her.

She looked uncomfortable. Eugenides turned to the guard beside him and cursed. He turned back to the queen, still cursing. The soldiers on either side of her looked shocked.

"You think I'm going to throw myself off the roof?" he asked.

She did. The people in his family tended to die in falls. His mother, even his grandfather. When the palsy in his hands had grown so severe that he could no longer feed himself, he'd been unable to climb to the roof, and he'd tumbled over the railing at the top of one of the back staircases. It hadn't been a hard fall, but enough to kill an old man.

"You started a war without mentioning it," Eugenides snarled. "You have my rooms watched, and I'm not *allowed* on the roof. What do I find out next?" He pushed past her and the soldiers. He walked backward away from her. "Tell me you've enrolled me as an apprentice bookkeeper. You bought a lovely house for me in the suburbs. You have a marriage arranged with a nice girl who doesn't mind *cripples!*" he shouted. He had reached the corner and disappeared from sight still shouting. He was making enough noise to wake every sleeper in that wing of the palace, and he didn't care. "I can't wait to hear!" He spaced his last words out and finally was finished. There was no sound, not even that of his receding footsteps.

The queen sighed and dismissed the soldiers who'd accompanied her.

"Shall I go back to watching his door, Your Majesty?" Galen's assistant asked.

"Yes," she answered heavily. "Watch him as carefully as you can."

Returning to her room, she sighed again. The accusation about the arranged marriage had been a home shot. It was a good thing Eugenides hadn't realized it yet.

In the morning the magus knocked at the library door and entered without waiting for an invitation. Eugenides, still in the clothes he'd worn the day before, looked up once from the fireplace and then ignored him.

"My king sent me, you understand," the magus said, sitting in the armchair opposite the Thief. "Our ambassador has reported that you were no longer a threat, but Sounis is wary when you are involved. He wanted me to gather a second opinion."

Eugenides ignored him.

"I have to go. I can hardly stay longer. My king isn't going to declare war until Attolia has the pass under her control. The narrow ascent will make the attack costly for her, but Eddis has only a small army to hold the pass. She has no real defenses outside the natural terrain. When her army is gone, my king will attack from Sounis. If Eddis surrendered . . . it would be better. You can see that, can't you, Gen?"

Eugenides didn't look at him and didn't speak, not even to point out to the magus that only very close friends were entitled to call him by the shortened form of his name.

"Gen, sitting in here isn't going to help anything. You can talk sense to Eddis. Maybe you aren't a Thief anymore, but you could still do something."

Eugenides lifted his head, but only to look into the middle distance beyond the walls of the library. The magus sighed and stood up. He patted Eugenides once on the shoulder and left without seeing how the Thief's eyes narrowed, watching him go.

He returned to his king in Sounis and told him he thought the Thief was no longer a danger to anyone, except perhaps himself. The best course of action was to join Attolia and seize Eddis. Sounis was delighted.

He was in his private dining room, reclining on a couch as he picked at a late meal. As the magus talked, servants moved in and out carrying trays with tempting delicacies, most of which the king ate. The trays were offered to the magus, and he selected enough to avoid offense.

"And when Eddis has surrendered, you think we will be able to hold all of it?" the king asked.

"Attolia's army will be wasted trying to secure the pass. You should be able to take it from her fairly easily. By then she will be deeply enmeshed with the Mede, trying to hold some power in her own country. Neither of them will have time to squabble over Eddis. If you secure Eddis quickly, you will be strong enough to outface the Mede when he tries to expand beyond Attolia."

"But our chances to take Attolia will be gone."

"For the present, yes."

"What exactly do you mean by 'the present'?" the king asked.

"Perhaps the next hundred years," the magus answered, and the king snorted in irritation.

"I thought you might mean that. Let's keep our predictions to my lifetime, shall we?"

"There's little chance the Medes would lose their grip on Attolia within your lifetime, Your Majesty," the magus said stiffly. "Remember that Eddis will not be assimilated immediately. It will take at least a year to reorganize the various ministries under Sounisian control."

The king flashed his magus a dark look. "Let us hope my lifetime is not so brief," he said.

"Of course not, Your Majesty," the magus murmured. "The reorganization of the government will be only one of many steps. Eddis has a superb fighting force. You will want to integrate it into your own forces without diminishing its worth."

"Eddis should have married me," Sounis said abruptly. "Do you think she still might?"

"It would be in our interests, Sire."

"Ours, but not hers?"

"Eddis has been independent for a long time, Your Majesty. They will not give up easily."

"They will give up in the end, though," said Sounis confidently, picking over the tray beside him for the pastry of his choice.

"Oh, yes," the magus agreed, as confident. "They are a small country with few resources outside their mines and their trees. Sounis will have them in the end." When the king dismissed him, he returned to his study to make careful notes for the history he was writing of the war the Sounisians had fought centuries before while struggling to stay free of the powerful invaders from the Peninsula. He hoped to use the knowledge he acquired in the exercise to aid him in a more successful defense against the Mede.

"What of the Thief?" the queen of Attolia asked. Her ambassador and his staff were still confined to their rooms in Eddis's palace, but there were those willing to pass information to Attolia. Their reports were unreliable, but they were all her secretary had to answer his queen's persistent questions.

"No one has seen the Thief," the secretary of the archives told her. "He no longer comes down to dinner."

"Reassuring news," the queen said.

"Surely he is in no way a threat, Your Majesty?" Relius asked, puzzled by her continued interest in the crippled Thief of Eddis.

"I don't think he is a threat, Relius, but he bears watching. To be certain that he was no threat, I should have had both his hands cut off and probably his feet, too." She thought for a moment about the words of the Thief's grandfather and corrected herself. "To be entirely certain, I should have hanged him, but the traditional punishment seems to have been effective so far. Do watch him. If there's any sign that he has come out of his internal exile, I want to know about it."

Relius's spies continued to report that the Thief had retreated to his rooms and admitted no one, not even his father. His queen never attempted a visit. She never spoke of him, and evidently no one else at court dared to. Those who needed the books or scrolls from the library made their selections and carried them away to read elsewhere. There were not many scholars in Eddis.

Galen alone forced himself on Eugenides. He had a key to the door connecting Eugenides's retreat to the library, and Eugenides could hardly barricade himself in. Galen, however, was not one of Relius's informants. Relius knew that he left increasing amounts of lethium for the Thief, and that was

all. Not even the servants, leaving food in the library and returning to collect empty trays, saw Eugenides.

He remained in his rooms as the winter eased and the
spring came.

Snow gradually turned to rain in the mountains, and twisting ropes of solid ice melted into eager streams of bone-
chilling water that hurried down the mountain slopes toward
their elder sister, the Seperchia River. In the pass that the
Seperchia cut between the Hephestial Mountains and the
coastal range, the streams were forced into narrow ditches and
crossed the roadway there in stone-sided culverts. A temporary
dam of branches in one culvert caused the water to back and
deepen. When a stone shifted in its bed, the swirling water ate
at the ground behind it. No one reset the stone, no one prevented the damage from spreading. The ground collapsed;
stone and bank were washed away, with more stones following, knocked loose and dragged along by the flood.

Elsewhere Eddis's royal engineers diverted the water more
deliberately, eroding years of careful work that had gone into
maintaining the road that ran from Attolia's capital, through
Eddis, to the capital city of Sounis, carrying most of the trade
between the three countries. In some places whole sections of
the road disappeared in heaving muddy landslides, and the
engineers, torn between satisfaction and anguish, reported to
the queen that no army would reach the heights of the pass
quickly.

chapter 8

SPRING CAME EARLIER on the coast than it did in the mountains, and Sounis's summer was already near when the king's magus woke one morning in the last hour before dawn with his ears ringing to find his room awash in moonlight. There was a sound like thunder still lingering in the air, and he left his bed to look out the window.

"There isn't much to see from here," said a voice behind him. "You need a view of the harbor."

The magus turned to look for the Thief of Eddis and saw a shadow standing in a corner out of the moonlight.

"Eugenides," he said. He had recognized the voice.

"Yes."

"What have you done?"

"Not much yet," answered the Thief from the darkness. "I remain fairly limited in my physical activities." He held up his right arm, and the magus started before realizing that the hand he saw had to be a wooden one, concealed by a glove.

Another booming explosion filled the air, and the magus turned back to the window but could see only a glare reflecting on the whitewashed walls of the buildings below.

"I had to send someone else to light the fuses," Eugenides said behind him.

"Fuses?" asked the magus, with a sick feeling.

"In the powder magazines of your warships," Eugenides explained.

"Powder magazines?"

"You sound like the chorus in a play," said Eugenides.

"And the play is a tragedy, I suppose?"

"A farce," Eugenides suggested, and the magus winced.

"How many?" he asked.

"How many of your ships are burning? Four," said Eugenides. "Five if the *Eleutheria* catches when the *Hesperides* burns. She probably will."

"The *Principia*?" The *Principia* was the largest ship in the navy. She carried more guns than two of the smaller ships put together.

"Oh, yes," said Eugenides, "she's definitely gone."

The magus looked out again at the flickering reflections from the fires as his king's navy burned in the harbor.

"The sailors are all ashore for the Navy Festival," he said.

"Celebrating their naval superiority and control over most of the islands in the middle sea," agreed Eugenides. "Sounis outdid himself this year with the free wine."

"Surely there was a guard on the ships, though," protested the magus.

"We put on our pretty Sounisian uniforms and paddled out there in a shore boat and told them they were relieved from duty by order of the king. Or rather, my loyal assistants did. I'm not much use in a rowboat these days."

The magus dropped his head into his hands. "We have no navy," he said. It was an exaggeration, but painfully close to the truth. His Majesty's best warships had collected in the harbor at Sounis for the yearly festival. Attolia had still not reached the top of the pass, Eddis's soldiers fought bitterly, and Sounis had wanted to fortify his citizens for the war ahead.

"You said I should do something." Eugenides smiled in the dark, twisting the knife of his revenge a little deeper into the magus.

"I did?"

"As you were leaving, after your extremely edifying visit in the spring. You said, 'You could still do something.' Your exact words."

"I meant talk your queen into surrendering, *not destroy our navy in its own harbor!*" the magus shouted.

The shadowy form of Eugenides held one finger to its lips. "Shh," he said.

"And my king?" the magus asked more quietly. "What have you done to my king?"

"He's as safe in his bed as he thinks he is. Although he's probably out of bed by now. We don't have much time."

"Time for what?" the magus asked.

"I didn't come to Sounis to blow up His Majesty's warships. I told you someone else had to do that."

"What did you come for if not to murder my king?"

"I came to steal his magus."

"You can't," said the magus in question.

"I can steal anything," Eugenides corrected him. "Even with one hand." He took a step forward into the moonlight and waggled his fingers. The smile on his face made the magus feel worse, not better. "You shouldn't let the king choose your apprentices. Your most recent student, as we speak, is betraying your plans for the price of a good cloak. I would have given him more if he'd had the sense to ask for it."

"My plans?" said the magus, beginning to wonder if he was still asleep. The scene in the moonlit bedchamber had all the discontinuity of a dream.

"Your plans to blow up the king's navy."

"Aaah," said the magus, catching on, "I'm working for Eddis?"

"Oh, gods, no. You're working for Attolia. You have been all along. Poor Ambiades found out, and that's why you got rid of him. Pol, too."

"Not even Sounis would believe that," the magus protested.

"He will for long enough," said Eugenides. "Think of it as stealing not you but the king's faith in you."

"And what happens to me without the king's faith?"

"If you're smart, you leave Sounis," said Eugenides. "Quickly."

He waited while the magus thought. They both knew that Sounis was afraid of his advisor's power, that he chose poor apprentices for the magus to keep that power from growing, and that the king's heir had been sent to a teacher on the island Letnos to keep him far from the magus's influence.

They left the megaron through one of its smaller courtyards. The magus had a shoulder bag with three manuscripts inside, his silver comb, his razor, and his telescope, which he'd carried down to his room earlier in the evening after stargazing from the megaron's roof. Eugenides wouldn't let him go to his study and wouldn't let him carry any clothes.

"My history of the Invasion," he had protested. "It's in my study."

"You want people to think that you're going down to the harbor, not running for your life," Eugenides had told him. "Hurry, and you'll live to rewrite it."

Dressed as an apprentice, he walked behind the magus, keeping his wooden hand close to his side, and none of the guards looked twice at either of them. Once in the narrow streets outside the megaron, Eugenides led the way, hurrying through the old city and then down through the new city by back streets. He detoured into a quiet cul-de-sac where he'd left a bag hidden behind a stairway. Inside were two faded gray overshirts. He handed one to the magus and pulled the other over his head.

Crowds got thicker as they approached the harbor. Only the most dedicated revelers had been in the streets when the explosions began, but sailors sleeping on the floors of wineshops had dragged themselves out and were making their way, with the rest of the curious populace, down to the docks. Caught in the unexpected pedestrian traffic were the large wagons that moved through the city in the darkest hours of the night. They were forbidden to block the traffic during daylight hours. Dawn was approaching, and their drivers cursed as the horses moved a step at a time toward the market gate out of the city. The huge animals were normally placid, but the shouting, milling crowds unsettled them, and they jerked in their harnesses and their neighing rose above the sounds of people in the streets.

Pulling the magus by the material of his cloak, Eugenides worked his way along the line of wagons. He had almost reached the market gate itself when he found the wagon he was looking for and swung himself up onto the back of it. He seemed to the magus to move as easily with one hand as he had with two. He turned to help the magus as one of the men already sitting on the wagon bed spoke.

"That was a near thing," the man said as the wagon cleared the last of the congestion and picked up speed, rumbling through the torchlit tunnel under the city's wall. "I see you collected your prize."

"I did indeed," said Eugenides.

The wagon was only a few miles outside the city when it left the main road and bumped down narrower tracks to a farmhouse and a stable. Waiting by the stable were saddled horses, one for each of the occupants of the cart, excepting the magus and Eugenides.

Eugenides stood, with the magus beside him, as the horses

were mounted. Each of the riders nodded once to him as they rode away.

Then the riders were gone. Only Eugenides and the magus were left, and the man quietly unharnessing the cart horses. The farmhouse beside them was dark, the yard was quiet. The sky was pink and blue with the dawn, and the air was still. One of the horses sighed and stamped one huge hoof in the dust. The Thief disappeared into the stable through the open double doors and reappeared a few moments later, having removed the false hand and replaced it with a hook. He was stooped over the crosstree of a sleek messenger's chariot that he handled easily, even with one hand. He saw the magus staring and smiled.

"You see how well planned this adventure is," he said. "I arrange not only a cart but a chariot as well. Timos will drive us."

Timos led the cart horses into the stable and reappeared with a matched pair of racing horses. They were beautiful animals, graceful and excited in the morning air. Eugenides stepped back to give them plenty of room while Timos backed them to the chariot and began to fix their traces. When Timos was done and had climbed into the chariot, Eugenides stepped up as well and waved for the magus to join him.

The messenger's chariot was light and well balanced. The magus, stepping onto the woven leather flooring, felt it give under his feet. He braced himself, as he saw Eugenides was doing, and held on very tightly as the horses jumped forward and the chariot whirled around the corner of the farmhouse and back down the rutted tracks to the main road. Once on the main road, Timos let the horses choose their pace, and fields, farmhouses, olive groves, whole villages passed in a jostled blur. The horses never slowed until the sun was high overhead and Timos pulled them up at an inn. New horses were hitched into place while the three travelers stood by the chariot waiting. These, too, moved like the wind until Timos again pulled up at another inn.

There'd been no chance to ask questions when the horses were changed, and talking was out of the question in the jolting chariot.

"We'll eat and then go," Eugenides said, indicating a table under a tree by the inn. The magus moved agreeably, but very slowly, toward the shade.

"Tired?" Eugenides asked.

"Old," the magus answered. "Too old to be dragged out of my home by the machinations of someone I thought was a friend."

Eugenides stopped to look over his shoulder. "Who told Sounis that now was the time to take Eddis? Who told him to ally first with Attolia to conquer us? He'd be stomping around in Attolia's grain fields right now if it weren't for you, and you know it."

"True," the magus admitted mournfully.

"It would serve you right if I dragged you off to Eddis and locked you into a cell for the next fifty years."

The magus settled onto a bench and rested his head in his hands. "Whether I spend the rest of my life in comfort in Eddis or in jail won't be historically significant."

"If all you cared about was historical significance, you could have stayed in bed until the king's guard came for you."

The magus had been disposed to save his skin, but he knew there were greater things at stake. "Eugenides, if Sounis held Eddis, he could stop the Mede expansion and be prepared if an internal war ever arose in Attolia to drive them out. If he can't unite at least Sounis and Eddis, all three of these countries will be divided and swallowed in a historical eye blink. Even you can see that."

"One thing I see," Eugenides said, "is that everybody is always willing to throw someone else's country to the dogs. I don't have any desire to be overrun by the Medes, but I don't look forward to being overrun by Sounis either. And you don't need to worry about political naïveté. I would have much preferred to slit Sounis's throat while he slept, but his heir is hardly ready to inherit the kingdom, and we can't have a civil war in Sounis for the Mede to step in and resolve, can we? Our horses are ready." Hooking a bag that lay on the table, he held it in the air and dropped several small loaves of bread into it, then started across the courtyard to the chariot.

"Gen." The magus, still sitting on the bench, called him back.

Eugenides waited, looking at him over one shoulder.

"You've become quite ruthless in your old age," said the magus.

"I have."

If the magus was surprised when they turned off the road toward the main pass and raced inland, he didn't have the breath to ask any questions. He waited until the horses slowed and stopped on a curving stretch of empty road.

"Where are we going?"

"You are headed for a nice hunting lodge on the coastal side of the pass. I haven't left my rooms for weeks, so it would be awkward if I were seen riding up the pass with you. I'll go on foot from here and up the Oster path and then come down into the capital from the backcountry with fewer people to see me."

"If I am seen, there is no difficulty?"

"We're hoping you won't be seen, and if seen, not recognized. I'm a little more easy to distinguish, and we won't rely on luck to keep me from being noticed."

The magus looked up at the mountain and back at Eugenides.

"I made it down," the Thief said. "We'll see if I can get back up."

"There must be an easier way," said the magus. "Not that I personally would be unhappy to see you reduced to pulp on a rock pile at the base of a cliff," he added.

Eugenides smiled at the gibe, the first real smile the magus had seen from him.

"There are many easier ways, but not if I'm going to be home in a reasonable time. Enjoy the lodge. You'll have a guard, but they've been told to be pleasant to you. You are an honored guest," Eugenides said, stepping away from the chariot and nodding to the driver.

"For how long?" the magus asked as the driver turned the chariot in the narrow roadway.

Eugenides held up his arms in an elaborate shrug as the chariot jolted away.

When Attolia learned that Sounis's ships had been sunk in their harbor, she sent first for her master of spies.

There were rumors that the sabotage had been performed by a group of men dressed as Sounisian sailors returning to their ships to relieve the officers standing watch. They'd boarded the ships easily, and their access to the powder rooms had been simple. Still the queen wanted to know about the saboteurs. Had one been missing a hand?

"He hasn't left his room, Your Majesty."

"Are there servants who bring his food, get him dressed in the morning, take away his dirty clothes, empty his night jar? Are they in your pay? Is there anyone who can tell you that he has seen Eugenides in that room?"

"No, Your Majesty, but—"

"Then you can't be certain he's there, can you?"

"No, Your Majesty, but—"

"But what, Relius?"

The secretary took a careful breath. "There's no evidence, Your Majesty, that the Thief has left his rooms in the last few weeks. We have reliable reports that he argued with the queen and that she does not speak of him. Also, Your Majesty, this business involved several men, and in the past the Thief worked alone. We are not even certain that this was the work of Eddisians. The magus has disappeared, and his apprentice says that he conspired with us. We know that is incorrect, but that's all. We don't know who his masters are."

"Who else could they be?" the queen asked.

The secretary went on hesitantly, unsure of his ground. His queen had lately showered favors on her Mede ambassador, and he was reluctant to anger her. "There are the Medes to be considered, Your Majesty. A strong alliance between Sounis and Attolia is not to their advantage."

"True," said Attolia, sitting back in her throne. "We shall see where the magus turns up."

Within days of the destruction of Sounis's navy, pirates raided and burned two of the most important port cities on his islands. Piracy had grown increasingly common since the pass through Eddis had been closed to trade. Merchants carrying their goods by ship had been tempting targets, and any captain could reflag his ship to become a pirate at a moment's notice, only to change flags again and return home an honest merchant mariner.

These new pirates had worked alone and preyed on isolated sailing ships. No one expected them to join forces. Many of the islands hadn't yet learned of the destruction of the king's navy and hadn't taken even the most rudimentary precautions against sea raiders. Their harbors were open, and their towns guarded only by night watchmen patrolling the streets for drunks or thieves. The pirates had landed without warning, had looted the warehouses along the docks and burned them while many citizens were still sleeping in their beds. The citizens woke glad not to have been murdered in those beds. They sent outraged calls for assistance to their king only to hear that there was no navy to defend them and that the raiders had probably been not pirates, but Attolian warships under false flags.

With his remaining ships, Sounis attacked one of Attolia's smaller islands in revenge. More towns burned. Any hope of an alliance collapsed. Attolia regrouped her navy to defend herself from sea attack by Sounis but left the bulk of her army in the pass.

Reversing his earlier threats of war, Sounis turned to Eddis, asking for lumber for his shipyards. The ambassador from Eddis closeted himself with the king and revealed that Eddis had hired a master gunsmith in the fall and had retooled her foundries over the winter to produce cannon instead of the iron ingots she had been shipping to the Peninsula in the past. She was able to provide Sounis with the guns he needed to arm his new warships but expressed a reasonable reluctance to sell cannon that might be used against her. She demanded a show of good faith that Sounis would not ally again with Attolia.

Within a month of the disaster at the Navy Festival, the first lumbering grain wagons were on their way to Eddis to resupply the war-strained country, and Sounis's reduced navy had seized two of Attolia's most vulnerable islands. Chios and Sera were two prizes, small but wealthy in marble and artisans. They were bones of contention and had changed hands between the countries of Sounis and Attolia for hundreds of years. Once again the possessor of them, Sounis would not reform his alliance with Attolia if it meant surrendering them.

Attolia, with her navy intact, carried out her own attacks. She was willing to let Chios and Sera go. There were other islands of more strategic importance, and she turned her attention toward those. She took Capris and failed to take Anti-

Capris, its near neighbor, by only a narrow margin. Sounis lost two more of his warships.

At the suggestion of her Mede ambassador, she attacked Cymorene and secured its eastern end against Sounis. Cymorene was one of the largest of the islands, and she couldn't hope to control its mountainous interior without bringing in her army, but most of her land forces were still climbing the pass to Eddis. Eddis had hoped that the temptation of a weakened Sounis would draw them away, but Attolia continued to advance. Eddis harassed the army but was unwilling to waste her soldiers, her most precious resource. Even Attolia, with her population still unrecovered from the plague a generation before, had more men than Eddis. Her army moved steadily upward.

Sounis offered to send an army to reinforce Eddis, but she declined. Steadily losing ground in the islands, Sounis pressed Eddis for the cannon she had promised. He wanted to mount them on his island defenses until warships could be built. Two more of his supply shipments had arrived in Eddis, and she had little excuse to refuse.

The moon was down, and the hallways of the palace were lit by the glimmer of small lanterns at the intersections of corridors. The stone walls were dark and did little to reflect the light. The stone floors were covered in thin carpets. The queen of Eddis walked slowly to avoid tripping on unseen wrinkles. She walked slowly to avoid making any noise, and she walked slowly, with her head carefully held upright, to avoid the appearance of sneaking through her own palace, which was what she was doing. She wanted to talk privately to Eugenides and his father. Eugenides in his own mysterious way could arrive in her rooms at night in response to a message left with his food in the library. His father either had to be admitted by the queen's attendants or the queen had to leave the attendants and meet him elsewhere. They had agreed to meet in the library.

Eugenides was waiting for her. His father had not yet arrived.

Eddis closed the door behind her and turned. "We are discovered," she said with a rueful smile. "You were right, and I should have let you relay messages instead of trying to have a secret meeting."

"You don't look alarmed," Eugenides said. "Who saw you?"

"It was Therespides," said Eddis. "He ran into me creeping around a corner. I don't know which one of us was more surprised. Or embarrassed, for that matter."

"He guessed where you were going?"

"There's no one else in this part of the palace to be visiting. I think he was coming in from a visit down in the town."

"Why aren't you more worried?"

The queen looked down at him and smiled fondly. He had grown quite ruthless lately, but he still showed signs of naïveté from time to time. "You've heard that a liar thinks everyone else lies?"

"Yes."

"A thief thinks everyone else is stealing from him?"

"Go on—without derogatory comments about people of my profession, please."

"A philanderer thinks everyone else is philandering."

Eugenides looked blank for a moment. "Oh," he said.

"Practically incestuous," said the queen, and she bent down to kiss him on the forehead. "Not to mention a little matter of robbing the cradle. It will keep the court babbling for weeks, and I hope Sounis hears about it."

"I hardly fit into a cradle anymore, and anyone who'd believe we were amorously involved has to be crazy, but Sounis probably will hear it and believe it. Poor besotted fool."

"He's not besotted with me, just my throne."

"Besotted may not be the right word. Obsessed. And not just because he wants the throne. He wants you, though I'm not sure why."

"I'm glad you've remained a thief, Gen. As a courtly flatterer you lack something."

"It's the king's heir we should feel sorry for," Eugenides said. "Poor Sophos's heart will be breaking if he hears you love another."

Eddis laughed. "I doubt his feelings are deeply engaged."

"Rarely have I seen a more love-struck individual than the king's nephew," said Eugenides, with his hand on his heart to emphasize his sincerity.

Eddis settled herself into a chair. "It's Attolia who needs to keep thinking we don't speak, and I'm afraid Therespides has a direct line to the secretary of her archives."

"All these things I'm learning about Therespides tonight. Why don't you just drag him out in the snow and shoot him?"

Eddis shook her head, looking grave. "He's a reasonably good man and valuable in his own way. If he makes his gold selling gossip to Attolia, I don't mind. It's helpful to use him occasionally to carry erroneous information to Attolia. Still, I can hardly summon him to my throne at the morning session and say, 'Do please keep it a secret that I am meeting Eugenides in the dark of night.' Nor do I want to do it privately."

"You don't want him to be tempted?"

"Let's say that I would not like to rely on him and then be disappointed. At this point Therespides doesn't worry me."

"There are other spies you are more concerned about?"

"More than ever," said the queen. "Her army has retreated."

"She's retreating?" Eugenides sat forward in his chair.

"Not 'is retreating,' 'has retreated.' Like a cat jumping out of a bath." Eddis shook her head in admiration.

"She heard about the cannon?'

"She must have. I think she knew even before we told Sounis. In another two or three days we would have had the entire battery in place and would have been able to fire down on her. She must have known all along and been hoping to take the pass before the cannon were up on the mountain above her. It was a well-planned retreat, and her army is safely out of range now."

"Any chance that she'll drop the whole business? We've handed her naval superiority. Would taking back her islands as well as Mesos and Ianathicos satisfy her?"

Eddis shook her head. "Your father thinks not, and I agree with him. The islands have moved from empire to empire too many times to be considered a dependable possession by anyone. If we remain allied with Sounis, he is going to want those cannon. If we give him the cannon, she'll march her army back up the pass." She sighed. "I'd hoped to wipe out a large enough portion of her army that she'd have no chance of taking the pass with what was left—even if we did give this year's cannon production to Sounis. Sounis is pressing hard. I want to talk to your father about it without having the entire council looking on."

She leaned forward and dragged her chair closer to the fire. "We may as well fetch the magus out of hiding," she said. "Will you come with me?"

"On a horse?"

"You can ride in a carriage if you like. I'll have to go on horseback so people can see me."

He could hardly be so rude as to ride in a closed coach if his queen was riding outside it. He'd have to go on a horse and let everyone have a good look at him, too.

"If you like." He sighed inwardly.

chapter 9

THE HUNTING RETREAT was a summer home for the rulers of
Eddis. It was shaped like a stone megaron, with a broad, high
porch across the front, supported on four pillars, but the pillars, like the rest of the building, were wood. There was a separate structure for the cooking, lest a runaway fire burn down
the entire residence. The food was carried on a dirt path from
the kitchen to the dining room. The second story held small
dark bedrooms with unglazed windows that looked out across
the overgrown meadow to the surrounding forests. In the winter the windows were covered with shutters and the building
was uninhabited.

It was not the palace of the wealthier lowlanders, but it held
happy memories for Eddis. She dropped off her horse and
strode up the steps and across the porch to the door. Inside
was an atrium with stairs to the second floor. Her Thief followed more slowly, stiff from the ride.

Eddis stood in the atrium, talking to a man on the balcony
above her. When the Thief came in behind her, Eddis
turned.

"Elon says the magus isn't here. He's out digging up
weeds."

"Oh? Any particular weeds?" Eugenides asked the valet,
cocking his head back to address the man.

"I'm sure I couldn't say that he has a preference. We've had them all, with roots and dirt, so he can draw pictures of them." The valet's tone was replete with grievance.

"I didn't know he was a botanist," Eddis said quietly to Eugenides.

"Neither did I," answered her Thief. "He's probably trying to develop a new poison to use on us both. When will he be back?" he called to Elon.

The valet shrugged eloquently.

"Not what I had foreseen," Eddis said wryly, "though I shouldn't have expected him to be here repining. I should have started a day later and sent a messenger ahead. Surely he is not followed around by a cohort of guards?" she asked the guard commander who had appeared at the door.

The commander explained that one guard had been assigned to follow the magus to be sure he didn't wander so far that he escaped back to Sounis. That guard was changed every day as the task of hiking after the magus was not an enviable one. The rest of the guards passed their days gambling with dice or hunting to fill the cook's pot.

"Well, I hope the pot is full," Eddis said. "Have a cook pack a picnic and provisions for the men, and we will ride out again once the magus has returned." The trumpeter was sent out to blow recall. The queen looked back to the valet. "You had better pack his things."

The valet nodded. "And the weeds?" he asked.

"I think we'll leave the weeds. We'll show him some nicer ones when we stop to eat."

When the magus appeared, trailed by a footsore guard, the queen asked if they should delay to give the magus time to rest. "We mustn't overtax a gentleman of your years," she said, teasing gently.

"I believe I am stout enough to be at your disposal, Your Majesty," the magus replied gravely, "though otherwise old and very feeble."

With a reputation as a soldier only just overweighed by his reputation as a scholar, he was surrounded by armed men who judged him neither old nor feeble and watched him very carefully. He was in the presence of their queen, and the relaxed camaraderie they'd shared with the magus during his stay at the summer residence was gone.

Led by the queen, the party started back through the coastal hills. They left their path to ride up a sloping meadow to the lip of a small valley, no more than a shallow cup between two rises. "A picnic for us, I think," said the queen. "The magus and Eugenides and I will eat in the clearing."

The valley before them was filled from side to side with a heavy carpet of vines. The few trees still standing had been engulfed. Their dead branches poked through the lush greenery of the suffocating creepers. A narrow dirt path led to a small clearing where a flat green patch of grass grew. There was room for the three to sit, but they would have to leave their horses.

"Your Majesty, please," the commander of her guard pleaded in an urgent undertone. The queen only smiled.

"I'm sure you will find a comfortable place around the rim of the valley," she said. The commander sighed and bowed his head to inevitability.

"As you wish," he said.

The magus carried the saddlebag with their meal in it down to the clearing, which turned out to be a fine carpet of moss, not grass. In places where the moss was thin, paving stones showed through. The tiny open space, entirely surrounded by vines, had once been a terrace or forecourt to a building. After he'd lowered the saddlebag to the ground, the magus went to look more closely at the vines. They had smooth stems and dark matte leaves. Their bright red blossoms were tissue-thin, the five petals crumpled around the stamen and pistils.

"Don't pick them," the queen warned. "Here they are sacred to the memory of Hespira, though they are dragged out as weeds anywhere else."

The magus straightened. "Hespira?" he said, puzzled. "I don't know Hespira. Is she the goddess of the temple?" He had seen under the vines the shattered ruins of a temple.

Eddis shook her head. Eugenides had stretched out on his back and closed his eyes. "Hespira's mother planted the vines that destroyed the temple," said Eddis.

"A rival goddess?" the magus asked.

"A mortal woman," Eddis answered as she settled herself on the moss and opened the saddlebag. "The goddess Meridite abducted her daughter."

"Is there a story that goes with this?"

"Oh, yes," said Eddis.

The magus glanced over at Eugenides, who opened his eyes long enough to say flatly, "Don't look at me. I've retired from storytelling."

"Eugenides, sit up and eat, and don't be cross," said Eddis.

"Am I cross?" Eugenides asked.

"Yes," said Eddis. "Magus, don't sit there. Sit on this side." She pointed to a place on the moss, and the magus sat, seeing no difference between it and the place he had chosen himself.

"She wants the commander to have a good shot at you," Eugenides pointed out with a touch of malice. He was still lying down, and his eyes were closed. The magus looked up to the rim of the valley to see the commander and several of his soldiers standing with their feet squarely planted and their crossbows trained on him. Two others were circling the rim of the valley in order to have the magus in their sights from the far side. The magus glanced at Eugenides. He hadn't needed to look to know they were there.

"I only want the commander not to worry himself," said

Eddis calmly. "He will fret if I am between him and the magus." The queen hadn't looked up to the hillside either.

"What about the magus fretting?" Eugenides asked, and Eddis lifted her head from the package she was unwrapping to look at her guest.

"Don't be alarmed," she reassured him. "They are only being cautious, not bloodthirsty."

"It would be one way to prove your loyalty to your king," Eugenides said.

"A fatal way," observed the magus.

"True, but they can't be too careful," said Eugenides. "It might be worth it to you to clear your name. Did you miss the subtle negotiations at the edge of the valley? The commander didn't want to be left behind. He didn't want the queen alone in the valley with you."

The magus had heard the exchange without understanding its significance. He pointed out what was obvious to him: "But we aren't alone." Eugenides lay on the moss less than a man's-length away.

"You may as well be. I never would have been considered a match for a soldier of your reputation," said Eugenides. Unspoken was the assumption that he was no longer a match for anyone. There was a dryness to his words that was almost, but not quite, bitterness.

The queen explained. She spoke quietly, but her words had sharp edges nonetheless. "In his life Eugenides has gone to great lengths to portray himself as a noncombatant, so people assume he is. He has to live with the fruits of his labors and sometimes finds them unsweet. Sit up and eat," she said to her Thief, and this time he levered himself into a sitting position.

He ate with his left hand. The hook on the end of his arm lay at rest in his lap.

"When do you wear the hook and when do you wear the

false hand?" the magus asked with a straightforwardness that surprised the queen.

"The hand is less noticeable," Eugenides answered, unoffended. "But the hook has a number of uses, and the false hand isn't good for anything. So I teeter between vanity and function."

"And when you stop teetering, where will you be?" the magus asked.

Eugenides shrugged. "In the madhouse . . . or maybe in a nice home in the suburbs, keeping books."

The magus suspected that the very blandness of his voice covered over some ugliness the way a covering of leaves can hide a pit trap. The magus didn't risk falling. He changed the subject.

"Would you tell me the story of Hespira?" he asked Eddis.

Before she answered, Eddis looked up to check the position of the sun. "I'll tell it to you if you like. We have the time. Eugenides, if you are going to lie down again, put your head on my knee."

The magus lifted his eyebrows. The queen noticed that he raised both at the same time. Eugenides had lately taken to raising just one when he was being amused, and she wondered whom he was copying. Eugenides rested his head on her lap. Pensively she tried to brush away the crease between his brows. She knew the magus wondered at his bad temper.

"We are sending a message to the queen of Attolia," she explained, speaking to the magus though she continued to look down at Eugenides. "My guards will see how fond I have grown of my Thief, and gossip. The gossip will carry to Attolian spies, who will report to Relius, Attolia's master of spies, and he will carry the news to her."

"Her secretary of the archives," murmured the magus.

"Hmm?" asked the queen.

"Secretary of the archives, Relius. Master of spies is so—"

"Accurate?"

"Overly direct," said the magus.

Eddis laughed.

"Attolia has been unaware of Eugenides's activity?" asked the magus.

"As has Sounis," said the queen, "until now."

"And what has happened to change that, if I may ask? I had a most relaxing stay in your lodge, but not an informative one."

"Yes, I didn't know you had an interest in botany," said Eddis.

"I don't really. I have a friend who does. He isn't well enough to travel and relies on acquaintances to send him samples and drawings. And how is your war progressing?" he asked, declining to be sidetracked by scholarly inquiry.

Eddis smiled. "Seeing himself betrayed by Attolia, Sounis has been most kind in relieving the strain of Attolia's embargo on Eddis. We have received several shipments of grain and other necessities in exchange for a promised delivery of cannon, which I regret to say we are going to be unable to deliver."

"So you turn a two-way war into a three-way one?"

"A war we would lose to a war we might survive."

"Why not take Sounis as an ally against Attolia and fight a war you might win?" the magus asked.

"Because as an ally Sounis would expect to bring his army across Eddis, and that will never happen while I reign," said Eddis with absolute conviction.

"I see," said the magus. "And for the duration of this war . . . ?" he asked.

"You will be a prisoner in Eddis," said the queen. "I am sorry. We will try to make you comfortable."

The magus bowed his head politely.

"The goddess Meridite had a son by a blacksmith. You know Meridite?"

"Yes," said the magus.

"Good," said the queen, and began her story.

The goddess Meridite had a son by a blacksmith. It was an unusual union, and some say that she was tricked into it by the other gods, but whatever she thought of the father, she seemed fond of the son. His name was Horreon, and she watched over him as he grew up. The blacksmith had no wife, and so father and son lived alone, and Meridite visited from time to time to see how the boy was growing. He worked by his father's side, learning his trade from a very early age. He had a gift, no doubt from his mother. Everything he made was the finest of its kind. When he was young, he made horse-shoes lighter and stronger than anyone else's. His blades were sharper; his swords never broke.

His father was a surly man to begin with and grew more so, jealous of his son. Finally Horreon left the blacksmithing trade and became an armorer. His forge he set up deep in the caves of Hephestia's Sacred Mountain. He used the heat from its fires to work the metal and chained a monster to his forge to drive the bellows to blow up the flames. The shades traveling to the underworld and those summoned back by sacrifice to provide prophecies were said to stop on their way to speak with him.

Though he was served by the lesser spirits of the mountain, he had no human company, or anyway very little. His armor was said to preserve the wearer from any attack, but it took a brave man to venture into the caves to request his work, and there were not many. Those that chose to venture into the caves had to find a guide, a spirit or a shade, to lead them to Horreon's forge.

One day, his mother came down to visit him and found

him alone and melancholy. He had sent away the lesser spirits and was sitting by his forge, idly tapping his hammer and watching the sparks fly up. She asked him what grieved him, ready to put it right, and he told her he wanted a wife. Surely, she said, he could have any he chose.

But what wife would choose him? he asked. The goddess looked at him, and it was true. He was not attractive, no more than his father had been. He was short, and his arms and shoulders were massive with the strength of his work. His brow was low; no doubt his eyebrows nearly joined as he scowled into his fires. As a child, standing at his father's side, he'd been scarred by the sparks that flew from the anvil. Where the wounds had been sooty, the scars were black. His face was pockmarked, as were his hands and his arms. He lived his life in the dark so that his eyes would be able to distinguish to a degree the colors of heated metal. What wife would choose to live with him?

What matter if she chose or not? said the goddess. The wife he chose would have him. She was the goddess Meridite, and she would see his wishes granted.

His wish was for a wife who chose him, he said. He had no heart for an unwilling wife. The goddess Meridite kissed her son on his black brow and went away.

She spent some time looking for a girl both pretty and well mannered and willing to live in a dark hole but found none. She remembered that a pretty face is not the best indicator of a tractable wife and looked among the ugly girls, but not even an ugly girl would marry a man who was pockmarked, who worked in the dark with spirits and monsters. No father would let his daughter go to such a husband, so Meridite turned back to the pretty girls and looked for one with no father to protect her. Now the prettiest of the girls was the daughter of Callia, who was a widow and a priestess of Proas. You know Proas? Yes, that's right, the god of green and growing things.

One day, as the girl walked the road between the temple of Proas and her home, the goddess Meridite saw her. Appearing at a bend in the road, Meridite called out to the girl, and the girl turned. Meridite looked her over carefully and could see no flaw that would make her an unsuitable wife. The goddess held out her hands and took the girl's. "Beautiful child, can you sing?"

"Yes, Goddess," Hespira answered.

Meridite was a little cross to be identified as an immortal so readily. She pouted. "You know me?" she said.

"Yes, Goddess," said Hespira.

"Then you know I have a son?"

"Yes, Goddess." Hespira knew she had any number of sons and waited to hear which one the goddess spoke of. She was patient. It is the gift of all the followers of Proas, and no doubt she had learned it from her mother. She was also clever. If the goddess had looked beyond Hespira's beauty, she would have seen this, but she didn't look.

"Horreon. He's ill, very likely he will die." Meridite sighed.

"I am sorry," said Hespira, though Meridite didn't seem overly concerned. Meridite only thought it would seem unlikely that she was looking for a wife for her son if he was supposed to be on the verge of death.

"He asked me to find someone to sing to him," said Meridite. "Will you come? "

One does not refuse a goddess. Hespira agreed but asked if she might send a message to her mother. Meridite consented. She called a dove to bear the message, but once the bird was out of sight, it dropped to the ground dead, and so the message disappeared.

"Come to my temple first," said Meridite, and offered Hespira food. She declined. The goddess pouted, and Hespira agreed to have something to drink. When the goddess wasn't looking, she carefully tipped the drink into the basket she carried. Then, quite cheerful, Meridite took Hespira down into the mountain along the twisting black caves in total darkness. Hespira was frightened. She had not reckoned on being so hopelessly lost. She wondered if her mother was looking for her.

Her mother had waited until the end of the day, and as the sun was setting, she had walked the road between the temple and her home, calling her daughter's name. When there was no answer, she had gone from door to door, asking at each house. The people there could only shake their heads and say that they hadn't seen the girl.

Meridite, confident that the drink she had given Hespira would leave her ready to fall in love with Horreon when she saw him, gave up any pretense that he was ill. Her son had wanted a willing wife, and lo, Meridite had made one willing. She smiled in the darkness, pleased with her gift to her son.

She brought the girl to the edge of the cave where the forge was and left her. Suddenly alone in the dark, Hespira stopped at the entrance and stood looking into the space before her. The cave was empty of minions. There were no spirits; the fire was quiet; the chained monster slept curled at Horreon's feet. Horreon himself sat on the stones at the lip of the forge. The fire was dim, and by its light he was gently tapping a bit of metal he had heated. Each time he tapped the metal, sparks flew up into the air. Glowing with their own light, they danced in front of the forge, swinging in circles and dipping in sequence like the dancers at a festival.

"They are lovely," said Hespira from the entranceway, and Horreon looked up, startled.

"If you have no light, you have come a long way in the dark," he said. "Are you a shade?"

"No," said Hespira. "I am a living maid." She stepped forward, carefully picking her way across the rough ground of the cave floor.

At the sound of her voice the monster by the forge awoke and slunk toward her, his chain rattling out behind him. He was black and the size of a large dog, with leathery black wings that whispered as they dragged behind him and claws that scrabbled against the stone beneath him. Hespira hesitated. Surely Horreon could have no reputation as an armorer if all of his customers were eaten. Bravely she held one hand forward as she would to a strange dog, and the bat-winged creature lifted its head and a forked tongue licked out once and then twice to brush her skin before the monster turned back to the forge and lay down again while Horreon looked on.

"You wish armor for your lover or your brother?" he asked.

"No," said Hespira. "Your mother brought me."

Horreon scowled suddenly, his brows drawing down, and Hespira's heart quailed.

"And why did my mother bring you?" Horreon asked.

"She said you had asked for someone to sing to you," Hespira answered.

Horreon still looked suspicious, but he scowled less.

"Sing, then," he said gruffly.

Hespira stopped in the middle of the floor. After a moment she opened her mouth and sang the nanny song about the boy who was rude and got not and the boy who was good and got much.

Horreon grunted. "Forgive me my rudeness," he said.

"I may," Hespira said.

Horreon looked her over, reevaluating what he saw. "When might you forgive me?" he asked.

"When I have a chair to sit in, and a pillow," said Hespira, "and light to see with whom I speak."

Horreon laughed. It was a rumble in his chest that Hespira didn't at first recognize. Then the armorer stood and bowed and offered her his arm, and together they stepped across the cave to a stair and door that led to a room lit with lamps where there was a single chair.

"No pillow," Hespira pointed out.

Horreon stuck his head out the door and bellowed in a voice that seemed likely to split the stone walls around them, "A *pillow!*" and a moment later he reached into the hallway and pulled back an embroidered pillow. He closed the door, then saw Hespira's look of reproach and opened it again to thank whoever or whatever lingered in the hall. Horreon brought the pillow and placed it in the back of the chair, then offered the chair to Hespira. She sat. Horreon sat at her feet, and they smiled at each other.

Callia searched and found no sign of her daughter. Finally she went to the temple of her god and made a sacrifice and begged him to tell her what had become of Hespira. The god sent her into the forest to await an answer. There she saw the trees twisting, their branches dipping and reaching like hands passing a burden until finally the dead dove dropped at her feet. She bent and collected the message from its leg and knew where Hespira had gone. She went to the caves in the Hephestial Mountain and searched through them for Horreon's forge, but mortals cannot find the forge without a guide, and she had none. She wandered through the darkness bearing a small lamp and calling her daughter. She could hear Hespira singing somewhere in the dark, but the sound of her voice was carried through the caverns and gave her no direction. Her daughter, in the rooms with Horreon, could not hear her calling. Horreon heard and for a moment was silent. Hespira asked him what was the matter.

"Nothing," he said. Already he was unable to bear parting with Hespira, right or wrong. Reluctantly he sent the shades to drive her mother away. Terrified, the woman fled. Stumbling out of the caves and falling to the ground in the moonlight, she sobbed for her lost child. She went back to the temple of her god and sacrificed again, begging him to restore her daughter, but he answered that the gods could not bicker over what befell mortals. This was not a helpful response, but not unexpected either. Hespira's mother pointed out that she was not any mortal; she was his priestess and surely deserved his protection. Proas only reminded her that as his priestess she had gifts that she might use to address the difficulty herself.

Hespira's mother went away and waited as the long, cold winter passed. Horreon and Hespira were happy together in the dim light under the mountain. Hespira was unaware of time passing, thinking that she spent an evening there in the room by the forge, but Horreon knew. Hiding it from Hespira, he fretted. Already he loved her as he had never loved anything in his life. His father had been a cold man, jealous of his son. His mother granted his wishes from time to time, but otherwise he had rarely seen her. All his life he had known the forge and the colors of hot metal and little else. Now he wanted Hespira and no one and nothing else.

Hespira told him stories of the world, stories of kings and queens in their palaces, plain stories about her neighbors bickering over missing chickens and the disappearing melons from one neighbor's garden, ordinary things that he soaked up like the sunshine. She sang to him, and he listened, content.

In the springtime Hespira's mother wrapped her head in a shawl and bent her back under a tray of seedlings and came to Meridite's temple here in this valley. It was the favorite of Meridite, graceful in its proportions, protected from the wind, with a forecourt surrounded by a garden almost as lovely as the gardens around the temple of Proas. Hespira's mother came as a supplicant and offered to add her seedlings to the garden. She planted them carefully around the base of the temple, the first of the vines that grow here now. She had nurtured them from fall through the winter and invested them with the gift of growing that she had from Proas. The vines, when they were planted, quickly grew, and the tiny rootlets clung to the temple walls and slipped between the stones to loosen the mortar. When Meridite saw the damage they were doing, she ordered her priests to pull them down. But the priests could not, and the vines grew higher. The facing stones began to fall, and Meridite came to blast the vines herself and realized she could not overcome the gift of Proas.

Irked, she went to Proas and demanded he remove the vines, but Proas declined. They were none of his doing, the vines on Meridite's favorite temple. She must find the cause if she wanted a solution. So Meridite sought out the priestess of Proas and commanded her to remove the vines, but the priestess told the goddess the vines would die when her daughter was returned to her.

Meridite was much taken aback. Mortals do not challenge the gods. Only once had a mortal dared and he'd been driven insane for his insolence.

"Your daughter?" Meridite couldn't guess whom she meant.

"Hespira," said the mother.

The goddess's mouth opened in an O of surprise. "That lovely girl," she said. "She's very happy, you know," said Meridite, hoping to placate the woman.

"Then I hope you will be happy with your shattered temple," said the priestess, and turned her back on the goddess to go back through her doorway.

"Dear, dear," said Meridite. She loved her son, but she loved her temple more.

"Come out again, you wretched woman," said the goddess, "and we will go collect her together." So the goddess and the girl's mother went to the caves of the Hephestial Mountain.

In a pool of light cast by a lamp, Horreon sat on a footstool listening to Hespira sing. She sang about the rain dropping in the spring and the grass greening, and Horreon bowed his head. "Would you miss the rain?" he asked in a low voice.

"Yes," said Hespira.

"And the sun?"

"Yes," said Hespira.

"Will you leave me to return to the sun and the rain?"

"No," she answered. "I will stay."

Horreon took her in his arms. Her head lay on his shoulder, and he cupped it with one large hand the way a mother cradles her child and knew that he could not keep her.

"My mother brought you," he said.

"I chose to come," said Hespira.

"Did she bring you here from your home, or did she take you to her temple first?"

"She brought me to her temple first."

"And did you eat there?"

"No," said Hespira, smiling into his shoulder that he would think her foolish enough to eat at his mother's table.

Horreon didn't ask if she drank anything. He couldn't bear to ask and hear the answer, and he saw no need of it.

"Come," he said, and led Hespira through the caverns to the cave that opened onto the mountainside.

There they met the goddess and Hespira's mother. Hespira's mother ran to her, taking her daughter in her arms. Horreon looked away. He released Hespira's hand, but she clung to his.

"Did you worry?" she asked her mother.

"It is a year you have been gone," her mother told her.

"It was an evening, no more," protested Hespira. She turned to look at Horreon, and he looked down in shame.

He said, "This close to the Sacred Mountain, time ebbs and flows. A current can carry you forward a year in an eye blink if you choose."

"And you chose?" Hespira accused, and Horreon nodded.

He'd meant to carry her forward a hundred years, out of the reach of her mother forever, but had changed his mind.

"Didn't she suit you?" Meridite said. Looking at the girl carefully for the first time, she saw that she was not just pretty, she was clever. Who wants a clever girl? "Just as well," said Meridite, "that her mother wants her back."

"She suited too well, Mother," said Horreon, and Meridite was startled to see that he was angry and that he was angry at her.

"You were bringing her back," the goddess said.

"I was letting her go," said Horreon, and he turned back toward his cave, but Hespira still held him.

"Well, if you like her, keep her," Meridite snapped. "What's one temple to me? Just because it is my favorite, don't think I can't do without it."

"I asked for a woman who chose to be my wife," said Horreon.

"I chose," said Hespira.

"See," said Meridite.

"She ate nothing in your temple, Mother," said Horreon. "What did she drink?"

Meridite flushed as only a goddess can.

"Nothing," said Hespira, tugging at Horreon's hand until he turned to look at her. "Nothing," she assured him. "I tipped it into the basket I carried."

"Oh," sniped Meridite, "you are clever." But Horreon only stood blinking like an owl in sunlight.

"I chose," Hespira said again, and Horreon believed her. So Hespira took leave of her mother and returned with him to the caves of the Sacred Mountain, and the vines of Hespira's mother grew over Meridite's temple. When Hespira left the mountain to visit her mother, as she did from time to time, the vines were dormant, but otherwise they grew and grew until the mortar was all picked to dust and the temple fell in on itself and nothing was left but a pile of stones covered in green leaves and red flowers.

As for Hespira and Horreon, they were mortals, but who knows how time passes at the skirt of Hephestia's Sacred Mountain? Many believe they live still, and miners claim to hear her voice, singing to him behind the sounds of their picks.

The magus was quiet when the story was done. He looked at Eddis with new admiration. She sat cross-legged with the open packages of food around her, quite comfortable but then a little embarrassed by his regard.

"And Hespira's mother?" the magus asked finally. "Did she miss her daughter?"

"Oh, she grew used to the idea," said Eddis. "Mothers must."

"Alternatively, she lost her mind and wandered the caves of the mountain, endlessly calling for her daughter, and *that's* what the miners hear," said Eugenides without opening his eyes.

"There are a number of different ways to tell the story," Eddis admitted.

"I didn't realize that so much of the teller could be invested in the stories," the magus said. He was used to the dry records of scholarship without the voice of the storyteller shaping and changing the words to suit an audience and a particular view of the world. He'd heard Eugenides tell his stories, but hadn't realized the Thief's interpretations were more than a personal aberration.

"Go on," said Eugenides with a smile, his eyes still closed. "Tell my queen she's debasing the old myths created by superior storytellers centuries ago."

"I wouldn't dare," said the magus, shaking his head.

"Surely they tell stories like these everywhere?" the queen asked. "You must have heard them from your nurse when you were a boy."

The magus shook his head. Eugenides nudged the queen. He knew that the magus had been raised by strangers when his family had died of the plague. He had been apprenticed very young, at his own request, to a scholar in the city, and when his scholarly training had not at first proven lucrative enough to support him, he had taken to soldiering. There had likely not been time for stories in his youth.

After a pause the queen asked, "How will you occupy yourself, Magus, during your stay?"

"Perhaps I will collect more stories," the magus answered with a smile.

"What about your history of the Invasion?" Eugenides asked.

"As most of it remains in Sounis, my work on it will necessarily be curtailed," said the magus, frowning at him.

"I could fetch it for you," Eugenides offered.

"You will not!" The magus and the queen spoke together.

Eugenides smiled again, pleased to have gotten a rise out of both of them.

"Better I should recopy it from scratch," said the magus.

"You may have the library to work in," said the queen graciously.

Eugenides opened his eyes at last and started to sit up. "What? In my library? Have him underfoot every day?"

"My library," the queen reminded her Thief.

"You've only yourself to blame," the magus pointed out, smiling at the way the tables had turned.

"Agh," said Eugenides, lying back down and covering his face with his arm.

Eddis smiled, relieved that his bad temper had passed for the time being.

"Your Majesty?" The secretary of the archives waited in the doorway for Attolia to recognize him.

She was being disturbed at a late supper she was enjoying by herself, having been too busy to eat during the day. The Mede ambassador had tried to join her, but she'd soothed his feathers and sent him away, pleading an indisposition that would allow her only clear soup and bread. "And poor food makes for poor company, Nahuseresh," she'd warned, only half joking, and he had politely excused himself. He liked meat with his meals, and Attolia knew it. She had just dipped a little bread into her soup when Relius knocked and entered.

"What is it?" she asked.

"The king's magus of Sounis. He's been located."

"And?"

"He's in Eddis, Your Majesty. He was evidently in a hunting lodge in the coastal province."

She waited. Only Sounis would be surprised to hear of his move to the capital. She didn't think Relius would have interrupted her meal for a small bit of unsurprising news.

"The queen of Eddis collected him personally," Relius said. "She and her Thief. They evidently picnicked on the way back. They are reported to be . . . close." It was the mildest term to describe the gossip that was current in the Eddisian court. Probably the affair was one of long standing and his spies had been unaware of it. If the queen of Eddis and her Thief had been pretending to be at odds with each other, it could only have been to conceal his efforts on her behalf: the destruction of Sounis's navy and the removal of his magus.

"Get out," the queen ordered abruptly.

The servants and the secretary waited outside the closed doors of the private dining room, listening to the sounds of china shattering as the dinner dishes were swept off the table and onto the floor, followed by nearby amphoras and one of the heavy carved dining chairs as the usually cold-blooded queen picked it off the ground and threw it. The silverware from the table rang for a few moments after bouncing on the tiles. When it was quiet, the servants knocked and entered, careful not to creep in. The queen did not appreciate creeping. Attolia was once again in her chair, having righted it herself. Her hands were in her lap, and her face was impassive. She was thinking. As the servants righted the dining table and cleared away the mess, she tried to assess the danger that Eugenides had become.

There was a new magus in Sounis to carry the news to the king. He didn't think his tenure in the position would be lasting, and he sorely hoped to leave the post with his neck intact.

"He was working for Eddis, then," the king said.

The new magus hesitated for a moment, weighing his dedication to truth against his desire not to irritate the already testy king. He was a scholar dragged into this new position by the king's command. He was not a courtier. Against his better judgment, he chose truth.

"I believe not, Your Majesty," he said reluctantly.

"Not working for Eddis? Then what the hell is he doing there? Vacationing?"

"I believe he is not there entirely of his own volition, Your Majesty."

"What's that mean?" the king asked impatiently.

"The apprentice that reported meeting an Attolian outside the magus's rooms, I think he was mistaken."

"That's obvious enough or my magus would be in Attolia, wouldn't he?" the king snapped.

The new magus pressed on. "He was deliberately misled, Your Majesty. I think it was an Eddisian who intended to be taken as an Attolian and that he gave that apprentice gold to betray my predecessor for the purpose of misdirection."

"If you can't say that more clearly, I can find someone else who can," the king warned.

The new magus struggled on. "The apprentice assumed

that the Attolians had used the magus for their purposes and finished with him, that they wanted the magus betrayed and eliminated. On the contrary, I think my predecessor was quite innocent. The Thief of Eddis himself gave the apprentice the gold and did so because only if my predecessor was afraid for his life could he be induced to flee to Eddis."

"Eugenides? In the megaron?" Sounis had been angry enough when his magus's apprentice had come to tell him that the magus allowed Attolian spies to wander through his hallways. That Eugenides had been in the palace was chilling. "What the hell was he doing, then?" the king snarled.

"Well, stealing your magus, sir."

The king sat blinking in his chair. Then he jumped to his feet, shouting for an officer of his guard.

chapter 10

THE MORNING AFTER he and the queen returned from their journey across Eddis to collect the magus, Eugenides rose early, his body aching. He rode poorly with one hand, though no worse than he had ridden with two. The queen had been content to go at a walk. People had come out on the streets of the city and down from their farms to stand by the road and watch them pass. They hadn't cheered their queen. They weren't a cheering population, but they'd smiled, and waved, pleased as much by the sight of Eugenides as of Eddis. Eugenides had wished for the ground to open and swallow him. Thinking of the stares, he shuddered.

When his bare feet touched the cold floor, he shuddered again. The mornings were brisk in the mountains. He muttered curses under his breath as he rummaged with his hand through the neatly folded shirts in his wardrobe. His father's valet tidied things whenever Eugenides turned his back, and in the days he'd been away in Sounis a number of his rattier belongings had disappeared entirely.

"Oh, how inconspicuous I will be when next I am in Attolia," he said out loud, "dressed in Eddisian formalwear with gold frogs on the front." He cursed again when he couldn't find his sword without moving every last thing off the shelf across the bottom of the wardrobe. He left what he'd moved in a pile on the floor. It made the room seem more like his own.

"I should just go back to sleep," he grumbled, but he dragged out the sword and the sheath as well as the belt and tossed them onto his unmade bed, leaving oil stains on the covers. Someone had made sure the sword wouldn't rust while he wasn't using it. He opened the curtains to his room and complained—to himself; there wasn't anyone else to listen—that it was still dark outside, but he couldn't ignore the sunshine glowing on the peaks of the mountains across the valley. Only when he sat at his desk and reached for the hook and the metal and leather cup that fitted over the stump of his right wrist was he quiet. He sat for a moment, holding it in his hand before he put it back, and looked for the cotton sleeve he put over his arm before the prosthetic.

He found the sleeve, but couldn't find the small clasp that clipped the fabric to itself and kept the sleeve fitting snugly. He remembered that he'd dropped it undressing the night before and hadn't heard it hit the floor. It was lost therefore in the pattern of the wool carpet in front of the fire and would probably take half an hour to find. Sighing, he pulled open a drawer in the desk and ran his fingers through the clutter inside until he found a substitute. He pinned on the sleeve and carefully smoothed the wrinkles from it before he gritted his teeth and pushed his arm into the leather interior of the base of the hook. It was a tight fit, in order to give him some ability to catch and pull things. If he wore it too long, the skin of his arm was white and bloodless when the hook came off, and though he'd grown calluses where it pinched, he often had blisters.

More bothersome were the phantom pains he still had in a hand that was no longer there. He woke sometimes in the night to an ache in his right palm where he'd injured it trying to escape Attolia. The injury had never had a chance to heal. Eugenides expected the pain of it would plague him until he was dead. He didn't like to think about the missing hand, but he sometimes caught himself reaching with his left hand to rub his right when it felt sore.

Grumbling again, he pushed his stocking feet into boots that he'd had made when he found his old boots had gotten too small over the previous winter, hung his sword belt and sword over his shoulder, and took himself down to the armorer's courtyard, where trainees and soldiers alike were stretching their muscles and checking their weapons before beginning their exercises. The armorer's forge was open on two sides to the courtyard, and Eugenides went there to drop his sword on a bench.

The armorer nodded. "You'll need a new one," he said. "Balance won't be right in that." The courtyard had fallen silent.

"Do you have a practice sword I could use?" Eugenides asked, his back to the silence.

The armorer nodded and pulled one down from the racks on the wall.

As Eugenides took the sword, someone stepped into the shed behind him, and he turned to see his father.

Eugenides nodded a greeting. His father waved him out onto the training ground. As they walked together, Eugenides noticed his father's stare.

"Do you think she'll not notice?" his father finally asked.

"Notice what?" said Eugenides innocently.

"Her missing fibula pin with the rubies and gold beads pinning up your sleeve."

"Garnets and gold beads."

"The man said they were rubies."

"They say there's no hope for liars and fools in this world."

"And where does that leave you?" his father asked pointedly.

Eugenides laughed. "In possession of the queen's garnet fibula pin, and serve her right. I told her not to wear it with that orange scarf from Ebla. Is it always so quiet down here?" he asked.

Busy noises filled the open court, and the grim smile of the minister of war passed almost too quickly to be seen.

"You'll start with the basic exercises."

"If you say so," Eugenides said, radiating reluctance.

"I do," said his father.

Much later, covered in sweat, Eugenides was cursing comfortably. The stiffness of the horseback ride had been replaced by more current aches and pains. "I'd forgotten how much I hated this," he said.

His father replied, "If you wouldn't overwork yourself the first day, you might be less sore."

Eugenides looked up at the sky, where the sun was clearing the top of the palace's high wall. "It's late," he said, surprised. The courtyard around them was empty. Even the armorer had banked his fire and disappeared. "No wonder I want my breakfast."

The minister of war shook his head. He'd known from the first that his youngest son, for all his complaints, had the concentration and the patience to be a great swordsman. They were the same virtues Eugenides's grandfather had admired in him. The minister of war still regretted, privately, that his son hadn't been willing to be a soldier and had to remind himself that Eugenides might still have lost his hand. Neither profession was a safe one.

When the queen met with her council in the map room, Eugenides attended. There were surprised looks from the members of the council, most of whom were unaware that the Thief's reclusion had been a sham. As it was no longer possible to pretend that he was not at her service, his queen had asked him to hear the advice of her counselors for himself, rather than repeated secondhand. His official duties, however, were nebulous. He was not a minister and did not sit at the table. He settled into a seat against the wall.

By leaning forward slightly and looking between two of the men seated at the table, Eddis could watch him. Halfway through the meeting, he leaned his chair back against the map painted on the wall behind him and closed his eyes.

The maps depicted Sounis and the islands off the coast. Eddis and Attolia were represented, as well as more distant countries. The farther the countries from Eddis, the less accurate the maps. They had been painted more than a hundred years earlier and were more decorative than useful. The more useful maps were painstakingly inked on large sheets of vellum and laid out on various tables around the room.

The queen rubbed her temples and summarized the reports before her. "The cannon will not be delivered to Sounis. He has heard about the magus and knows that it was not Attolia that sabotaged his navy. His soldiers tried to seize the last delivery of grain and supplies just inside the pass. They couldn't recover the wagons, so they ran them into the river there. I am sorry we couldn't get those supplies up the mountain, but we have the other shipments, and we will keep the cannon."

She drummed her fingers on the arm of her chair and went on. "Sounis is going to empty his treasury to buy ships. Without our cannon, I don't know how he will arm them except to look for an ally who will provide both ships and firepower. We can hope he won't find one.

"Attolia has taken every advantange of her naval superiority over Sounis. I am sure you have all heard the rumors that she has retaken Chios and Sera. She's taken Thicos as well. We could hope that this would keep her happy, but there's no sign that she's moving her army away from the base of the pass. The peace emissary we sent was rebuffed. There will be no trade with Attolia or with Sounis, and we can expect a hard winter.

"The late-summer windstorms will be here soon. After that, with the navies in harbors, I think we'll need to be prepared to defend ourselves on all fronts until the winter snows close the pass."

"The neutral islands?" someone in the council asked. "Will Attolia seize those as well?"

"It depends on how well her naval battles go and how strong she's feeling. A neutral territory is an asset to both sides if they are evenly divided; it's a safe harbor they don't actually have to defend. If Attolia continues to have the upper hand, she may seize the neutrals. They've been warned not to resist, and we'll hope for the best."

"And the pirates?" another counselor asked.

"Neither side has the resources right now to patrol the sea lanes. Piracy is continuing to grow at a rate that I am sure surprises no one here." There were a few chuckles from around the table. They weren't surprised.

One by one, the ministers presented their reports on the distribution of the grain, the consumption of resources, the disposition of the armed forces, and the other vital statistics of her nation. When the meeting was over, they stood, bowed courteously, and left their queen to consider the information.

Eugenides remained, his chair still tipped back and his eyes still closed. Eddis sat watching him. His eyebrows were drawn together, and there was a sharp crease between them, which meant that his arm probably hurt him. He never mentioned any discomfort and snapped if anyone asked him about it. Otherwise he had grown very polite and very withdrawn. He rarely began conversation on his own, and people hesitated to speak to him when the crease in his brow deepened to a scowl, betraying the pain his arm caused him on bad days.

Eddis wasn't sure that Eugenides still dedicated offerings to his god. Certainly no one complained to her anymore of missing earrings or other baubles. Eddis had noticed her fibula pin reappearing on Eugenides's sleeve, but that had disappeared before he left for Attolia the final time. Eddis had heard several people, out of the thief's hearing, lamenting the loss of his acerbic comments on the court but found that she missed his grin more. He still smiled from time to time, his smiles sweeter for their infrequency, but he no longer grinned.

She sighed. "Attolia has an excellent advisor," she said.

Eugenides opened one eye and then closed it again.

"Who?" he asked.

"The Medean ambassador. I'm sure he told her to take Thicos and to attack Cymorene. It's not of much strategic importance to her, but it will be to the Medes if they control a territory on this side of the Middle Sea. Evidently, Attolia and the Mede are as close as you and I are rumored to be."

"Ornon said she would have hanged me but for him," Eugenides said. Ornon was the ambassador Eddis had sent to Attolia on her Thief's behalf.

"You don't remember yourself?"

Eugenides shook his head. "That part's very hazy," he said.

Eddis didn't ask what memories were clearer. She could guess.

"I suppose I am indebted to him, then," she said.

The front two legs of his chair dropped to the floor abruptly, and he opened his eyes to glare at her. She'd offended him.

"Am I supposed to wish that you were dead, Gen?" she asked.

They stared at each other. Finally he raised his chin and said, "No, you are not supposed to wish that I were dead, and no, you are not supposed to feel indebted to that Mede bastard, and no, I don't need a lecture on self-pity, and I don't want to hear about all the people in this country who lose their hands or their feet to frostbite every winter."

He propped his chair back against the wall behind him and crossed his arms, looking sullen.

"Touchy today, Gen?"

He sighed. "Oh, shut up."

"How many people in a given winter lose a hand or foot to frostbite?" she asked gently.

"Not that many. Usually it's just the fingers and toes that go. Quite a few of those, though."

"Galen told you?"

"Mmm-hm."

"How tactful of him."

Eugenides smiled painfully. "I asked him."

Eddis smiled painfully back.

"What are you thinking when you look like that?" Eugenides asked.

"I'm thinking of murdering the queen of Attolia," Eddis admitted.

Eugenides stood up and turned his back on her to look out one of the deeply set, narrow windows. "I hate that Mede," he said.

"Gen, it was *Attolia* that cut off your hand, wasn't it?" Eddis asked.

Eugenides shrugged. "Would we be at war if I had been hanged?" he asked.

"Yes," said Eddis. Truthfulness made her add, "Maybe."

"Can you deny this started the war, then?" Eugenides held up his mutilated arm.

"No." Eddis had to concede the point. "But as I said, Attolia cut off your hand."

"Because of the Mede," Eugenides answered. "If he hadn't spoken, she would have hanged me. Ornon had her angry enough to have me drawn and quartered and be done. Not," he added, truthful in turn, "that I would have enjoyed being drawn and quartered."

"And could the Mede have known he was inciting a war?" Eddis asked.

"Oh, yes," said the Thief.

Eddis was quiet, looking down at the table in front of her, covered with reports on casualties and the cost of the war with Attolia. "Then I will not consider myself in his debt." She looked over the stacks of paper that detailed her remaining resources, the size of her army, the supply of food, the ammunition. "He's got troopships sailing in the straits," she said. "They are like crows waiting to fall on the bodies. I wonder if Attolia knows."

Attolia knew. She'd known before they left their own harbor that they were being provisioned to patrol her coast. She knew how many of them there were and how heavily they were manned and how many cannon they carried. She knew that her barons were as well informed. They were quiet these days, like little birds hiding in the shrubbery when the fox passes by. She was fortunate, she also knew, that the Mede emperor had sent her an ambassador who was physically as well as politically attractive. Her court knew she had short patience for flattery, and she rarely heard it, but Nahuseresh's she accepted with smiles, delighting in the compliments he showered on her. Better than his compliments was the consternation on the faces of her barons as they watched her dipping her eyes at him and looking up from under her lashes, just the way she had seen her youngest attendants flirting with their lovers. Attolia was enjoying the Mede's company very much. She was happy to have him think her a womanly instead of a warrior queen. When he escorted her, she was receptive to his verbal sallies, a complacent object of his suggestive caresses as he linked arms with her and held her a little closer than was appropriate. She hoped no one told Nahuseresh how she'd treated the last person who'd tried to flatter her, though perhaps if someone did, the Mede would only be more confident of his appeal.

Her attendants all agreed with her assessment of the Mede's physical appearance. She listened to their chatter in the mornings and the evenings as they dressed her and arranged her hair. Attolia permitted them their gossip so long as they were discreet. She enjoyed their chatter, though she never took any part.

"They say the Mede has ordered a new tunic woven with gold in the thread and precious stones sewn in around the collar."

"They say he has several sets of emeralds and his valet sews them onto whichever clothes he chooses in the morning."

"He should buy some other stones," Phresine said. She was the oldest of the queen's attendants and sat by the window with a needle pinched in her lips while she arranged the hem she was darning in one of the queen's dresses. She took the needle out. "Something that goes better with rubies," she said, glancing over at her queen, whose rubies were being carefully braided into her hair.

It was a daring attendant who risked a sly gibe at her mistress, but there could be no doubt that Attolia smiled on the Mede, that she permitted him to hold her hands at greetings a trifle longer than was proper, that he called her "dear queen" and sometimes just "my dear."

"Something that goes better with his beard," said one of the younger women with a titter. Her rash words provoked an uncomfortable silence. The attendants looked to their queen.

"Chloe," said Attolia.

"Your Majesty?"

"Go fetch something for me."

"What would you like, Your Majesty?"

"I don't know. Go find out."

"Yes, Your Majesty," Chloe whispered, and hurried away.

The talk turned to safer topics after her departure.

chapter 11

THE COUNTRY OF Eddis prayed, and as if in answer, the Etesian winds came late. Sounis used what remained of his navy to ferry his army out to the islands to defend those that he could. Attolia attacked relentlessly and secured one island after another. The Mede whispered advice in her ear, and she listened carefully. She had always been a careful listener, and it was easy for the Mede to see evidence of his advice carried out. He was an astute general, and Attolia appreciated that.

"Does she know about the ships?" Kamet asked him.

"I doubt it," said the Mede. "What intelligence she has she directs toward her barons, trying to keep them on their leashes. She has very little vision outside her tiny country, and doesn't seem much interested in the affairs of the wider world. I begin to think she owes her throne to the very barons she suspects of treason. I don't know who else keeps her in power."

"You will ask her about an embassy on Cymorene? We will need that as a staging ground."

"I have asked her already. She is wary and has put me off, but I will win her over in time. It will be no trouble to convince her that the embassy will be small and harmless, existing only to supply the occasional messenger ship between our benevolent empire and hers."

"We still need cause to land here on the mainland."

"We'll have it," said the ambassador. "There is no need to hurry, and once we are fixed here, we will be unmovable."

When the Etesians finally came, Sounis withdrew his troops from the islands, leaving them to defend themselves in the unlikely event that Attolia would risk her own navy by attacking during the season of windstorms. He collected his navy in his safest harbors and turned his attention toward his land-based enemy, Eddis. Attolia did the same.

The mountains defended Eddis better than any army could have, but there were gaps in their protection. The Irkes Forest was a stretch of pines that covered one of the gradual rises into the mountains. When Sounis had tried to move an army through the forest, Eddis had threatened to burn the trees around them. Sounis had withdrawn. With the sea war temporarily stalled, Sounis returned to the Irkes and burned it himself and then advanced through the ashes.

The mountains were more uniform on the Attolian border. The newly forged cannon at the pass prevented Attolia's army from attacking there. The only other access for an army was the canyon where the Aracthus River had once cut its way down the mountainside to join the Seperchia. When the Hamiathes Reservoir had been constructed, the river had been diverted to a new course and joined the Seperchia farther downstream. The former riverbed and the road that ran along it were defended by a heavily fortified gate at the bottom of the mountains, and that gate was further defended by the chasm of the Seperchia River between it and Attolia.

Unable to move an army into Eddis, Attolia sent small raiding parties up the side of the mountain under cover of darkness to attack farms in the isolated mountain valleys. Many of the farms were deserted, the men fighting in Eddis's army, the families moved to the safety of the capital city, leaving the farms to be burned out by Attolia's raiders.

The overabundance of sheep that had crowded the capital the winter before was gone, many of them moved back to the pastures of the coastal provinces, but many more of them slaughtered to feed the population. Offerings burned in every temple as the people prayed for the rains to come to wash their enemies off the mountains and the snows to lock them out for the winter.

When the weather finally turned cold, Attolia called in her raiders. Sounis, having lost the battle for the Irkes, withdrew his army, and Eddis drew her breath at last. Exhausted soldiers returned to their families to rest. In the iron mines the work went on, unremittingly, as they pressed for the ore to make Her Majesty's cannon to supplement those few that were mounted above what remained of the Irkes. The rains fell on the ashes of the pines and washed them away. The water cut furrows into the gentle slopes until the walls of the furrows collapsed and ditches grew in their places and the gradual rises were carved into painful hillocks and ravines that would slow any army that fought its way uphill. The streams below ran red with the dirt as if filled with blood.

In Eddis's capital the palace filled again with lords and barons and Eddis's officers in their embroidered tunics. Bright candles lit the ceremonial hall during formal dinners as Eddis attempted a show of peacetime rituals.

One day in the winter a doctor from one of the military hospitals came to see Eugenides. In the late afternoon of the same day a page brought a message to Eddis, and she excused herself from a meeting with the master of her foundry and climbed the stairs to the roof of the palace. There were wide walks along the walls where the court strolled on fine days. Eugenides sat on a parapet. Eddis approached but stopped about five feet from him. She didn't want to startle him. His feet dangled in space four stories off the ground.

He turned his head slightly, enough to see her in the corner of his eye. "Do you still have people following me?" he asked. "Am I not allowed to sit on the roof on a nice day?"

"It isn't a nice day," Eddis answered shortly. It was in fact bitterly cold. Flurries of snow blew in the wind. "You've been here more than an hour, and you are making the guards nervous." She settled on the low stones beside him.

"You heard what happened?" Eugenides asked.

"I heard one of the doctors from the War Hospital asked you to visit the wards and you went with him."

"He took me to visit the amputees."

"Oh."

"Because the cannon blow men apart and because the doctors sew the open edges closed—"

"Eugenides—"

"—because of course we wouldn't want soldiers to die just because they are missing such nonessentials as arms or legs."

He was looking out over the valley. Across from them was Hephestia's Sacred Mountain, rising above all others with the Hamiathes Reservoir on one shoulder. "That damned doctor asked me to visit the wounded. Then he trotted me out in front of all those broken-apart men as if to say, 'See, here is the Thief of Eddis; losing a hand hasn't bothered him.' As if I were a sacred relic to restore them and they could then jump out of their beds and lead happy lives forever after."

"Eugenides—"

"Well, I patted every one of them on the shoulder like some sort of priest, and then I went outside and threw up." He leaned forward a little to look down between his toes to the hillside far below him. Eddis, sitting with her feet inside the wall, refrained from plucking at his sleeve to pull him back. Telling the Thief to mind his balance was like telling a master swordsman not to cut himself.

"That doctor," Eugenides muttered. "Why didn't he say,

'See, here is the failed Thief of Eddis and the cause of all your misery'?"

"Gen," Eddis said firmly, "this war is not your fault."

"Whose is it, then? I fell into Attolia's trap."

"I sent you there."

"I fell and you sent me. She set the trap and sprang it because Sounis hounded her, and Sounis hounded her with the support of the magus, who fears the Mede, and the Mede emperor, I suppose, is under his own pressures. So whom finally *do* we blame for this war? The gods?"

He looked up into the cloud-filled sky. Eddis laid a warning hand on his arm.

"Oh, I'll watch my tongue," said Eugenides. "I have learned how, and I don't want the clouds to part and Moira to arrive on a band of sunlight to tell me to shut up, but I wish I knew if we're at war and people are dying because the gods choose to have it so. Is this the will of the Great Goddess, that Eddis be destroyed?"

Eddis shook her head. "We are Hephestia's people still. I believe that. Beyond that I don't know. Nothing I've ever learned from a priest makes me think I know just what the gods are or what they can accomplish, but, Gen, I know my decisions are my own responsibility. If I am the pawn of the gods, it is because they know me so well, not because they make up my mind for me." She remembered the properties of the stone of Hamiathes and said, "We can't ask the gods to explain themselves, and I, for one, don't want to."

Eugenides looked thoughtful, remembering his own experience with Hamiathes's Gift, and nodded his agreement.

They had both been quiet for a while before Eddis spoke again. Her words surprised Gen. "You aren't the boy hero anymore," she said.

"Was I ever?" he asked, raising one eyebrow.

She smiled, wondering again where he had picked up that particular facial expression. "Oh, certainly you were the golden boy," she said. "You kept the entire population amused. And since you brought Sounis to his knees, you've been the darling of the court as well."

"The magus said something along those lines. All that glory, and I missed it," Eugenides said mournfully.

Eddis laughed and leaned closer to put one arm around his shoulder.

Eugenides thought it over. "Not the darling of our dear cousins," he pointed out.

"Even them," said Eddis. "They were as angry as anyone else when . . . you came home." She stumbled, close to the sensitive subject of his missing hand. He referred to it occasionally, sometimes lightly. He'd joked that it couldn't possibly affect his riding for the worse, but he still flinched visibly sometimes when it was mentioned by anyone else, and she knew he hated to talk about it.

Sitting together in the cold, they both thought of the cousins who had died since the war began. Stepsis, Chlorus, Sosias in the raiding party at the very beginning. Timos had died stopping Attolia's advance up the main pass the previous spring. Two others, Cleon and Hermander, had been wounded in those battles and had died of infection over the summer. Others had died after the Irkes Forest burned. Eddis remembered them in the first few days after Eugenides had been brought home to the palace. No one had been more eager than they to avenge their Thief.

"I think they felt it was their prerogative to hold you face-down in a water butt and no one else should dare touch you. Therespides is going to admire you, albeit grudgingly, for the rest of his life."

"I thought you said that was all over. I missed it."

"I only said that you weren't a boy hero. You've grown now. People will expect even more of you—that you can steal a magus and bring Sounis to his knees again and do it with one hand."

"One hand, maybe, but a hand full of your best soldiers. How much credit can I take for that?"

"All of it," said Eddis. "It wouldn't have happened but for you. You deserve all the credit—or the blame, some might say—otherwise Attolia wouldn't be so frightened of you."

Eugenides looked over at her, surprised.

"Oh, yes, she's afraid. She'll take Sounis in the spring or by summer. We'll offer peace again, and she'll take it if she can, because she's afraid of what you might do once Sounis is no longer occupying our attention."

Eugenides continued to look nonplussed, and Eddis nodded her head. "I wish she would give up this war now, but I can see that her barons would eat her alive. Still, she is not so foolish that she would continue a war once she had some victory to appease them. And after Sounis's defeat at Irkes Forest, she knows that our soldiers are as good as their reputation." She said quietly then, "Gen, you are a sacred relic to the men in that hospital."

"Are you telling me in your gentle way to stop whining?"

"Yes."

"I don't feel like a hero. I feel like an idiot."

"I think heroes generally do, but those men believe in you."

"I did wait until I was outside before I threw up."

In the spring the rains came. The trees bloomed in the lowlands. The snows melted in Eddis, and the floodwaters kept every access to the mountain country closed. The people of Eddis prayed for the rain to never stop even as they trudged through mud to their knees and longed for fresh greens. Attolia and Sounis worked their fields before turning back to their war making. Eddis watched to see if they would attack each other or move again against the mountains.

The rains continued. Sounis bypassed any attempt to retake the islands he had lost to Attolia and instead moved in a surprise attack on Thegmis, almost in the harbor of Attolia's capital city. The queen was not in her capital. Communications failed, her generals blundered, and Thegmis fell.

Sounis controlled the island, but he'd lost his last large ship in the attack and had no means to resupply his troops or to withdraw them. Attolia blockaded the island with her own navy and waited. Sounis offered to make peace, but Attolia, with the upper hand, rejected his offers. In the mountains Eddis and her minister of war hoped that Sounis was being stupid without the advice of his magus, but they worried.

"He's not this much of a fool," said Eddis.

"Have you talked to the magus?" her minister of war asked.

"I did. He is not much help, and that may be deliberate, but he says he doesn't know what Sounis is planning."

"We shall wait then and see," said the minister.

In the evenings, before dinner was served, the court gathered in the old throne room. Four officers who had already drained several cups of watered wine joked about the threats of the queen of Attolia, lately reported by Eddisian spies. In a sudden silence, their words carried over the crowd. ". . . send him into the afterlife blind, deaf, and with his tongue cut out as well . . ."

Eyes turned to Eugenides, standing across the room in a group with several of his uncles. Everyone knew that Attolia had been speaking about him. Eugenides turned to the crowd and ducked his head. "I was so looking forward to my next visit," he said with mock chagrin, and, chuckling, people returned to their conversations. Eddis, from where she stood near the hearth, watched the Thief carefully, but he turned back to his uncles with an impenetrably bland expression. The queen gestured to her steward and directed him in a low voice to reorder the seating at dinner.

Later, from the head of the table, Eddis watched Eugenides take his place with his father to one side of him and Agape, the youngest daughter of the baron Phoros, on the other. The queen was too far away to hear what he said as he sat down, but Agape answered, and they seemed to get on well. Eddis sent up a small prayer under her breath and turned to speak with her own seatmates.

"You seem to be burdened with my company more often than you deserve," Eugenides was saying.

"They're afraid you might snap at anyone else," Agape answered with a serious expression.

Eugenides looked startled. "No one could snap at you," he said.

"Yes," said Agape, still very serious. "I'm much too sweet."

Eugenides laughed outright, and Agape's grave expression gave way to a smile. She was the youngest of four sisters and the loveliest as well. The others had allowed a certain shrewishness of character to distort their good looks, but Agape was a great favorite at the court for her kindness and her wit.

"Are you in a dreadful mood?" she asked, laying a hand over Eugenides's. "Your father warned me that you might be."

Eugenides glanced at his father, who was staring down at his plate and didn't look up, though he had certainly heard.

"Yes," said Eugenides, turning back to Agape, "a dreadful mood. You should swap seats with your sister Hegite. She and I deserve each other this evening."

"You are unkind to poor Hegite."

"I would be if she were sitting next to me."

Agape smiled. "I suppose it is lucky she is not, then," she said.

"I think luck has nothing to do with it," Eugenides answered, glancing at his queen, "but with a dinner companion as lovely as you, I won't complain. Are you singing at the festival?"

They talked then about the upcoming festival, which would end with the rites of Hephestia and an entire day and night of singing by the temple chorus and by selected soloists. Agape had sung the year before and said she would sing again, spending the next few weeks in seclusion in the temple grounds while she practiced.

Midway through dinner Eugenides lifted his wine cup and looked down into it.

"Something is the matter with this cup," he said.

"What is it?" Agape asked.

"I can't get anybody to fill it." He had several times caught the eye of a wine bearer only to have the boy glance away, pretending not to have seen him. "Excuse me," he said to Agape as he turned and leaned across his father. It was an awkward reach as he had to use his left hand. He accomplished it gracefully and removed his father's wine cup, leaving his own in its place.

"There," he said, "I'm sure you can get it filled." He challenged his father with a look, and the older man nodded.

"I'm sure I can," he said, and signaled to a wine bearer. The boy came with the ewer and poured out the wine. Eugenides drained the cup he'd taken from his father and held it up. The boy hesitated and looked to the minister of war.

"Demos," Eugenides said, "stop looking at my father, and fill my wine cup." The minister of war turned to look across the room. Demos filled the cup. Eugenides drained it. "Now fill it again," he said, and the boy did as he was told while the minister of war sat stiffly, turned away.

"Good lad," said Eugenides. "Now keep an eye on that cup because I don't want it empty again this evening, understood?"

"Yes, sir," the boy said as he backed away.

"You *are* in a dreadful mood," Agape said.

"I am," said Eugenides. "And telling me I can't have wine with my dinner will only make it worse."

"Being drunk is much better," Agape agreed.

Eugenides looked at her sharply. "Agape, I think you are trespassing."

"Yes."

"But you're not going to stop?"

"No." She smiled, and Eugenides, in spite of his foul mood, smiled back. Capitulating for the moment, he didn't touch the wine cup again. After dinner he excused himself politely and disappeared. When his father looked for him, he hadn't joined any of the small groups around the ceremonial hall for after-dinner conversation. Nor had anyone seen him go upstairs to his room.

With a jug of unwatered wine, he stepped across a courtyard of rain-washed pavement to the guard barracks. The wine, he knew, would ensure his welcome and few questions. Hours later he returned to the central palace and the library. He stopped unsteadily in the doorway when he saw the magus inside, bent over the papers on the table they'd agreed would be his for the duration of his stay in Eddis.

"I stayed up late just to be sure you were gone," Eugenides said, yawning.

"Unlike your father, I am certainly not waiting up for you," said the magus dryly. "I have work I prefer to do uninterrupted."

"Was my father here?"

"Until half an hour ago. It was like having a basilisk in the room."

Eugenides laughed as he crossed the library to his room. "I'm glad I missed him," he said.

The magus, taking note of his unsteadiness, agreed. "I'm glad you missed him, too."

"And will your muse keep you working all night?" Eugenides asked.

"It might," the magus answered.

"Not if you can only work uninterrupted," the Thief said cryptically as he closed his door.

The magus had meant to work just a few moments more, but after the interruption he fell back into his thoughts and was still in the library when Eugenides's hoarse screams began. He put down his pen and listened.

He was a soldier as well as a scholar, and he was not unfamiliar with the sound of men screaming. He pinched the bridge of his nose between his thumb and his fingers. Then, reluctantly, he stood and walked to the door of Eugenides's room and banged on it. He banged hard and for a long time before the screaming subsided. There was silence, then, until finally the bolt was thrown and Eugenides opened the door to look out. The side of his face was creased with sleep and his hair was damp with sweat.

"Just bad dreams," he said quietly.

"Come sit by the fire?" the magus asked.

Eugenides staggered out into the light and sat in a chair and groaned. "Oh, my head," he said.

"That will be more effective than a lecture from your father," said the magus, amused.

Eugenides disagreed. "You've never heard my father lecture."

"Do you want to talk about them?" the magus asked, sitting in a chair nearby.

"The lectures? Not really. He never says much, but it's always to the point."

"The screaming nightmares."

"Oh," said the Thief. "No. I don't want to talk about them."

"The weather, then?"

"No, thank you. Not the harvest either," said Eugenides. "Tell me why the king of Sounis wants to marry the queen of Eddis." He'd asked the magus the same question before.

"The political importance of the marriage is obvious," the magus answered.

Eugenides shook his head but did it carefully in consideration of the pain left when the numbness caused by too much wine had faded. "I don't mean the political advantages. He wants more than that."

"Eddis is brilliant, Gen. She's very young, almost as young as yourself, and she is already a successful leader and a gifted ruler. Her legal reforms have changed Eddis more in seven years than anyone would have thought possible when she took the throne. And on a personal level she is quite . . . magnetic."

"She's ugly," Eugenides objected.

The magus hesitated. "Perhaps not the conventional ideal of physical beauty."

"She's short, she's broad-shouldered, and hawk-faced with a broken nose. I would say no, she is not an ideal."

"She has a lovely smile," the magus countered.

"Oh, yes," Eugenides agreed. "I've seen men fall on their knees and beg to walk across hot coals for her after one of those smiles."

The magus shrugged. "I suppose my king would like one for himself," he said simply.

Eugenides nodded and stared into the fire. "Agape," he said.

"Hmm?" asked the magus, puzzled at the abrupt change in topic.

"Agape, the queen's cousin. She and the queen are much alike."

"Your cousin, too, isn't she?"

"Oh, you know how it is, we're all cousins here," Eugenides said, still staring at the fire. "The connections are different. Agape is the daughter of the queen's mother's sister, and I am related to the queen through my father, who is her father's brother. Agape's grandfather was mine's half brother, I think." He waved his hand, dismissing genealogies. "We have special priests who keep track of these things and spend months figuring out who can marry whom. Agape's much more closely related to the queen than to me, and she is very much like her."

"She is," the magus agreed.

"Maybe you could get Sounis to marry her?" Eugenides suggested.

"Perhaps."

"Poor Agape," Eugenides said wistfully.

"He's not an entirely irredeemable character," the magus said, defending his king.

"I'm sure not," Eugenides said agreeably, "but he's caused a lot of bloodshed wanting a woman he can't have."

"Not a new thing in the history of the world," the magus said.

"No," Eugenides responded thoughtfully, "and maybe I should be more sympathetic, but I think I will just go back to bed."

"Shall I stay?" the magus asked.

"No," said Eugenides. "I am going to give up on wine as a soporific and take some of Galen's lethium." He gave a sketchy good-night wave with his left hand and disappeared into his room.

In the morning he asked for a private audience with the queen and scheduled it with her chamberlain, a highly unusual chain of events. In general, if he wanted to talk to her, he just did, and if he wanted to speak privately, he appeared at her elbow when no one else was near, whenever and wherever that might be. After weeks of silence, barricaded in his library after the magus's first visit, he'd woken her in the middle of the night in her bedchamber, while her attendants slept on undisturbed nearby, and asked to borrow several men and a chariot in order to destroy Sounis's navy.

Now Eddis met with him in one of the small interview rooms in a newer part of the palace. It was an official receiving room and had a throne in it raised three steps off the floor. She always felt as if she were perching like a bird rather than sitting like a monarch on this particular throne. She looked down at her Thief.

"You're requesting my permission to run away and hide?" she asked.

Eugenides winced, but he then nodded. He stood before her dressed in his most formal tunic with his hair newly clipped and his chin carefully shaven. "Yes," he admitted. "I am requesting your permission to run away and hide."

"Eugenides, we can't afford to have you disappear in a fit of despair just now."

"Do I look sunk in despair?" he asked, holding his arms out from his sides.

"I assume you're hiding it to maintain pretenses."

"It's worse than despair I am hiding," he said, sounding suddenly very bleak.

"Is there something worse?" she asked.

"Oh, yes." He shifted his weight and looked around the empty room. He turned away from her and appeared to take a great interest in the interlocking gold squares painted around the walls near the ceiling. "I'm terrified," he admitted.

Eddis thought he was joking and laughed. He glanced at her and away again, and she stopped.

He crossed his arms over his chest and, still facing away

from her, spoke to the wall. "Those men in the hall last night . . ."

"They were joking."

"I know they were joking. I'm not laughing," he snapped, and caught himself. His head dropped forward, and he addressed himself again to the wall. "The only thing I want to do right now is bolt the door to my room and hide under the covers. I'd do it, too, but then I might fall asleep, and I can't risk that. So much," he said bitterly, "for the hero of Eddis."

He brushed his hair off his face, then tucked his hand back under his arm. "I remember when they brought me up the mountain. Parts of the trip. I remember thinking that nothing else, nothing worse, would happen, because I was home. Then I heard Galen telling you that if it was glower in my eyes, I'd be blind." He was shaking his head. Eddis had to make an effort to stop shaking hers. "And I stand around listening to people *laugh* at the idea that I might end up deaf and dumb as well."

He started to pace. "Her following stroke is as good as her attack," he said. "I'm too frightened to leave my room, much less to be of any use to my queen."

"You're not in your room now."

"No, I'm doing my best not to look like a mountain hare frozen in one spot by terror, but I don't know how long I can keep it up, and that's why we didn't have this discussion at your morning session with half the court looking on."

He stopped pacing abruptly and turned his back on his queen in order to sit on the dais at her feet. He pulled his knees up and hunched over them. "Bleh," he said, disgusted with himself.

Looking down at him, Eddis could see that his tunic had grown too small and pulled across his shoulders. She remembered his many comments on her ill-fitting clothing, and she made a note to tell him at a more appropriate moment to get a new overshirt made. He had the money. All the proceeds from the ten hijacked Attolian caravans she had given over to him.

"Eugenides," she said, picking her words carefully, "you're letting yourself be upset by talk. Empty threats. She wouldn't do any of those things."

"You wouldn't think so, but she cut out the tongue of that traitor Maleveras and left him in a cage in the courtyard for a week before she had him executed."

"She'd been queen for less than a year. He'd talked half of her barons into deserting her, while pretending to be an ally, and his sedition nearly dethroned her. By the time she discovered his treachery, she had very little real power and not many options. If she hadn't done something to deter other warmongers, she would have lost the throne."

"And that baron who was robbing the treasury. She cut off his hand, too, didn't she?"

"She had him executed. I would have done the same if I'd found one of my tax collectors funding a revolt out of my own treasury. She had his hand cut off posthumously to display for effect. I don't *think* I would have done that, but I've never been in that situation."

Eugenides turned to stare at her over his shoulder. "You are defending her," he pointed out.

The queen of Eddis hissed in displeasure. "I don't want to. She's vicious, she's barbaric, and I think by this time edging toward insane, but I'm forcing myself to be honest. She has not indulged in atrocities for personal pleasure," she said firmly. "Or for personal revenge. She has used them as deterrents to defend her throne."

She picked her words carefully before she went on. "It's not the way I would like to think I would defend my throne, but in prosecuting this war against her I find myself . . . not commendable. I wouldn't have started a war to avenge you, Gen, or even to rescue you. Still, I wonder, what opportunity for diplomacy did I miss, and did I overlook it because I was angry on your behalf?"

Eugenides had lain on his back on the lowest step to the throne, with his legs crossed at the ankle and his arms still folded across his chest. The cuff and hook he wore were inlaid with gold to match the gold piping on his collar and the embroidery on the sleeves of his overshirt. It was like him, if he had to have a thing, to have the fanciest of its kind. Eddis thought he looked like a well-dressed funerary ornament. Eugenides turned his head to look at her and lay without speaking for the space of three or four breaths.

"If she doesn't indulge in torture for personal pleasure, why didn't she do the sensible thing and hang me?" he asked quietly. It was an unanswerable question. He followed it with another. "If she catches me again, what better deterrent than me could she wish to have at her disposal?"

Eddis hesitated. In the past Attolia had shown that she would stop at nothing to defend her throne. How much of a threat had Eugenides been to Attolia? Not much, Eddis thought, but who measures? She considered carefully before she spoke. "If she ever had you again, she'd kill you immediately. She was a fool to do otherwise, but, Eugenides"—she leaned over to meet his gaze directly—"she won't have you."

Eugenides covered his face with his arm. "I tell myself that, and I think I believe it, until I go to sleep. I tell myself that she isn't—that she wouldn't do those things. But I am afraid that she would," he whispered. "And then I wish she'd hanged me. I wish in my god's name that she'd hanged me, and I *hate* that Mede." He laughed, and Eddis winced.

"So," he said, his voice under control again, "may I have your permission to disappear until I look less like a frightened rabbit? Because I don't think I can keep up appearances here."

"How long?" Eddis asked.

"A few days, maybe ten."

"Ten?"

"Maybe."

"Take as much time as you need," Eddis said heavily. "I'll say I've sent you out to the coastal provinces."

That was better than he'd hoped, but Eugenides didn't say so. He pulled himself upright and stood to bow to his queen. Then he went away.

He was gone ten days and returned early in the morning of the eleventh. Eddis saw him at the back of the throne room during her morning sessions. He looked tired but relaxed. He watched while she dealt with the business at hand: who should get relief money, the care of the orphans and widows of soldiers, what was to be done with burned-out farms. Attolia and Sounis seemed content for the moment to war against each other, but Eddis had to have her tiny amounts of arable land planted carefully or her people wouldn't have the food to withstand another winter without trade. Sounis's troops were still blockaded on Thegmis. He was offering a peace negotiation. Attolia was still rejecting it.

The following week brought the news that Sounis had negotiated the purchase of ships from an anonymous continental power willing to support his war with Attolia. The ships were scheduled to be delivered in time to break the blockade of Thegmis and to support a land invasion before the arrival of the summer windstorms. With one stroke Sounis had doubled the size of his navy and Attolia had lost her opportunity to make peace.

"He knew he had the ships coming when he attacked Thegmis," said Eddis.

"Almost certainly."

*　*　*

The minister of war spoke to Eddis's council. "Attolia is fighting not only Sounis but her barons as well. She can't command in person the land battle and direct the navy at the same time, and her new-model generals can't run a war if her barons are going to work against Attolia's interests. The defeat at Thegmis was entirely due to the interference of the baron Stadicos with Attolia's orders. Sounis is already organizing to take back the islands that he's lost. He'll begin as soon as the new ships for his navy are delivered. If he controls the islands, Attolia will be hard pressed to stop a land invasion."

"She's an astute strategist. Are you sure that Sounis will re-take the islands, even with superior firepower?" someone asked.

The minister of war shrugged. "Who's to say? Sounis is not a subtle thinker, but he's not a fool either. Lately we had hoped that Attolia would take Sounis and be content once he was no longer a threat to her throne, whereas Sounis's goal has been to expand his hegemony. If he controls Attolia, he may still pursue war with Eddis, attacking us on two fronts. The only relief we could hope for would be the time it would take him to solidify his control over his new territory.

"However, the Mede presence off the coast is the real danger, and it has intensified. It's doubtful that Sounis could in the near term execute so crushing a victory that he could capture the queen. If the queen flees to the Mede, they will make every effort to restore her to her throne as their puppet. They will have the excuse they need to land in force on this coast, and they will likely overrun Sounis and then Eddis as well. Even if they refrain from a direct attack, our situation will only worsen without an outlet for regular trade. So for us, the very worst possible outcome would be Attolia's going to the Mede for help."

The queen asked for comment, and talk went on all morning as every detail of the war was reexamined.

"Your Majesty," said her Thief at last. He'd never spoken before at a council meeting, and those at the table turned to look at him in surprise.

"Our goal has been to dethrone Attolia without inviting in the Mede. If the instability of her rule were eliminated and Attolia had a government more stable but inimical to the Mede, it could mean an alliance between Eddis and Attolia that would drive back Sounis."

"Yes," Eddis agreed.

"I think," Eugenides said quietly, "that I could eliminate the instability of the Attolian queen."

"Go on," said Eddis, and her council listened as Eugenides talked.

"Attolia isn't in the capital. She is at Ephrata on the coast. There's no real castle there. It's a fortified megaron in the old style, which means it's not as easy for me to move through as her palace is, for example, or the megaron in Sounis's capital. However, Ephrata is not well defended. Sounis doesn't yet have a navy to attack her by sea, and she has the lower ridges of the coastal hills as well as the Seperchia between her and the base of the pass from Eddis. Our army would have to break the blockade at the bottom of the pass and cross the river and those hills to reach her. She's not much worried about an assault, and she keeps only a minimal garrison of her private guard at Ephrata."

The council looked at him expectantly, holding their collective breath.

"If I could get into Ephrata, I could remove the queen."

In the past he wouldn't have needed help, and it would have been a matter for him and the queen to discuss alone. Now he spoke to her entire council and its individual members looked not at him but at their hands, or cast quick glances at one another, all of them remembering a younger Eugenides who'd sworn he'd never be a soldier and wanted nothing to do with the business of killing people.

"We would need a force large enough to seize Ephrata," Eugenides said.

"How could we seize Ephrata?" one of the men at the table asked. "You just said she has her entire army camped between us and the Seperchia."

Eugenides explained. As the intricacy of his plan unfolded, it became indisputably clear where he had been for the ten days he'd been away. The queen watched him with her eyes narrowed as he talked about taking a small force down to Attolia and bypassing her army camped at the Seperchia.

"She has border patrols along the base of the mountains." One of the generals welcome at Eddis's council meetings spoke up. "How would you get any significant group of soldiers past those without alerting her?"

"She doesn't patrol the dystopia."

"For obvious reasons." The dystopia was the black, rocky ground left behind by the eruptions of the Sacred Mountain. The ground was fertile but too rough to cultivate and too dry. Its only regular water source was the unnavigable Aracthus River, which flowed down from the shoulder of the Sacred Mountain and directly across the dystopia to the fields between it and the banks of the much larger Seperchia River.

"How do you propose to get to the dystopia without being seen and then get across it?" the general asked.

Eugenides looked at his father.

"The Aracthus?" his father asked.

Eugenides nodded without speaking.

"What's the garrison at Ephrata?" the minister of war asked.

"Fifty men," Eugenides answered, and waited.

After a pause for thought his father nodded. "It could be done," he said at last.

Eugenides turned back to the general. "You see," he argued, "by taking a smaller force, we can avoid the Attolian army. We can seize the megaron without meaning to hold it because once the queen is gone, the megaron is irrelevant."

"And you're sure she's there?"

"I am."

"And that she would be there when we attacked?"

"That could be determined."

Before anyone else could speak, the queen cleared her throat. All eyes except Eugenides's turned to her. He looked at the floor.

"If you would please excuse us," the queen said very quietly, "I will speak to my Thief."

Unsure at the cause of her anger, her council hastily collected its papers and disappeared. Eddis looked across the empty table.

"Fifty men," she said.

"Yes."

"You counted?"

"As best I could."

Eddis waved her hand at the empty seats around the table. "They think I sent you. They think you went to Attolia on my orders. I gave you permission to run away and hide, not to go creeping around Attolia's megaron so that she can catch you again. Are you out of your *mind*?" she shouted, standing up, scattering the papers piled in front of her, knocking a pen so that it dripped ink in fuzzy black dots onto the tabletop.

"I was afraid. I couldn't just sit here being afraid and doing nothing about it."

"So you did this? Damn you, Eugenides. What would I have done if she'd caught you?"

"I was in the woods watching people go in and out of the megaron. I wasn't anywhere near her."

"That's as close as you went? The woods?"

Eugenides hesitated. "I went into the town once."

Eddis stared at him and waited.

"And I scouted the outer walls of the megaron."

"What would I have done," Eddis repeated in a low voice, more anguished than her shouting, "what would I have done if she'd caught you and cut you to pieces and sent the pieces back to me?"

"Buried them," said Eugenides.

Eddis sat back against her throne and crossed her arms. She looked at Eugenides a long time while he waited patiently.

"Now you want to go back," she said.

"Yes."

"Eugenides, this is like seeing a child burn himself on a pot and then say he'd like to try climbing into the fire next."

"I'm not a child," the Thief said.

"We can send someone else," Eddis said, ignoring him while she considered alternatives.

"There isn't anyone else," Eugenides said firmly, interrupting her thoughts. "And I want to do this."

"I won't believe that. If this is truly what you want, I should have you locked up until you come to your senses. There has to be someone else."

"No," said Eugenides.

"Yes," said his queen.

"Who?" Eugenides asked.

"Gen," Eddis was forced into admitting, "it would be worse than losing you to have you do this and become like her."

He came and sat on the footstool by her chair. "I am your Thief. As you pointed out once before, I am a member of your royal family. There is no one else to send. And, My Queen, I do want this." He looked up at her. "I can't tell you why. She may be a fiend from hell to make me feel this way, but even if

I have to hate myself for the rest of my life, this is what I want." He shook his head, perhaps in self-contempt, and shrugged. "I dream about her at night."

Eddis looked down at him and said dryly, "We have heard you screaming."

He laughed, a sharp sound like wood splintering, then said, "I can't do this except at your direction." He leaned back against her legs and turned his head to look up at her. "My Queen," he said softly, "you can't tell me I am a grown-up hero and still keep me tied to you like a little boy. Let me go."

"Oh, Gen. When I said Eddis expected more of you, I didn't mean this."

She sat and looked at her hands for a long time.

"All right," she said at last. "Go and steal the queen of Attolia."

chapter 12

*I*T TOOK TIME to prepare for Eugenides's plan. The spring rains fell. Eddis grew green with the luminescence of new growth against a pearl gray sky. Independent traders slipped into the tiny harbors of the Eddis coast, and their small shipments were carried up the cliffs to the coastal province. In the capital the women and the men too old for fighting sewed the quilted tunics that were the uniform of the soldiers. The soldiers trained, Eugenides's cousin Crodes, who served as the queen's messenger, spent hours every day practicing his pronunciation, and Eugenides, for his part, took riding lessons, griping bitterly all the while.

One night in her megaron at Ephrata, the queen of Attolia retired late to her rooms. She had pored for hours over the papers on her writing desk, and she had written page after page to add to them, sealing her messages with wax and the imprint of the ring on her finger, one of the many seals she used. The royal messengers would be busy in the morning, each of them with a leather bag to carry marked with the royal insignia. Some would ride across Attolia, and some would board the small, fast ships that waited in Ephrata's harbor.

She was tired. She sat, almost too weary to keep her head lifted as Phresine gently combed the tangles out of her hair and twisted it into the single braid the queen wore when she slept. As Phresine combed out the long hair, she teased the queen about the shadows under her eyes.

"You will wear yourself to the bone. Your beauty will be gone, and your suitors will lose interest."

"It's a mask, Phresine. The suitors haven't any interest in me."

"Well, your mask will be gone soon if you don't take better care."

"Only to be replaced with another."

"And that one?"

"Power. What men like best for themselves and least in their women."

"Then you must marry before your beauty is gone, mustn't you?" Phresine stepped carefully on dangerous ground. It didn't pay to grow too familiar with Her Majesty. Phresine had never seen the queen lose her temper, but her censure was not to be taken lightly. She was unfailingly polite to her women, and kind in a formal way. Perhaps because she never allowed anyone too close, any sign of trust or confidence from her was highly prized by her attendants. Still, she ruled her court and her country with an inflexible hand. Pausing in her work, Phresine considered that for all she knew, the queen was as ruthless as she seemed, and Phresine valued her position too much to risk it by letting her tongue wag.

"Phresine," the queen said without turning her head to look at her attendant, "I can read your mind."

Phresine moved her hands, stilled during her thoughts, back to their tasks. "Then you know there's no harm in old Phresine," she said.

When Phresine was gone, the room was quiet except for the ceaseless sound of waves that came through the open window. The narrow slice of moon inched across the sky until it shone onto her carpet, and Attolia was still awake. She got out of bed, lifting her robe from where it was draped by the bedside. A year earlier an attendant would have been hovering, ready to serve a restless queen, but the queen had long since ordered them out of her chambers at night. She could get her own water if she was thirsty. She wanted to be alone.

She pushed her arms into the wide sleeves of the robe and wrapped it around herself, then dragged a chair to sit in the moonlight by the window. "Damn him," she cursed under her breath, "damn him, damn him, damn him," as if her curses could weigh down the Thief of Eddis like stones piled one on top of another until he was overcome.

She sighed and tried to organize her thoughts. If she was going to be awake, there were still problems of strategy to address. The Mede ambassador was persistent in his attentions. A close relative of the emperor and a brother of the emperor's heir, he was not an unlikely suitor. It was no doubt why he had been chosen as ambassador. She wished he wouldn't grease his beard so dramatically. The scent of the oil he used was overwhelming.

Her thoughts circled back to the scent of the hair oil she'd used as a child. She'd broken the last amphora of it and then never used it again. That same day her older brother had died falling from his horse, and the familiar earth had seemed to shift under her feet. Suddenly her world had changed, and she was a different person with new rooms in the palace, a new view from her windows, the comforting presence of her nurse replaced by the aloof faces of unfamiliar attendants. Not just a princess of the royal house to be married agreeably in a few years, she was the princess whose husband would be the next king of Attolia. Her dead mother's jewelry was collected from her father's concubines and brought to her. The combs in her hair were more ornamental, the earrings in her ears heavier, and her hair oils more expensively scented.

Within the month her father had chosen her husband, selling her to the son of his most powerful baron in exchange for a peaceful end to his reign. Sitting in her chair in the moonlight, Attolia thought back over the year of her engagement, which she had spent, as custom demanded, with the family of her future husband. Surrounded by strangers, completely isolated from any ally, she'd listened as her fiancé and his father talked over their plans to destroy the king and to wring whatever power and riches they could from her throne, sucking her country dry to feed their appetites.

Sitting in her corner, quietly spinning thread on her spindle or embroidering the collars on her fiancé's shirts, she'd listened to him as he struggled to follow his father's convoluted plans, gloating at every opportunity for treason and character assassination. It was her fiancé who gave her the name shadow princess. As quiet and as dull as a shadow he called her, and it was true. Caught in an abrupt adolescence, she was too tall and ungraceful. Her face was long, and as she schooled it carefully to keep it free of expression, she looked plain and not bright. Beside her in the corner the other ladies cast down their eyes demurely and flaunted for her benefit the gold earrings and bracelets her fiancé left with them after his visits. A shadow princess he'd called her, and someday, he'd said, a shadow queen.

Attolia had had few trinkets of her own, but as she sat quietly moving her needle through the embroidery, she had thought very carefully about the royal jewelry that would someday be at her disposal. She listened to her future father-in-law's plans and made plans of her own. She collected leaves, one by one, from the coleus bushes in the garden. They grew in hedges along the walks around the villa. She tied the leaves into a knot in one of her sashes and hung the sash in her wardrobe. Six weeks before she was supposed to return to the castle to prepare for her wedding, the news came that her father was dead. Her fiancé stopped in her rooms with a face so full of mock solemnity it was an insult and told her that her father had been poisoned by some unknown assassin. The princess felt her own face had turned to a stone mask. She fled to her bedroom and waited there for the tears to come, but none did. Finally she had decided that none were called for. Hadn't he gotten what he bargained for? Hadn't he reached the end of his reign without war?

She returned to the capital, where she was watched by her fiancé's spies, but not closely. She was the shadow princess, dull and quiet. She waited with every appearance of passivity as a funeral was arranged for her father and a wedding for herself. Then, at the wedding feast, while the lords and ladies of her court looked on, Attolia poisoned her bridegroom.

He'd had a porcine habit of eating her food when he'd finished his own. When his wine cup was empty, he would reach without comment for hers, having noted if she'd sampled it first. She sat through her wedding feast with her lips stinging from the poison of the powdered coleus leaf that had touched them as she pretended to drink, then watched as he took her wine, as casually as he had taken her country, and choked on it and died.

The lords of Attolia had turned on one another then, searching for the assassin, and the queen had retired to her rooms and waited while the barons wrangled over who would be the next king. Late that night she was finally summoned to meet the man who'd managed through threats and promises to gain the allies to proclaim himself king. Her hands clenched still when she remembered the disdain of the servingwoman sent to fetch her. The barons had looked Attolia over, she remembered, the way she had seen men looking at slave girls, and one man had laughed when she had crossed the room to sit on the throne. That same man had ordered her to be ready to marry him in the morning. She'd nodded stiffly, her face impassive, and the captain of her guard had raised his crossbow and shot the claimant for her hand through the heart.

The response had its calculated effect. In the stunned silence that followed, she divided the property of the dead baron among his competitors and informed them that the next king of Attolia would be her choice, not theirs. She then retired to allow them time to absorb the new reality of her rule: the guards around them, the hostages she held, and the army she controlled.

They hadn't called her the shadow queen then. The royal jewelry was the only resource she'd had, that and the knowledge she'd gained listening to the father of her fiancé as he'd tried to hammer into the head of his dull son the complicated intrigue necessary to seize the throne.

She had judged the men and women around her and doled her treasure out carefully. The golden bees—earrings the color of honey that were older than the monarchy—and brooches and fibula pins, ruby earrings and gold necklets and bracelets had all been dropped one by one into carefully chosen hands. Over the previous year she'd learned all she needed to know about her father's most powerful barons, and while they squabbled about who might be the next king, she'd made herself queen.

She had kept her bargains with the officers in her army, promoting them outside their feudal hierarchy, making a new-model army that answered to her and not to the divisive barons. She'd used her new army to destroy her erstwhile father-in-law and again taken the property of her opponents to placate her barons and enrich her supporters.

The stone mask over her feelings grew heavier and heavier as she was forced to more and more extreme measures to hold her throne. Surrounded by people who hated or feared her, she trusted no one and told herself that she didn't need to. Once, just after she'd seized her throne, she'd summoned an old nurse back to be an attendant, and the woman had refused to come to the palace. Enraged, Attolia had ridden out to the village where the woman lived, intending to see her arrested for refusing her queen's faith in her.

The nurse, who'd been young when she'd served Attolia, had grown to middle age. She'd married and had children. She stood in the court of her farmhouse, looking up to her queen, and asked, "Where are my children? Where is my husband, Your Majesty?"

Attolia had not registered their absence, had not cared until the woman pointed it out.

The nurse stepped closer to the queen and explained. "Two men came to the house saying they would keep my children safe while I served the queen. Did you send them?"

Mute, Attolia had shaken her head.

"I did not think you had. For now, my husband has the children and hides with them, but will any of them be safe if I serve you? And can you trust me if you cannot keep them from harm?"

She had reached up to lay a hand on Attolia's knee, a gesture of supplication, and comfort as well, and Attolia had shaken her head.

"Your Majesty, you are searching for your nurse, to trust with your life, but she's gone. There is no one you can trust here." Attolia had turned her horse and ridden away.

That year she'd had a gold headband made, set with rubies, to wear in her hair in place of the royal jewelry. It was a copy of the headband worn by the famous statue of the goddess Hephestia in the main temple in Eddis. Hephestia had ruled the old gods as Attolia intended to rule her barons, alone.

She had replaced the golden bees and the rest of the royal gems, buying them back from the people she'd bribed with them, sometimes buying replacements for pieces that couldn't be recovered, but she continued to wear the headband every day to remind her subjects of her authority. At night it lay in a velvet-lined case near her bed.

One morning, she'd found it moved slightly from its resting spot and beside it a pair of matching ruby earrings. She'd thought at first that it was some flattery delivered with the connivance of one of her attendants, perhaps from the newly arrived ambassador of Medea, or one of her court currying favor, but before she could interrogate the women of her chamber, a nagging suspicion grew that it was not a gift of flattery, but the Thief of Eddis laughing at her again. She never wore the rubies. They were kept in their own velvet case beside the one that held the headband.

In the moonlight she sighed again and climbed stiffly out of her chair and went to look at them. She opened the case and flicked them across the velvet lining with the nail of her forefinger, resisting touching them as if they might be hot. She snapped the case closed, laid her robe over a chair, and went back to bed and finally to sleep.

"She's retaken Thegmis." Nahuseresh sat in his office, tapping the edge of a folded message against his knee.

Kamet stopped in the doorway. "Will you have the excuse you need to land?" he asked.

Nahuseresh picked a letter from the emperor off the secretary's desk. The emperor wanted news of progress and would not be pleased to hear that Thegmis was once again safe in Attolia's hands. The ambassador didn't answer his secretary's question but spoke his thoughts aloud.

"I haven't seen enough of her generals. She is clever enough to hide them from me, sending this one away as she speaks to that one, never leaving an opportunity for me to study them. If I knew which one planned the retaking of Thegmis, I could kill him and cripple her. She'd offer us anything then, desperate for help."

"And if you can't identify the generals that she depends on, and you can't cut off her military support, what then?" Kamet asked. "The emperor will not start a war with the Continental Powers. They are bound by treaty to defend this coast if you attack it."

"We'll have our invitation, one way or another, and once invited in, we will be hard to send home again," said the Mede. "But, Kamet, I've noticed in you a distressing tendency to err in your pronouns of late. You say 'if you attack,' instead of 'if *we* attack.'"

The secretary dropped his eyes and held very still. "Forgive me," he said.

"Of course," said the Mede. He looked through narrowed lids at his secretary. "Are you tempted by the barbarian indulgences, Kamet?"

The slave shook his head slightly, still looking at the table in front of him. "I hope I have not made you angry." He glanced up and dared a self-effacing smile.

"Good heavens," said Nahuseresh. "Kamet, you're lovestruck."

Kamet dropped his eyes again. "She's very beautiful," he said in his own defense.

Nahuseresh laughed. "She is. She has beauty even those cats in the imperial court would admire, but I hadn't expected to see you fall victim to a pretty face."

The secretary shrugged, too wise to say that he sympathized with the barbarian queen as her choices grew fewer and her freedom slipped away.

chapter 13

*T*HE ROYAL ENGINEER watched the water pouring through the sluice of the dam at the Hamiathes Reservoir and reported his measurements to the queen of Eddis. With the heavy spring rains and the snowmelt from the mountains, the gates of the reservoir remained open. To close them would risk their destruction.

When the water flow slackened, it was already summer in the lowland countries and Attolia and Sounis continued their war, leaving Eddis penned in by part of Attolia's army at one side of the mountain pass and by Sounis's army at the other. Attolia retreated from the islands Sounis attacked, waiting patiently for her opponent to make a mistake. Finally the engineer reported that it would be safe to shut the gates on the flow of the Aracthus, reducing the river to a small stream, at least for the length of a day, or a night, without risking damage to the dam. Eddis's army ordered itself for a march from the top of the main pass down to Attolia, leaving a smaller force to defend the main bridge in the event that Sounis decided to attack Eddis while her troops were committed elsewhere.

Campfires at night betrayed the size of the Eddisian force massing against Attolia, and her army in turn began its preparations. Attolia had expected that Eddis must make some effort to drive back her enemies or face starvation the following winter.

"She has made no alliance with Sounis? You are certain?" she asked the secretary of her archives.

"Nothing is ever certain, Your Majesty." Relius had grown more cautious since the renaissance of the Thief of Eddis. "But if Sounis has made any agreements with Eddis, no one else knows of them. That is not to say that he will miss an opportunity to attack once you are involved in a land war."

"We can hold the coast," Attolia said, unworried, "and if we lose the islands, we will eventually gain them back again. So long as we hold Thegmis and Solon, he can't easily pursue a land war. Eddis has made a tactical error, I think, if she believes that we will be pinched in a vise between her and Sounis."

"Will you use the Mede's ships to keep Sounis's navy away?"

Attolia shook her head. "No. We don't need their help for this."

As the sun was setting, the engineer at the Hamiathes Reservoir ordered the main sluice gates on the dam lowered and watched carefully as the work was accomplished. The water strained against the wooden gates and forced its way in jets through the narrow gaps between the sluices, but the gates held. The royal messenger took the news to the palace, and the men waiting there began to move. Eddis spoke one last time to the general and the officers in charge of the men, and to her Thief. When she had given them their last instructions, she sent them on their way. She recalled the Thief as he reached the steps up to the door.

"My Queen?" He turned back, unsure what she required.

"Only for that," said Eddis.

Eugenides smiled and bowed his head. "My Queen," he said again, perhaps for the last time. Then he was gone.

Behind the last rush of the Aracthus, with their feet wet in the persistent trickle from the reservoir, a line of soldiers began their difficult journey in darkness, many glancing over their shoulders at the dam behind them until it disappeared from sight.

Because any torches might have been seen for miles across Attolia and reported to the capital, the stream of men twisted down the mountain in single file with only the light provided by the full moon. The canyon of the empty riverbed rose on either side. There were few breaks in the slick stone walls, and the shadows had a solidity that deceived the inattentive. The riverbed under their feet was rocky and uneven, and many were burdened with ladders as well as their weapons and gear. Those in the rear struggled with block and tackle, roughly squared wooden beams, wooden carriages and cannon.

From time to time they passed an officer looking up the river and counting minutes on a pocket watch. The men cast anxious looks up the river themselves and waded as quickly as they were able through waters that were sometimes as deep as their waist. Eugenides stayed just ahead of the cannon and worried no less than the queen's soldiers.

All of them sighed with relief when they reached the stopping place at the end of the first night. Those soldiers with ladders set them against the walls of the canyon, and others grouped themselves in lines to climb out of the water. Still others, more eager to be out of the riverbed, scrambled up the steep banks on their own. Once out of the canyon, the soldiers settled, as comfortably as they could, on a narrow shelf that ran along the edge of the Aracthus. The river, cutting its way down the mountains, had twisted around an outcropping of stone that had resisted erosion. The outcropping cut off the view of Attolia and hid the soldiers from any observers below.

Xenophon, who was in nominal charge of the expeditionary force, stood at the lip above the Aracthus and watched as the men climbed and the equipment was hauled up. The last man had reached the safety of the shelf above the river and the ladders had been lifted and stacked when a flare fired from the reservoir above lit the sky for a brief moment. It was a green flare, to say that the gates had been opened as planned, not a red one to say that they had failed and that all the destructive force of the river was already rushing downward.

Xenophon looked for Eugenides. He had resisted as hard as he decently could being put in command of the Thief. He had pointed out to his sovereign, with glibness taking the place of tact, that the thief had never so far as he knew been in the command of anyone. The queen had only smiled and assured him that Eugenides had promised to be tractable. Xenophon had had to yield with what grace he could muster, but Eugenides had been as good as his word throughout the planning stages of the campaign, and Xenophon had begun to eye him with cautious approval.

The Thief was sitting farther along the edge of the canyon with a watch in his hand, trying to read its face by moonlight.

"One of your brother's?" Xenophon asked when he'd walked up behind him.

"Yes," the Thief said. "He made it for me."

"And the time?"

"Late, sir. They've held the water back half an hour, and we used up that half hour getting here. It must have taken longer to get the last men on their way."

"That's not unexpected. They'll plan the safety margins accordingly on the next stages."

Then they waited, and in time the waters of the Aracthus

rose beside them, relieving the pressure on the sluice gates and catching up with the water that had gone before. The Aracthus often crested in the late evenings, swollen by the runoff from snow melting in the mountains, and the Eddisians hoped the rising and dropping water level wouldn't be noticed in the lowlands, where the irrigation channels had been destroyed by flooding and were not being rebuilt since they might be flooded again.

They waited through the day, those who could sleeping, the rest watching the blue sky for the first sign of clouds. A summer rainfall wouldn't threaten the dam behind them, but if clouds obscured the moon, the rocky riverbed would be impossible to navigate.

When the sun had set and the sky was dark, the waters trickled away, and the soldiers climbed down and moved on.

At the end of the second night of the march, Xenophon stood in the riverbed, looking up at the sheer walls on either side of him. "I can't see a damn thing," he said.

"There's one," Eugenides said, pointing to a black oblong in the cliffside, a hole in the stone suspicious for its squareness. "The others are right there in a row."

Xenophon waved to the men with the ladders, and they lifted and set them near the holes carved in the stone walls. Working carefully, with a great deal of swearing, they were able to lift into place a series of beams across the chasm of the riverbed. It was at its narrowest just above its steepest drop. Below the falls, the soldiers would have room to march beside the river, but the dawn was nearing, and they couldn't get down the cliffside in time to escape the rush of the Aracthus's waters. Nor could they get out of the riverbed. Even if they'd had the means to climb the steep walls of the canyon, once outside it, they would have been exposed on the hillside, visible to anyone below.

The beams fit, not neatly but effectively, into narrow holes carved into the stone.

"How long have these been here?" Xenophon asked the Thief, who shrugged his shoulders.

"You'd have to ask my father. They are a military resource, and I knew of them only by accident. I read a reference to them in a scroll that was a hundred and fifty years old," he said. "There was some unrest with Attolia then, and the king had sentinels posted here. The cuts were already made."

"And you're sure they are above the level of the river in flood?"

"They were a hundred and fifty years ago," said Eugenides wickedly.

Xenophon beetled his brows and frowned at the Thief. "I had your father's word that those orifices existed and would support beams across the chasm and that the beams so supported would be above the level of the river."

Eugenides relented. "We sent a stonemason down to check them to be sure they hadn't eroded. They all seem to be well above the high-water line."

Xenophon looked up at the structure that had taken form over his head. Nets stretched between the beams made a series of platforms. "Time to climb up, I suppose." He glanced at the Thief and then away, refraining at the last moment from asking if Eugenides could make the climb unassisted. Obviously he could if he had gotten up the ladders the night before. The Thief was wet to the neck, so he must have fallen at least once on the way down the river, but so had almost everyone. Those soldiers not engaged in the work of stringing the nets overhead stood in water up to their knees and shivered.

Eugenides had seen Xenophon's look and guessed its meaning. He stiffened, and Xenophon winced. He hadn't meant to offend. The general turned away and started ordering his soldiers into their positions. This was the second set of platforms, and there was still one more set to be put into place downstream.

Later, as the first light of dawn was showing in the sky, Xenophon carefully crossed the net of the platform under him and sat beside Eugenides. He was impressed with the young man's ability to keep up with the rest of his soldiers and was hesitating over how or whether to put this into words when the Thief spoke.

"I thought a messenger was to be sent down from the platforms upstream when the cannon barrels and carriages were secure," he said.

"They probably weren't sure he could get down the rocky part before the water hit. The canyon's too deep here to see the flare," Xenophon said.

"I think the water is at its height," Eugenides was saying just as a sudden thud shook the platform.

With the rest of the soldiers, Xenophon clutched the rope net under him. Only the Thief didn't. He leaned forward instead to look down into the river.

"What was it?" the general asked.

"I'm not sure," Eugenides replied. "It was big. It might have been a tree trunk that's been freed by the changing water pattern." He sounded uncertain. "It might have been one of the cannon," he said. "It didn't hit the beam directly. It was a glancing blow."

They sat thinking about what a direct blow would have done to the wooden supports for their nets.

The queen of Attolia stirred in her sleep and woke. She sat up slowly, blinking away the last traces of an unpleasant dream, and looked around the room. She could see by the light of a small lamp left burning on the nightstand, but there were dark corners the light didn't penetrate. There was a shadow behind the wardrobe, a deeper one at the edge of the window curtains. She sat up against her pillows. She pulled the bedclothes up as far as they would go and suppressed a perverse wish to have her old nurse come to chase away the darkness, perverse because she didn't know if she wanted the shadows to be empty or not. She sat watching until the day dawned and the shadows lightened and were gone.

When the last glimmer in the sky had faded, and the waters of the Aracthus had drained away, the men on the banks climbed stiffly down into the damp riverbed. A messenger from upstream reported that three of the cannon barrels they transported had been unsecured when the waters of the Aracthus swept down the canyon. They'd lost sixteen men when two of the loose barrels had destroyed the support for a platform down river from Eugenides and Xenophon. Four of the twenty camped on the platform had managed to grasp the supports of a platform farther downstream and had been plucked out of the floodwaters. Of the rest of the men there was no sign.

The cannon were found at the edge of the pool at the base of the last great waterfall before the Aracthus reached the dystopia. Two of them were split and unusable. The third Xenophon decided was still worth the difficulty of transporting. He had snorted when he'd seen them by the bank and said, "Thank the gods we don't have to dig them off the bottom." The pool was deep, deepest where the waters of the river dropped into it. The bottom was invisible in the darkness, and retrieving cast-iron cannon from the depths would have been impossible.

Where the ground was level, the gorge was wider, and there was room for the soldiers to camp in relative comfort for the day. There were no fires, but the men took dry uniform tunics and pants from the waterproofed bags they'd carried on their shoulders and put them on. When the sun set, Xenophon began the cautious advance across the dystopia. Once again the cannon moved impossibly slowly, and the soldiers dragging them cursed.

"Attolia's border patrols won't come this far?" Xenophon checked with Eugenides. He needn't have, these details had been discussed in Eddis, but Eugenides was happy to reassure him, glad that the responsibility of leadership was Xenophon's, not his.

"I doubt they'll bring their horses into the dystopia without good cause, certainly not at night," he said.

Xenophon was relieved that the Thief no longer seemed offended by the general's gaffe the night before. "This is the stupidest plan that I have ever in my career participated in," he said.

"I love stupid plans," said Eugenides. "How long will it take to get across the dystopia?"

"Twice as long as it would take without those worthless cannon of yours."

Eugenides laughed.

Once the Eddisians reached the edge of the dystopia they were surrounded by the trees called the Sea of Olives that grew along the base of the Hephestial Mountains in Attolia. They regrouped into orderly units and rested. They made no fires, and the olive trees hid them from view. In the afternoon their officers directed the soldiers onto one of the narrow tracks that led through the groves, and they began their march toward the Seperchia. Before they reached the road, they met up with a horse trader. A sharp-faced man, he looked likely to drive hard bargains, but he surrendered his horses to the Eddisians, taking nothing in return, and disappeared between the olives to return to Eddis.

The horses were hitched to the gun carriages. Then the Eddisians moved on, under Xenophon's cautious direction, from the narrow track to a road and down the road to a small town on the river. The townspeople stared incuriously at the soldiers in the heavily quilted tunics that were their uniform and their armor. All of them were colored the celestial blue and yellow of Attolia's army. The disguised Eddisians moved through the town to the docks where four ships waited to receive them. Wordlessly the soldiers were directed by their officers up the gangplanks and onto the riverboats. The men managing cannon muttered directions under their breaths, to hide their Eddisian accents, as they unhitched the horses and shifted the cannon barrels to the edge of a dock, where they were loaded with the aid of a block and tackle onto one of the ships.

Eugenides watched, unable to interfere, but he whispered to Xenophon, "Please the gods, no one is going to notice that you just put twelve cannon onto one riverboat."

Xenophon winced, but he also was unable to interfere. His orders or a soldier's response might give away their identity. They weren't the only soldiers in the town, and it was urgent that they leave it as quickly as possible. Within the hour they were gone, the boats moving down the river with the current, while Eddis's agent, who had procured the boats, reported to Xenophon. He was a merchant and a citizen of one of the city-states on the peninsula, with no particular loyalty to Attolia or to Eddis. His loyalty was to his own treasury, and he would remain with the Eddisians until their need for secrecy was over.

The ships were stocked with food, and each had a bricked hearth in which to cook. On each ship, hot coffee was poured into the soldiers' cups, and they made themselves comfortable for the trip. They would not risk a stop on the shore until it was time to disembark.

chapter 14

IN EPHRATA, ATTOLIA sat relaxed on the large chair on the dais that served as her throne when she was in residence. Until the current war with her neighbors, her visits had been rare. Ephrata was a small castle. As with so many of Sounis's and Attolia's strongholds, the one large room that had been the entirety of some minor prince's home had come to be the main hall of a fortified residence. The word *megaron*, which had originally described a building consisting of only one room, had changed to mean both this style of stronghold and the large hall inside.

There was a harbor nearby, but it was small and not well protected during the summer windstorms, so the tiny town on its shore had never prospered. Now it suited the queen's purpose well, allowing her to be close to her army as it blockaded the pass to Eddis and to communicate with her ships as they moved in and out of the harbor at her orders. None of the ships stayed long. Her navy was not so large that she could keep a fighting ship inactive at Ephrata, and so the poor harbor posed little danger to her fleet. All her larger ships sailed with her fleet, between the islands. She relied on a few fast messenger ships to carry orders to her sailors, but she had sent two out the day before, one of them carrying her secretary of the archives back to the capital to keep an eye on events there for his queen, and the harbor was empty.

Seated on her throne, Attolia listened to reports from her army and from Relius's spies. The spies reported mainly on her own army—at least on its hereditary officers—but they also confirmed the reports that the Eddisian army had camped just within the pass.

Attolia believed it was a tactical error and was pleased. Eddis had moved her army beyond the protecting fire of her cannon, and she wouldn't easily be able to retreat up the narrow pass. Attolia's army was the larger and the better equipped. She was on the verge of summoning her officers for a council of war when the Medean ambassador was announced. The queen dismissed the men before her and smiled at the Mede.

"Your Majesty hardly needs interrupt her business for me," he said as he came forward.

"The business can wait for my pleasure, Nahuseresh. I had thought you were many miles away in the capital."

"It was too dull to bear any longer without you," he said, bowing over her hand. "And too terribly suspenseful to know that you were here perhaps in direst need of my assistance." He said it with a smile, as if to assure her that he joked, that he had complete confidence in her ability to direct her army and her barons to Eddis's defeat.

"It is good to have a friend nearby," said the queen, squeezing his hand before releasing it. "But the greatest aid you can give me is your company." She knew the warships of the Mede emperor cruised the open water just beyond the outer islands, waiting to come to her assistance.

"For that honor," the Mede said, "no distance is too far to travel." Standing up, he looked curiously around the great room and for a moment glanced behind him. The queen reinforced his subtle hint with a nod at one of the attendants, and a chair was brought forward.

"Your Majesty is most gracious," said Nahuseresh as he sat.

"But not well served by your steward, I think." He looked with disapproval at the room. Its walls were undecorated except for an interlocking pattern painted near the ceiling. The pattern on its painted floor was darkened with age and indistinct.

"It's very old," the queen said with a smile. "This was an Attolian megaron, a fortified room on a hilltop, when your emperor's present palace was an empty plot of land in the Sidosians' territory."

The Mede ambassador preferred beauty to age. He didn't say so, but the queen knew it. Perhaps because she was Attolia and it was her megaron, she preferred it to the splendors of the Mede palaces with the glazed tile walls and the gold-topped pillars.

The Mede changed the subject. "Eddis overreaches herself at last?"

"Perhaps."

"And your barons, you are wary of treachery?"

"More wary of stupidity." Attolia dismissed the war and her barons with a wave of her hand. "Tell me, how was your journey here?"

The Mede had traveled by ship and had landed down the coast only a few miles away at the port of Rhea, but he told Attolia in convincing detail about the poor quality of the roads between Ephrata and the capital and the even poorer quality of the springs in his carriage.

"Poor Nahuseresh," said the queen, "to suffer so much for my sake." She laid a languid hand in his.

"At least I was fortunate to arrive before the rain."

"Is it going to rain? I have been immured in this hall with tiresome people all day and have not seen the sky."

"Yes," said Nahuseresh, "it will certainly rain."

The clouds had not yet dropped low enough to occlude the view from the mountains, and Eddis's watchers had seen the

Mede ship land. They reported the landing as well as the weather to their queen where she was camped in her tent above her army.

"Attolia would not hurry to attack in the rain," said Eddis. "We can hope for something heavier than the usual summer drizzle, and perhaps she will call her barons to her to receive their instructions." She worried that the queen might leave her megaron in order to oversee the disposition of her army. "So long as she is in the megaron, I think the Mede, on his own, will not complicate Eugenides's plans."

The queen of Attolia was waiting impatiently for the last of the barons that she had summoned to arrive when the captain of her guard, Teleus, entered the room and stepped to her side. He bent down to speak quietly in the queen's ear. The message took some time to deliver, and she sat immobile while she listened, her eyes narrowed in concentration. When he was done, she stood without explanation. Everyone else at the council table stood as well, while the queen left the room.

She reached the steps down to the courtyard as a group of exhausted horses was led away. There were six mud-splattered soldiers surrounded by a larger group of curious onlookers. Seeing the queen, the onlookers melted away. The muddy soldiers pulled themselves to attention, and one of them stepped forward.

"The royal messenger?" the queen asked.

Her guard captain, standing just behind her, answered, "He was struck by a crossbow quarrel just at the edge of the forest."

"And the message he carried?" the queen asked the lieutenant of the small group.

"We went back for the message bag, Your Majesty," he said, speaking carefully. He handed the leather messenger bag, stamped with the royal crest, to Teleus, who reached forward to take it.

"Well done," the queen praised him. She took the bag and opened it, withdrew the folded paper inside, and handed the bag back to Teleus. Attolia glanced at the signet on the seal only a moment before she cracked the wax and began to read the message. She looked up when she was finished.

"Send them to the barracks and come inside," she said to her guard captain, and started back up the steps to the porch of the megaron.

The lieutenant bowed to Teleus and nodded to his men, directing them toward the doorway that led from the courtyard to the guard barracks. Teleus saw that the lieutenant was familiar with Ephrata and left him to settle his soldiers himself. He followed the queen.

Nahuseresh saw them pass and took note of the message bag swinging from Teleus's hand. He raised his eyebrows in surprise. He thought he had closed off every road to Ephrata and accounted for every royal messenger.

In an anteroom to the counsel chamber, Attolia turned to Teleus. "Send for Hopsis from the capital," she said. "And call back Relius, too. Baron Efkis has betrayed us. One of his officers reports that he has allowed an army of Eddisians coming down the Seperchia to land on this side of the river. They are probably in the woods already."

"There are no messenger ships in the harbor," Teleus said. "The one due today hasn't arrived. The next isn't due until tomorrow."

The queen swore with a ferocity that would have stunned her Medean ambassador. "Get one of the fishing boats from the village," she said. "There should be a fast ship at Rhea down the coast."

"How could the Eddisians have come down to the Seperchia without being sighted?" Teleus asked.

"More treachery," said the queen, flicking a shoulder in a

brief shrug. "I would not have thought it of the officers in the blockade at the bridge by the Old Aracthus Gate, but if they were overwhelmed and there were no survivors, the Eddisians might have got through without warning." She cursed again. "The messenger reported cannon," she said.

"We can't hold against cannon," Teleus protested. "We'll have to send to the army for rescue."

"You must try, Teleus," said the queen. "But I believe it is already too late."

She went to the wall above the gate of the castle to look out over the field to the forested ridge that lay between her and the Seperchia River. The woods that covered the ridge had grown down to the far edge of the fields. The fields themselves were no more than the garden patches for the megaron and the nearby village. The Eddisians would be able to fire from the cover of the trees and would direct all the force of their cannon into the poorly maintained walls of the megaron. Her captain pointed out the body of her messenger still lying on the road in the fading light of the day.

"You can't get the body?" she asked.

The captain shook his head. "The Eddisian crossbowmen have the gates covered. We tried sending messengers out to the village, but they were unable to get through the crossbow fire and came back."

The queen nodded. She had feared as much. "If we could get a boat out, we could send someone down the coast to Rhea, but I think we have to assume that the baron holds Rhea as well," she said.

She and Teleus were silent, watching the men moving in the woods.

"They can't bombard the castle without Piloxides's hearing the guns," the queen said abruptly. "He'll come then."

"True," said the guard. This hadn't occurred to him.

"So we need only to hold out until Piloxides reaches us."

They watched the edge of the woods as the darkness fell and the Eddisians camping there laboriously moved their cannon into position. They could hear the cursing and make out the men straining. One cannon broke away from its handlers and rolled down into an irrigation ditch at the side of the fields. Eddisians risking crossbow fire from Ephrata's walls hurried down to reattach ropes, and they painfully winched the cannon back uphill.

"Eleven cannon," the captain counted. "They'll be in position to fire by morning."

Thunder rumbled distantly, and they both looked up at the clouds. "A summer storm," said the queen.

"That's unusual," remarked Teleus.

Thunder rumbled again, and they were silent, listening.

"Those are Piloxides's guns," said the queen at last. "The Eddisians must be attacking from the pass. He's not going to hear anything over that." She looked again toward the dark trees.

"Surrender," she said.

"Your Majesty?" Teleus was taken by surprise.

"They can have the megaron," Attolia said bitterly, "and all my barons as well. Piloxides will retake it in the end. Tell them we will surrender in the morning." She turned to her guard captain with a grim smile. "I am sorry to leave you, Teleus. You understand, I won't be here when the Eddisians take over?"

"I understand, Your Majesty." Teleus bowed.

"Make the arrangements," the queen said, and went down from the wall.

While Teleus signaled the Eddisians, she returned to her room and dismissed her attendants. Hastily she collected a few necessities and a heavy cloak, then sat down to write out several letters. When it was finished, she called in the guard stationed outside the door and sent him to find his captain.

Once he was gone, and the corridor outside empty, she left her rooms and hurried to a small locked door, for which she had a key. Behind the door a twisting staircase spiraled down. Carefully waiting until the halls were empty, the queen moved through the small stronghold to another door and another staircase that led to deeper hallways cut into the rock of the outcropping on which the megaron stood.

She'd brought a lamp but didn't need it. Lamps already burned in the hallway sconces, lit by the guardsman Teleus had sent ahead of her. She saw no one until she reached the door she sought. Beside it, Teleus's guard was waiting. He'd heard her footsteps and had pulled himself to attention by the time she approached. If he thought the situation was irregular, nothing in his manner showed it. Staring at the wall opposite him, he presented the queen with a view of his ear and awaited her orders.

"The boat is ready?"

"Yes, Your Majesty." The boat was always ready.

She unlocked the door herself, and the guard followed her through. On the far side the air was chilly and damp and dark. They were in a cave under the megaron that opened onto the harbor. They could hear the water washing against the dock in front of them, and through the mouth of the cave the queen could make out the white tops of the waves in the darkness. The light from the doorway behind them lit the dock, and Attolia didn't bother with her lamp. A boat waited, its sails wrapped against its mast. It was not a large boat, just large enough to hold two, but Attolia was confident it would serve her purpose. She didn't expect to sail far. She would go to the Medes and worry later how to extricate herself from their assistance and how to explain to Nahuseresh that there hadn't been room for him to accompany her. She walked down the dock, careful in the dim light, and stopped when she reached the boat. The tie lines were long and allowed it to float several feet out in the water. She gestured for the guard to pull the boat in. Out of the corner of her eye she saw him drop obediently to one knee and reach over the water. The hook in place of his missing right hand thunked quietly into the wooden hull.

Teleus stood above the gate and looked down at the Eddisian standing below him. He'd expected someone on a horse and was surprised when the soldier had stepped out of the cover of the trees and walked across the fields to the megaron.

"You wish to surrender?" the man shouted.

"In the morning," Teleus answered.

"Fair enough. Will you leave your dead until then?" The royal messenger was lying in the road as the darkness gathered.

"We'll bring him in tonight with your permission," Teleus said.

"I'll tell my general," the soldier said, and waved one hand up at Teleus before turning back to the forest.

"Let me go, sir," said a voice at Teleus's elbow. He turned and recognized the lieutenant who had come in with the messenger's bag. "He was a friend," the soldier said. "I'll go get him."

"Very well," said Teleus.

A little later the guard was standing beside one of the pillars that supported the wide porch of the megaron and saw the lieutenant on horseback waiting while the gate from the courtyard was opened. He was accompanied by four others, the rest of the messenger's guard but one. Annoyed, he remarked to no one in particular that it didn't take five men to collect a body. He started down the steps from the porch, but the gate opened, and the riders disappeared through it. He waited in the courtyard, meaning to speak to the lieutenant when he returned. When he heard the shouting on the wall, he rushed up the stairs to the lookout above the gate. Staring into the twilight, he saw no one on the road. The horsemen and the body of the messenger were gone.

"The messenger?" he asked.

"Jumped up the moment they got near," the guard said. "No more dead than I am. One of the riders took him up behind, and they rode into the woods."

Teleus stared. Five men. The messenger's guard minus one. "Follow me," he commanded the nearby guard, and ran back down the rampart stairs even faster than he had climbed them.

chapter 15

_A_TTOLIA TURNED TO look at him, where he kneeled watching her face. He'd grown, she realized. Boys did often grow in one last leap just as they became men, but her spies either hadn't noticed or hadn't thought to tell her. He was not quite her height, but with his hair cropped short under his helmet, she hadn't looked twice at him when she had seen him with the other muddy soldiers in the courtyard earlier. He'd had a false hand then, instead of a hook. She supposed he'd covered it with riding gloves. The greatest change in him was not his height, nor the length of his hair, but the expression on his face. He looked at her as impassively as she knew she looked at him. She could feel the immobile mask of her own face. She thought that if she searched for the guardsman Teleus had sent to escort her, she would find him nearby, not unconscious, not bound and gagged, but dead.

"You've changed," said Attolia.

"So I have been told. Into the boat, Your Majesty," said Eugenides with a nod of his head. He still squatted there next to the boat, within easy striking distance. The black water was near to hand to receive her body.

Attolia remembered his face as it had looked the first time she examined it closely, when he'd been in her castle on the Seperchia, bleeding from a sword wound. He'd smiled at her—the satisfied smile of an archer whose shot had gone home—when he'd told her that she was more beautiful than Eddis but less kind. Attolia didn't think he would smile at her again, not even to gloat. She hesitated another moment and then stepped into the boat. It rocked under her, and she sat down quickly, facing backward, on a wooden bench that stretched from side to side close to the mast. She pulled her cloak tighter to ward off the chill.

"Where there's life, there's hope, Your Majesty?" Eugenides asked, his voice expressionless. Attolia didn't answer. She fixed her gaze on the centerboard case in front of her, while the Thief used the knife-edge along the inside of the hook to slice through the line that bound the sail of the boat. The boom dropped beside her, the sail flapped free. Eugenides untied the boat and, holding its bowline, walked it toward the end of the dock. Distantly they heard shouting. Eugenides picked up speed, beginning to trot. The boat moved quickly through the water, and as it passed the end of the dock, Eugenides stepped in at the stern. The boat rocked again. Attolia clutched the front edge of her seat. Men spilled through the doorway behind them, but the boat was already out from under the overhang of the megaron's foundation and into the wind. It heeled abruptly as the sail filled, and Attolia shifted her weight. Eugenides dropped into the seat at the stern and laid his hook over the boat's tiller to steer. He adjusted the sail with his hand and the boat picked up more speed, leaving the cavern behind. By the time Attolia's soldiers reached the end of the dock, the boat was out of reach, its occupants invisible in the darkness.

The water in the harbor was choppy, and the little boat seemed to jump from wave to wave. Attolia felt the spray hitting her back and was thankful that the closely woven wool of the cloak repelled most of the water. She huddled inside it.

They left the harbor and sailed out into the dark sea. When Eugenides turned the boat to follow the coast toward Eddis, the wind was behind them and he was a dark mass in the stern. Over his shoulder Attolia watched the lights of the megaron fade until they disappeared entirely behind the rocks of a headland. They sailed on, the water slowly soaking through the back of Attolia's cloak as it splashed over the bow behind her.

Eugenides asked, "Do you swim, Your Majesty?"

"No," she answered shortly.

When Teleus led the soldiers up from the cavern below the megaron, he met the Mede, waiting at the top of the stairs.

"Perhaps you would like to tell me what caused this furor, guard?" the Mede asked, and Teleus hesitated, but could see no justification in not reporting the abduction of the queen. The Mede smiled grimly.

"How very clever of the Thief of Eddis. No doubt he is drowning her as we speak," said the Mede. "Perhaps drowning himself as well, if he means to sail down the coast on a cloudy night with no moon to guide him." Nahuseresh didn't seem to mind much the idea of the queen drowning. Teleus watched him, eyes narrowed.

"We have to get a message to the army at the pass," Teleus said.

"Why?" asked the Mede, raising his eyebrows in surprise. "To start the arrangements for a state funeral?"

"She might not be dead," Teleus snarled.

"True," Nahuseresh agreed thoughtfully. "That's true. I had better leave you to your task. Please excuse me, guard. I have some dinner waiting for me in my rooms, I think."

"Your Majesty." Eugenides spoke many hours later. "You'll want to bend your head, I'm going to jibe."

Attolia opened her eyes and looked back toward him. The

wind had blown the clouds apart, and the moon shone on the water around her and on the high black cliffs not far away.

"The sail will swing across the boat quickly," Eugenides explained. "You don't want the boom to hit you."

Stiffly, Attolia hunched down. Eugenides moved the tiller to one side, and the boat lurched. The sail swept overhead and slammed hard at the end of its lines. The boat tilted and Attolia lunged for the high side, but Eugenides was already sitting on the rail, leaning backward to bring the boat level. The speed of the boat, once it had turned broadside to the wind, seemed twice what it had been before, and Attolia went on clutching the siderail as the boat charged toward sheer cliffs.

She was rigid, her fingers clenched as Eugenides steered between rocks topped with foaming white water and sailed directly toward the cliffs, in which she could see no break or variation. Then, as he adjusted the tiller again, she saw the narrow opening they aimed for. A minute later they were between its walls. The wind lessened, and the water was smooth, only rising and falling in gentle swells. The boat's momentum carried it forward as Eugenides carefully maneuvered it past hazards that she couldn't see.

Moving more and more slowly, they drifted into a tiny cove entirely surrounded by the high cliffs. There was no wind, and the water was smooth, reflecting the moon that shone overhead. The harbor was utterly quiet after the noise of the open sea.

Attolia settled herself again in the middle of the forward bench, staring again at the centerboard case.

"Your Majesty." Eugenides spoke quietly and waited until Attolia raised her eyes to look at him.

His face was still, his expression unreadable. Seeing it, Attolia remembered the day in the audience chamber when she had become queen in fact as well as in name. Her guard captain, Teleus's predecessor, had eliminated her overbearing suitor, and she'd left her barons to themselves to accept the reality of her rule and gone to her bedchamber—the last time she would go to that room instead of the royal apartments. She'd stood in front of the smooth silver mirror there and studied her face, reaching up to touch her skin, wondering if it could in truth be as hard as it appeared. She'd been frightened and sick in that audience chamber, with no assurance that the captain could or would hold to his promises, but none of her fear, or her revulsion, had shown on her face. She was the stone-faced queen, then and ever after. She had needed the mask to rule, and she had been glad to have it. She wondered if Eugenides was glad of his.

"You have a choice now," the Thief was saying. "Conscious or unconscious, you can go into the water. I have the boat pole to make certain you don't come out again." He nudged the pole lying at his feet. It rattled against the centerboard case, and hearing it, Attolia glanced down. The boat pole was five or six feet long and had two small hooks at the end. The hooks she could easily imagine catching in the folds of her clothes as Eugenides leaned on the pole to force her farther and farther under the surface.

She looked back at Eugenides impassively. She thought he had brought her a long way to drown her, but she knew that in his own field he was meticulous and supposed he wanted to be entirely sure of his results.

He made no move but instead spoke again. "Or you can offer me something I want more than I want to hold your head underwater until the last of your air is gone."

Attolia had thought her choice was to be conscious or unconscious when she breathed in the black water that would kill her; she couldn't imagine what Eugenides might want more than that. It was all she would have dreamed of in his place.

"I want to be king of Attolia," he said.

Attolia blinked. She looked around the tiny harbor and had to clear her throat with a cough before she spoke. "You've brought me to a place rather spare of witnesses if you want me to declare you my heir before I die."

"I wasn't proposing to become your heir," said the Thief.

"Then what?" asked Attolia.

"There's an easier way for a man to become king," said Eugenides, and waited for her to realize what he proposed.

Attolia stared at him. "You think I would marry you?" she asked in disbelief.

"If you object to marrying a man with one hand, you've only yourself to blame."

"And when did you grow into a man?" asked Attolia, lifting her eyebrow, her voice tinged with sarcasm.

Eugenides didn't rise to her bait. "It's your choice, Your Majesty," he said quietly.

"And if I choose to die here?" she asked.

The only sounds were the slap of ripples against the boat bottom and the susurration of the water against the base of the cliffs around them.

"Then Attolia collapses into civil war and the Medes come," Eugenides said at last. "They will rule Attolia, and Sounis as well, while Eddis retreats to her mountains."

"Eddis has no trade without Sounis and Attolia. She is not self-sustaining. If your queen destroys Attolia, she destroys herself."

"She has the pirates."

The queen looked again at the harbor around her, understanding perfectly how useful it was to a queen who had no official navy. "How resourceful of her. Of course she has the pirates. Can she control them?"

"Well enough to serve our purposes. Well enough to keep Eddis from starving."

"You hope."

Eugenides shrugged. "Eddis will have been a poor country for a long, long time before the Medes lose their grip on this coast, but there will be an Eddis long after Sounis and Attolia are gone. We have our mountains to keep us."

"And if I choose not to die?"

"Then I will escort you to my queen to begin negotiations for a marriage contract. Together the armies of Eddis and Attolia can keep the Mede off this coast and force Sounis to make peace as well."

"And you would be king in Attolia?"

"Yes."

"And I would be queen still."

"You would rule. I will not interfere, but you will accept Eddisian advisors."

"Then I watch my country bled dry to pay Eddis tribute, its treasury drained, its taxes raised, its peasants enslaved, and the barons again the true rulers of the country, free to do as they please so long as the king is fed?"

"Do you care," asked Eugenides, "so long as the queen is fed as well?"

"Yes," Attolia hissed, and leaned forward with her hands clenched.

Eugenides remained impassive. Attolia could see him in the moonlight but couldn't guess if he was pleased to have elicited a reaction from her. She sat back on her bench and composed herself.

"Yes, I care. It is my country."

The Thief thought carefully before he spoke. "If I am king, there will be peace with Eddis but no tribute."

The queen sniffed in disbelief, then sat hunched over, wrapping her hands in the fabric of her dress to warm them while she thought. She was cold and wet, and sitting across from Eugenides, she felt older than her years. Her bones ached. Eugenides, she was sure, was too young to have bones that ached. No matter what he thought of himself, he was hardly more than a boy. A boy without one hand. She reached up to push the wet hair out of her face, wondering when she had sunk so low that she had begun torturing boys. It was the question she'd asked herself night after night, lying awake in her bed or sitting in a chair by the window, watching the stars slowly move across the sky.

"I listened outside your cell door every night before I sent you back to Eddis," Attolia said abruptly.

Eugenides sat quietly, waiting for her to go on.

"The first night you cried," she said. She looked for a reaction but saw none.

She had lingered outside his cell, in the dim light of the lamps, alone because she'd sent away her escort while she listened. Alone, because she had known, even then, that she would turn on any guard who mocked the Thief's pain. He had cried in breathless, racking sobs that had gone on and on, long after she'd thought he would have exhausted himself. Finally he had slept, but the queen had not. The sound of his tears had kept her from sleep that night and woken her from nightmares since the evening she'd heard them.

"The second night you repeated the same words over and over. I think the fever had set in by then. Do you remember what you said?"

"No."

She knew every one of them. His voice, broken and stumbling, had filled her dreams until she had wept in her sleep, crying tears for him that she'd never been able to cry for her father or for herself. "Oxe Harbrea Sacrus Vax Dragga . . ." she began.

Eugenides's chin lifted as he recognized the opening words.

"It's the invocation of the Great Goddess at her spring festival," he said calmly, "calling her to the aid of those that need her. The words are archaic."

"She comes to the aid of those who need her? She didn't come to yours."

"You have a decision to make, Your Majesty." Eugenides reminded her. "And not much time to make it in."

It was quiet then, while Attolia thought, particularly about the Medean ambassador with his attractive face and his quick smile.

Eugenides waited. "Very well," the queen said, sitting up straight to look him in the eye. "Be king of Attolia. But never drink from my wine cup while you hope to live."

"There's an oar by the boat hook," Eugenides said, his voice devoid of triumph. "You'll have to paddle us to the dock." He steered, reaching across his body to use his hand instead of his hook, while she shifted on her seat in order to dip the paddle into the dark water and move the boat toward the tiny dock that jutted from the rocky beach at the base of the cliffs.

She had no skill with the paddle, and it was half an hour before they reached the dock. Attolia pulled the boat against it, and Eugenides stepped out. He turned and offered her his hand. Once she, too, was standing on the dock, he moved back several steps, closed his eyes, and stretched his arms up over his head to ease the stiffness in his shoulders. Attolia reached to pull from its fabric padding the knife she carried along her ribs, but it was gone. Gone as well were the ceremonial knife from her belt and even the tiny blade hidden in the twists of her hair.

She looked at Eugenides to see his eyes open and his hand holding all three knives, their blades spread in a fan. He tossed them one at a time into the air, catching each by the blade as it came down and tossing it up again, juggling them one-handed, then holding them out, handles first, to the queen. She hesitated, expecting him to pull them back, but he didn't move.

"Have all three," he said.

When she'd taken them, he pointed to a spot just below his heart.

"An upward stroke here," he said, "would be most efficient, but almost anywhere would do the job. You can push me into the water," he said. "I don't know if I can swim with one hand or not."

Attolia waited, sensing a trap. The moon disappeared behind a cloud. Eugenides was only a dark form against the darker water behind him. "Before you make a decision," he said, "I want you to know that I love you."

Attolia laughed. Eugenides flushed in the dark.

"I have been surrounded by liars all my life and never heard one lie like you," said Attolia, smiling.

"It's the truth." Eugenides shrugged.

"This is a feeling that's come upon you suddenly? Since our recent engagement?"

"No," said the Thief quietly. "When I stole Hamiathes's Gift, I loved you then. I didn't understand it. I thought you must be a fiend from hell," he admitted, cocking his head to one side, "but I already loved you."

He said, "Before he died, my grandfather used to bring me to your palace so that I could see it for myself. There was a party and dancing one night, and the palace was full of people. I went to the kitchen garden to hide because it should have been empty, but once I was inside, the door opened from the flower gardens, and you came in by yourself. I watched you walking between the rows of cabbages and then dancing under the orange trees. I was above you, in one of the trees."

Attolia stared. She remembered the night she danced under the orange trees. "And how old were you?" the queen asked. "Six?"

"Older than that," said Eugenides, smiling at the memory.

"Calf love," said the queen.

"Calf love doesn't usually survive amputation, Your Majesty."

"A good thing I cut off your hand, then, instead of cutting out your heart," said Attolia cruelly. "You think you still love me?"

"Yes."

"And you think I'll believe you?"

Eugenides shrugged. "You can kill me here, Your Majesty, and be done with this. Or you can believe me." He'd seen her in a pale dress dancing in the moonlight, pretending an entire troupe of dancers danced the harvest circle with her, her arms open to embrace the sisters and friends who existed only in her imagination, and he'd never seen anything so beautiful or so sad. He'd remembered that moment when he'd seen her flush at being called cruel. Afterward, when the magus offered to send him information more current than that in his own library, Eugenides had accepted gladly and read carefully, trying to see whether Attolia could be the monster in human guise she was accused of being, or only a woman who ruled without the support of her barons. In the end he had taken advice his grandfather had given him years before and gone to see for himself.

"I love you," he said. "You could believe me."

Attolia looked at him a moment longer, still holding the knife ready. Then she slid it back into its padded sleeve in the front of her dress and stepped forward. She laid one hand on his cheek. He stood as if he were frozen.

"This is what I believe," she said. "I believe that at the top of the stairs you have friends waiting, and if I climb those stairs without you, I will surely die at the top."

"There's the boat," Eugenides said quietly, not moving under the warmth of her hand.

"You didn't tie it to the dock, and it has floated away. If I did reach it, could I hope to paddle it past the rocks?'

"No."

"Then let us climb the stairs together," said the queen, and she turned away from him.

chapter 16

THE STEPS LEADING up from the beach were cut into the side of a fissure in the cliffs. From time to time wooden steps stretched across the fissure to carry them to better footing on the opposite side. Eugenides let the queen go first, that she might set the pace and that he might keep an eye on her. The climb warmed her and loosened her muscles, but her feet in their felt slippers were still wet and cold. Each step hit like a blow. She checked the knives in their places frequently. At the first turn, where a wooden bridge crossed to the far side of the narrow canyon, she turned to speak to Eugenides. He was below her, cautiously out of reach.

"You didn't suborn Efkis," she said.

"No," Eugenides answered, "that was a lie. There was no royal messenger. The lieutenant was my cousin Crodes. He has been practicing his Attolian accent for months. The royal messenger pouch we had from your embassy in Eddis."

"But you moved your men past Efkis's guard. And your cannon," she said. "Eleven cannon. How did you get those past?"

"They were wood."

"Wood?"

"Wood," said Eugenides. "Fake. We brought them all down the Seperchia on one boat and then threw them over the side at the end and floated them to shore."

"Bastard," Attolia said.

"Not that I know," Eugenides responded, and for a second a smile flickered on his face, the same sly smile of the successful archer that Attolia remembered. The smile disappeared in an instant.

Attolia turned to begin climbing again. She declined to look back at Eugenides. She climbed ferociously, spending her anger on the stairs. Eugenides followed, listening as her breath grew more labored, waiting for her to get tired and slow down. Having set the pace, the queen refused to reduce it. Struggling to breathe without panting, she kept climbing.

"Your Majesty," Eugenides said.

The queen stopped and swept around to stare down at him.

Eugenides had spoken before he'd thought of anything to say. He only wanted her to stop, hoping that when she began the climb again, she would go more slowly. He looked up at her, tongue-tied by her beauty and her scorn.

"I thought you might like the earrings," he said lamely.

It was as if he could hear the blood moving through her and could hear her flushing with rage.

She said venomously, "I might like the earrings? As much as I would like to marry a half-grown boy? A one-handed goat-foot?" She used the lowlanders' slang for the mountain people of Eddis. "When I am actually willing to marry you, I will wear your earrings. Don't wait for it, Thief."

She turned her back on Eugenides and started climbing again as fast as before.

"Your Majesty," he called.

"What now?"

"It's a long climb," he said, very subdued. "If you keep going like that, you're going to die of apoplexy before you reach the top."

"I'm sure I wouldn't be the first you drove to apoplexy,"

snapped Attolia, but resumed her climb at a slower pace. Eugenides followed, still a safe distance behind her.

They climbed in silence for another half an hour. They could see the end of the stairs above them when Eugenides succumbed to temptation and produced under his breath a credible imitation of a small goat bleating. Attolia heard him. Her head lifted, and she froze for a moment, her hands tightened into fists. She reached for the knives and again found them gone, though she had checked them in their sheaths several times during the climb. Murderously angry, she turned and started deliberately back down the stairs toward the Thief. Eugenides skipped backward step by step as the queen advanced.

"The more stairs we go down, the more stairs we have to climb up again, Your Majesty," Eugenides called.

The queen stopped. After years of intrigue and outright war with her barons, she knew when she was beaten. Without assistance she could not free herself from the Thief. His armed companions waited at the top of the cliff to escort her to her wedding, and there was no help at hand. She schooled herself to patience, always her best resource, and turned back to the climb.

When she reached the top of the stairs, the coastal hills hid the higher mountains beyond them. They were silhouetted against the lightening sky, but it was still dark, and the men before her were difficult to make out. She looked them over coolly. Most of them were in the uniform tunics of Eddis's soldiers, but she could see older men dressed in sober civilian clothes. The fat one, she thought to herself, was one of Eddis's ministers. She supposed the other old men were ministers as well. Eddis honored her with their company.

There was no sign of a camp. The horses and pack animals were staked in rows, their saddles on, their packs loaded.

The officers and ministers approached, variously grave or embarrassed. As they got closer, Attolia recognized more of them. Eddis's minister of trade, her minister of the exchequer. A little ahead of the other men was a man who was neither grave nor discomfited. He was absolutely poker-faced. With narrowed eyes, the queen recognized him as well, Eddis's own chamberlain, brought along to perform the obligatory introductions, which he did without a whisker's deviation from his usual palace style. Only once did he falter, looking over his shoulder.

"He said he wouldn't be here," one of the ministers said in a carrying whisper, and the chamberlain went on with the formal greetings of the queen of Eddis in absentia.

"And now?" the queen asked the open air.

"We'll move as quickly as we can across the hills to the Pricas Spring. There we will be able to cut down to the main pass," said Eugenides behind her. "There will be some hasty negotiations, and we'll be engaged, with your barons as witnesses."

"A dull ceremony," said the queen.

"We can have pomp and glitter at the wedding—and the coronation."

Attolia turned to give him a cold look. He smiled an equally cold smile and turned to the men who'd come to join them.

"No unexpected difficulties?" the minister of trade asked.

"No unexpected ones," Eugenides reported.

The chamberlain spoke to the Attolian queen. "Your Majesty, I regret that we cannot offer you any rest after what must have been an extremely tiring journey, but I am afraid we must reach the main pass with all possible speed. We have a horse for you, if you can ride?"

"I can," said Attolia, meaning that she would rather cooperate than be tied to a saddle.

The chamberlain cleared his throat. "If I may offer it, Your Majesty, I have a dry cloak for you."

"You may offer it," the queen said.

He glanced down at her feet. "We have dry shoes as well. If you will excuse me." He bowed politely and went away to fetch the cloak and soft leather boots as well. When he returned he knelt to remove her slippers and slipped the warm boots on in their place. They were a good fit, and the queen silently curled her cold toes in relief.

They helped her onto a horse that had been brought near as Eugenides stood farther away and watched. Attolia didn't look in his direction. She mounted the horse and was led away without once glancing back.

They climbed higher into the coastal hills and then turned to ride along a narrow trail. They spent the day in the saddle under hanging clouds. The coastal hills were less uniform than the sheer rise of the Hephestials inland of the Seperchia River. The path rose and dipped along the lifting shoulders of land. At nightfall they rode out onto the side of a hill overlooking Attolia and found a camp made on a terrace there. The camp was deserted except for a messenger left to report that Xenophon had encountered no difficulty in the retreat from Ephrata.

Attolia was shaking from exhaustion and accepted the help of one of the soldiers to dismount. He was an older man in uniform but had no tabs on his collar to indicate that he was an officer. He didn't seem much awed by being so close to a queen. Perhaps he served in his own queen's household. He looked oddly familiar, and she wondered if she had met him on some state occasion in Eddis or at her own palace in Attolia. His hands gripped her around the waist as she slid off the horse. They tightened, and for a moment she was irrationally frightened, caught by him, her feet dangling above the ground. His eyes were hard. She stared at him, and he dropped his gaze, then lowered her gently the last few inches to the ground.

She turned away from him and asked the minister who was near what would happen when they reached the queen of Eddis. "There will be negotiations, Your Majesty. I assume."

"On the subject of dowry?" the queen asked, lifting her eyebrow.

"I assume so, Your Majesty. Her Majesty's chamberlain will escort you to your tent." The minister excused himself. The older soldier had disappeared.

The largest tent was hers. The chamberlain led her to the doorway and stopped beside it to bow. He was punctilious in his politeness to the captured queen, and she thought perhaps the politeness was more hateful to her than scorn would have been. She hadn't seen Eugenides all day.

Inside the tent, for her comfort, there were rugs and cushions on a low sleeping couch. She was left alone. The guard waited outside. The queen stared at the empty tent for a moment. Had she been expecting company, she wondered, dinner guests, maybe, to eat the cold supper that waited on a tiny table by the bed? She crouched on the sleeping bench and ate. When she was done, she was almost too tired to stand but dragged herself up to go to the opening of the tent and pull aside the flap that covered it. The guard turned to eye her nervously. A young man not used to the presence of royalty, Attolia guessed.

"I want to see Eugenides," she said in her best regal manner.

The sentry offered to send a message to the Thief.

"Take me to him instead," Attolia commanded. "It's faster, and I am tired and want to rest after speaking to him."

The soldier hesitated, and glanced at a lighted tent beyond the queen's. Attolia started toward it. Let the sentry try to stop her by force if he dared. Making the best of an impossible situation, he hurried to get ahead of her. The doorway of the tent was open, and as Attolia approached, she looked past the sentry's shoulder into the warm light of the lamp hanging on the central tent post.

Eugenides sat on a low stool. The heavyset man kneeling in front of him was wearing the green trimmed tunic of a physician and was just easing the cuff off his arm. Eugenides's eyes were closed. As the cuff came free, he shuddered and dropped his head to rest on the other man's shoulder.

Attolia stood still, remembering that the night before she had thought that Eugenides was too young to have bones that ached.

"Eugenides." The sentry used his name, which was also his title.

"What?" the young man snapped as his head came up and he opened his eyes. He saw the queen standing beyond the doorway and froze for a moment, looking sick, before he turned stiffly to sweep up a towel from beside him and wrap it around the bare stump of his arm. He stood then and stepped toward the door cradling the arm, all expression wiped away from his face and his voice. "Can I help you, Your Majesty?" he asked politely.

"What has happened to the army under Piloxides?"

"I don't have news yet," said Eugenides. "The attack on Piloxides was a feint, meant to distract him. There was no complete engagement."

Attolia returned to her tent without speaking.

In her sleep she heard gentle rain falling on the roof of the tent and woke to shouting. Her legs were still wrapped in the blankets and she was just sitting up when Eugenides pushed the cloth away from the door and stepped into the tent. The lantern hanging in the tent had been left burning, and by its light she could see the sword unsheathed in his left hand.

"What luck you have," he said, stepping toward her.

She wouldn't cower. She lifted her chin as he crossed the tent toward her. When he reached her side, he did not raise the sword as she had expected. He bent down and kissed her briefly on the lips.

Shocked, she pulled her face away and kicked at the blankets binding her legs. By the time she was standing, livid with fury, Eugenides was gone, and the flap of the tent had dropped behind him. She stalked to the doorway to push the cloth aside.

The sentry, the same young man as before, stood outside. "Please stay in the tent, Your Majesty," he said more firmly than he'd spoken before, hopeful that she might obey.

Soldiers with their blades bare crossed in front of the tent at a run. Attolia stepped out of the doorway and let the door cloth fall behind her, cutting off most of the light from inside. It was raining again, though not hard. The moon was gone, and it was difficult to be sure what was happening. As her eyes adjusted, she could see men coming across a ridge that ran along the edge of the mountain terrace. "Who is it?" Attolia asked, her heart in her throat.

"Your Majesty, please go inside," the sentry said again, his voice raised.

Attolia stood her ground. Short of pushing her, the sentry couldn't get her back into the tent, and he looked no more willing to use force than previously. She saw the crests on the armored helmets of the soldiers coming over the ridge and her eyes widened. They were not her troops. They were Medes.

The Eddisian camp was in chaos as the soldiers in it rolled

out of their sleeping blankets, dragging their swords from their sheaths and snatching up their handshields before running toward the Medes in haphazard order. The Medes strode down the ridge in the orderly formation that had won their empire, the soldiers shoulder to shoulder, with their shields locked. They were perfectly organized into an overwhelming fighting unit, and Attolia looked away as they met the first line of Eddisians.

She had tried to explain the Eddisians once to Nahuseresh. He'd pressed her to commit her army to taking the pass up to Eddis, thinking that once they were past the danger of the cannon overlooking the gorge, they could easily sweep through to the top of the pass and win the mountain valleys. She'd refused, doubting that her army would succeed in fighting its way past the cannon without being eviscerated. Nahuseresh had attributed her reluctance to an entirely understandable female timidity. He didn't seem to understand that the people of Eddis had very little to do all winter beyond develop superior artisan skills and train for war.

As the Mede soldiers reached the first of the Eddisians, the Eddisians threw themselves onto their knees, leaving their backs unprotected as they cut the legs out from under the men at the front edge of the phalanx. More Eddisians, running up, threw themselves at the shields, pushing the Medes backward as their supporters pressed them forward. The first rush died, spitted on the swords of the Medes, but the orderly formation compressed and then collapsed. Swinging their swords, the remaining Eddisians drove into the chaos that had been a fighting unit. The Medes struggled to re-form, but they were overwhelmed. For a moment Attolia thought she saw Eugenides, but in the darkness she couldn't be sure.

Then the darkness was driven away by the light of a flare fired into the air on an arrow or crossbow quarrel. It drifted slowly to the ground, its light making it easy to distinguish the bare heads of the Eddisians from the crested helms of the Medes. By the painful light of the burning magnesium ball, Attolia picked out the Thief of Eddis. Beyond Eugenides, she saw the soldier who'd earlier helped her down from her horse. Though they were not close, as Attolia watched, she could see that he and the Thief fought in tandem. Eugenides pressed his opponent. When the man flinched backward, he stepped into the range of the other Eddisian, who spitted him neatly, then turned back to his own attacker. Together Eugenides and his partner had carved a hole deep into the remains of the Medes' fighting unit.

Then the Mede crossbows, in position above the fighting, began to fire by the light of their flare.

"Your Majesty will please go inside the tent." The sentry beside her was shouting. He'd lifted the flap of the door behind them, silhouetting them both against the light inside. He took her by the arm and pulled. Attolia shrugged him off, but his hand was already slipping away. She turned as he fell to the ground as a tree falls, a crossbow quarrel through his throat. Dark blood welled up to mix with the rain. His body spasmed and then was still.

The door cloth of the tent had fallen, and the light was gone, but the queen sidled out of the doorway and beyond the edge of the tent, so that she would not be visible against its lighter surface. From there she continued to watch the fighting. One Eddisian after another dropped in a rain of quarrels. Attolia scanned the melee for Eugenides but couldn't find him again.

"Peace," yelled a Mede from the hillside. "Peace now, Eddis." The remaining Eddisians fell back, lowering their swords. The Mede soldiers lowered theirs as well and waited.

Eugenides was there, shoulders heaving, sword in his hand,

as he used his forearm to push the wet hair off his forehead. The older man was beside him. He spoke, and Eugenides turned to face him. They stayed like that for a moment before Eugenides shook his head and turned away. He looked up the hillside to where the invisible crossbowmen of the Mede lurked.

"Peace!" he shouted into the air, and threw his sword down into the mud. The other Eddisians did the same. Peace and surrender to the Mede.

The gray-haired man spoke again, and Eugenides replied. Whatever he said made the older man give a sour laugh. Then they turned together to look at Attolia as if they could see her through the tent. She could see their pale faces, a little blurred by the rain. Eugenides said something else to the other man, who then nodded and stepped away, distancing himself from the Thief.

Beyond them a figure was silhouetted for a moment on the ridge. Attolia knew who it must be, stepping carefully down to the terrace now that the fighting was done, and she walked out into the open to meet him. When she reached the Mede ambassador, she laid both her hands in his and smiled.

"I have much to thank you for, Nahuseresh, more now than just the pleasure of your company."

"It is my honor, Your Majesty. I only wish I could have saved you the strain of your terrible journey." He bowed over her hands to kiss them both. Even in the rain, his hair lay neatly on his scalp. His cloak swept the tips of his polished boots where the raindrops seemed to sparkle in the torchlight.

She lifted her gaze from his boots back to his face as he straightened.

"A fine rescue," the queen said.

"I have landed my army at Rhea and ordered it to the base of the pass to Eddis to support your soldiers there. I can only hope that Her Majesty will forgive me," the Mede said, "for bringing my men uninvited through her territory."

Attolia squeezed his hands. "What alternative do I have?" she said lightly.

"An opportunity to serve you is a gift from the gods," said the Mede, bowing again.

She stiffened. "What gods?" Attolia asked.

"Yours, mine, what matter?" he said. He'd been joking, confident that the gods were a matter of superstition to her. "Maybe they've made a treaty, an example to us all."

The queen smiled again. "Perhaps they have," she said. She looked to where the Eddisians had been grouped, seeking out Eugenides. The Medes were moving through the group, separating out the officers and those men not in uniform. When they reached Eugenides, one made a comment that made the others laugh.

"Did you bring any manacles?" Attolia asked Nahuseresh.

"A few pairs," answered the Mede. "I think they won't be much use on your one-handed thief," he reminded her.

Annoyed at her thoughtlessness, Attolia pretended to be amused.

"I brought neck chains," Nahuseresh said.

"How clever you are. Chain him to two of the soldiers, will you? Two officers."

"As you wish," said Nahuseresh, and summoned one of his men with a wave of his hand. Attolia left him and stepped across the slick mud to Eugenides. The Mede soldiers had looped a rope around his upper arms and bound his arms to his sides. He stood slack-shouldered, staring at the ground, as they finished their knots and moved away.

As she approached, Eugenides lifted his head to look over the queen's shoulder at the Mede. He had guided Attolia in a number of the naval battles, Eugenides knew. He was liked by some of her barons, courteously hated by others, but respected by all of them. He flattered the queen of Attolia and directed the Mede ships that patrolled her coast as well as the soldiers on land. He didn't take part in the fighting itself, but who could doubt that he would be as competent at killing men as he was at everything else he undertook? So well suited to be a king, all he wanted was a kingdom, and he would condescend to take Attolia. Eugenides hated him.

As the queen approached, Eugenides dropped his eyes. He wanted, desperately, to be sick or to drop to his knees, cover his face with his hands—hand—and cry. If he didn't look the queen of Attolia in the face, he hoped to avoid doing either.

"Where there's life there's hope, Eugenides," Attolia said as she looked him over. His hair lay in damp tendrils on his forehead. The light rain beaded there and dropped onto his face. There was a spatter of mud across one cheek mixed with heavier drops of blood. She looked carefully for any injury but saw no signs and assumed it was someone else's blood. She stooped a little to see his eyes better and followed their direction. He was looking at the water runneling the mud by her left foot. She straightened.

"You'll be chained by the neck to two other prisoners," she told him. "If you and they live to reach my megaron at Ephrata, the other two will be safely returned, without ransom, to Eddis." Eugenides didn't move. His hope of heaven could have been in the dirt at her feet, so fixedly did he stare there. "Do you understand?" she asked.

"Yes," he answered.

"What will you do now?"

"Oh"—he tried unsuccessfully to keep the tremor out of his voice—"grovel, I suppose."

"I've heard you do that before," said Attolia, briefly amused in spite of herself.

Eugenides swallowed. "That was begging," he said with a better effort at lightness. "There wasn't much opportunity for groveling last . . . time." He stumbled, then added evenly, "I am very good at groveling."

"Anything to save your skin?" Attolia asked.

"Nothing is going to save my skin," Eugenides said flatly.

She gripped his chin between her thumb and forefinger. She felt the breath go out of him at her touch. He resisted for a moment and then gave in, raising his head to look her in the eye. Even in the red glow of the torches his face was pale. The muscles in his jaw jumped as he clenched his teeth. He was afraid.

Attolia wasn't surprised that the mask that hid his feelings was gone. His training hadn't been in fear and diplomacy; it had been in silence and stealth. As he looked at her, his eyes were bright with anguish. He had heard of her threats, as she had known he would. She could see that he had no expectations of mercy from her. No hope that she would be something other than ruthless and cruel.

Eugenides was afraid and he was a fool and he knew it. He had forgotten what it felt like to be at the mercy of the queen of Attolia. The blood pounded in his ears, and his entire body was rigid to fight the trembling in his knees. He was sick with it. He remembered that feeling but thought it had been caused then by the pain in his head. Now there was no pain, but the same feeling in the bottom of his stomach. He would beg, he knew, for any mercy she would show, but he thought there would be none. Even if she exacted no revenge for herself, she would exact it for her throne, and for the Mede, to show him that she had committed herself and her country to him. A shudder he couldn't stop shook the Thief. He would lose his sight, and his hearing, his power of speech before he finally died. Dead is dead, he had told himself over and over.

Dead is dead. But worse than dying was knowing that she would be the one to take those things from him. Because she hated him.

He could tell her he loved her. He ached to shout it out loud for the gods and everyone to hear. Little good it would do. Better to trust in the moon's promises than the word of the Thief of Eddis. He was famous in three countries for his lies. Why should she believe anything he said, when he was standing with Mede swords at his throat?

Attolia felt him tremble under her hand. For two years he had been trying to build his defenses against her, and in a moment she saw them all stripped away. Certain he could not stand against her, Attolia stepped back, forgetting that being defenseless didn't preclude attack.

Eugenides took a deep breath and let it go slowly. Then he lifted his chin toward Nahuseresh, who was stepping nearer, having delivered his orders to an underling. The Thief leaned closer to the queen to speak almost into her ear. "From shadow queen to puppet queen in one rule," he whispered. "That's very impressive. When he rules your country and he tells you he loves you, I hope you believe him."

He anticipated her blow and leaned back. Her hand only brushed his cheek in an entirely unsatisfying manner. "At least that's one lie I didn't tell you," Eugenides said.

As he opened his mouth to say more, Nahuseresh reached the queen's shoulder, and the queen struck again, this time boxing Eugenides's ear hard with her cupped hand. Eugenides staggered, slipped on the slick ground, and fell backward onto his bound arms. His face twisted in pain, and he bridged, arching his back to get his weight off his arms, then rolled onto his side. She hoped the fall would shut him up but considered kicking him to be sure. She had no desire to hear him protesting his undying love, but he was so very stubborn when you finally got down to some substance under all the lies. She wondered if his stubbornness always led him to make any bad situation worse.

"He insulted you?" Nahuseresh asked.

Attolia turned. "Not for the first time," she said, rubbing her hand, wiping away a speck of mud. She tucked her arm back through the Mede's and walked away.

chapter 17

_E_UGENIDES DIDN'T NOTICE who helped him up. When someone pushed an iron collar under his chin, he lifted his head
and stared up into the sky. The rain fell on his upturned face,
and he wondered if his gods were watching. The collar closed
with a heavy click, and a key was turned in the lock. There
was a rattling sound as a chain was run through its metal ring.
The chain dragged, and he leaned back automatically to keep
his balance. Following a sharp tug, he marched with the other
prisoners, crossing the slick mud without looking at it, staring
instead into a yawning black pit that he lowered himself into
one step at a time. He couldn't see, except to see the queen
dancing in her garden, couldn't think except of her dressed in
palest green with flowers embroidered around the neck of her
gown as she watched them cut off his hand. My God, he
thought, I am so frightened. O my God, if you will not save
me, make me less afraid. He fell on the steep trail.

He hit face first, and the stones in the mud cut into his
cheek. He had fallen so quickly that he'd dragged down the
two others chained with him. They at least could brace themselves with their chained hands as they tried to get to their
feet. Eugenides's arms were bound to his sides, and his feet,
seeking purchase, slid across the wet ground. One of the men
made it to his feet, but he rose too quickly. Eugenides choked
as the chain pulled hard against his collar, and his weight

pulled the other man off-balance to fall again. Somewhere in the dark and the rain around them, someone laughed. The man got to his feet again and this time, while still leaning down, helped Eugenides up. Once upright, Eugenides was facing Nahuseresh, who stood looking on, much amused. White-hot hatred burned through Eugenides. If he was still without hope, at least he could think clearly again.

"Sir," whispered the man beside him, "at the next cliff, we will jump with you."

Eugenides turned to look for the first time at the men chained on either side. Both men nodded to assure him that they were willing to sacrifice their lives, but Eugenides shook his head. Attolia had promised the two men would be safely returned to Eddis, and he believed her. If the two soldiers were not to die in the dungeons of Ephrata, he would not drag them to their deaths at the base of a cliff. Eddis would need every soldier if she was going to survive his failure. He shook his head again and wondered what had gone wrong, what mistake he had made.

By dawn they had reached the lower slopes of the hillside and were met by Medean soldiers with horses. Attolia looked through them for her own men.

Nahuseresh explained their absence. "Your guard captain chose to hold the megaron until our return," he told her. Attolia nodded. "I was surprised, I admit, at his timidity," the Mede said. "Perhaps he is more used to guarding than fighting."

"Perhaps," said Attolia. "Perhaps he only knew his presence would be unnecessary once you were here to protect me."

"Ah," said the Mede, "it may be that was it."

Or it may have been the numbers of Medean soldiers that Nahuseresh had left in the barbarian hovel to encourage Teleus not to step foot outside it. "We must talk, you and I, about the captain of your guard," Nahuseresh said to Attolia, putting an arm around her for comfort. "I was informed, you see, by a most remarkable woman where you would be. I would not otherwise, I fear, have been on hand to rescue you."

"A remarkable woman?" The queen looked at him sharply. Jealous? Nahuseresh wondered.

"Why, yes, to slip past Kamet, sleeping by my door, to wake me in my bed, she is most remarkable, don't you see?"

"I do. And did she shake you by the shoulder or just speak your name?"

"She spoke my name." The Mede looked at the queen, wondering how she had guessed.

Nahuseresh was a light sleeper, a matter of necessity for him, and when he'd opened his eyes in the darkness of his room and seen a moving flicker of white, he had been instantly alert, slipping his hand under his pillow for the long knife he kept there before he'd rolled quickly to one side. He'd found a woman standing calmly by his bed looking down at him. He had been puzzled to find her dressed in the dark robes of the queen's attendants and not in white and had glanced around the room seeking another assailant, but he and the woman had been alone, and he supposed the white he had seen had been a trick of the moonlight.

"Nahuseresh." She had said his name again. "Will you hear my message?"

It was an odd turn of phrase. Nahuseresh had not heard it before. Of course he would hear her message; was he not lying on the bed less than three feet from her? He had wanted to ask where she'd come from and what had become of Kamet, who should have been sleeping in the anteroom, but if all she brought was a message, he was willing to hear it.

"What is it?" he'd asked.

"The queen of Attolia is not drowned," the woman had said. "Eugenides will carry her into the coastal hills."

"Is that so?"

The woman had gone on placidly. "He will bring her to the Pricas Spring and from there down the watercourse of the Pricas to the Seperchia, where the queen of Eddis waits."

"And how do you know this?"

The woman had been silent.

"And why should I believe you?" Nahuseresh had asked.

"I do not ask you to believe me, only to hear my message," the attendant had answered, and smiled and inclined her head graciously.

Nahuseresh related her message to the Attolian queen. "She could only have known these things if she was a conspirator against you," he explained. "Or perhaps the lover of a conspirator," he added, "and if you look to see who that conspirator might be, I think you will find the captain of your guard a likely candidate. Who admitted the Eddisians to the megaron at Ephrata? Who allowed them to leave again? Who sent Eugenides to the dock and who was just a moment too late to reach you there?" he asked the queen.

"I see," said Attolia.

"I am sure you do," said Nahuseresh. "If it was Teleus's woman who told me of Eugenides's goal . . ."

"His goal?" Attolia asked sharply.

"The Pricas," the Mede said. The queen's attention seemed to be wandering, no doubt put into flight, Nahuseresh thought, by surprise at the idea of honest Teleus as a conspirator.

"Yes, of course," said Attolia. "If it was Teleus's lover, she would have learned of the plans from him."

"I summoned your attendants the next day, and she was not with them. They claimed no one was missing, but I am sure you will discover for yourself who is absent, and then you must let me deal with her."

"Surely she deserves a reward," said Attolia.

"You are mistaken." Nahuseresh corrected her gently. "Had she spoken earlier, she might have been rewarded. Now I will see that she gets what she deserves."

"I defer to you," Attolia said, subdued.

Nahuseresh smiled and held her close as he led her to her mount. He did not intend to relate the events that had followed the mysterious woman's departure. Having delivered her message, to be believed by Nahuseresh or not, she had left so quietly that he hadn't heard a door close behind her.

"Kamet!" he had yelled, and had been both relieved and irritated to hear the secretary scrambling out of his bed to answer.

"Master?" He'd stood in the doorway, rubbing sleep from his eyes.

"A fine watchdog you are. I thought you'd been stabbed or at least drugged," Nahuseresh had said, sliding his knife back under his pillow and flipping his covers aside. "We have had a visitor."

He had told Kamet about the woman's message. "Fetch the lens and a light so that we can signal our boat offshore. Do we have a map of the coastal province of Eddis?"

"Do you believe her?" Kamet had asked.

"I am not sure. I will look at the map before I make up my mind."

"But you might believe her?"

"It is not much to Eddis's advantage to have Attolia dead," Nahuseresh had said, thinking aloud as he was fitting his feet into his slippers. They were deerskin, lined with lamb's wool and one of the few luxuries he'd brought to the barbarian coast with him. "Her titular heir is not fond of the Mede, but he would not hold the throne long. If Eddis held the queen rather than killing her, and the Attolians were persuaded to answer to her puppeted commands, we could be driven off this shore, and between them, Eddis and the controlled Attolia could deal with Sounis."

"So what the woman said is plausible?"

"I don't know yet," his master had answered caustically. "You haven't brought me my map."

Kamet had laughed and gone to fetch it. Together they searched for a marker of the Pricas Spring.

"It will be close to the chasm of the pass," the Mede had muttered, running his index finger across the carefully inked lines. "If it weren't very close to the chasm, the watercourse would lead down the coastal hills to the sea, not into the river."

"There," said Kamet, pointing. His trained eyes had found the words before his master.

Looking at the map, measuring distances by eye, Nahuseresh had said, "It's plausible. The springwaters have cut a canyon down to the Seperchia. If Eugenides landed somewhere in here, he could move that distance in a day and on the next perhaps reach his queen."

"There are no landing sites marked," Kamet had countered.

"No doubt the Eddisians have landing spots on their rocky shores that they do not advertise to their neighbors."

"So you will believe the woman?"

Nahuseresh had stared into space for a while, thinking. "I would be a fool, I suppose, not to act as if I did."

"You will retrieve the queen?"

"We will certainly bring her back," his master had answered. "Whether she will be alive, I cannot say. Alive, she would be very grateful."

"If she dies, there will be an internal war for the throne," Kamet had said.

"And someone will surely wish for the assistance of our emperor," Nahuseresh had answered with a confident smile.

"Be careful what you wish for," Kamet had murmured under his breath.

Led by the Medean ambassador to a horse, Attolia permitted him to assist her into the saddle. Sitting above him, she still managed to gaze up from under her lashes. She felt a small glow of pleasure at her skill in imitating her attendant Chloe. "Will you have the prisoners chained and brought to the megaron, the main hall, for me?" the queen asked meekly.

"As you wish, my dear," Nahuseresh said.

"I want one of them to carry a message for me to Eddis. I'll pick one after I have my bath."

"You can't pick now?" he asked with a smile.

"After my bath," Attolia said, and Nahuseresh deferred with a bow.

There were olives to ride through and then a road to follow past the tiny village of Ephrata. The road ran along the top of the bluffs overlooking the sea, curving as the bluffs curved and then climbing the spur on which the megaron sat. From the village Attolia had seen the bodies hanging from the megaron's walls, but she didn't ask about them until she and Nahuseresh were riding beneath them, through the gate to the main courtyard.

"Alas, traitors," said Nahuseresh. "I know how you deal with criminals, and I knew you would not disapprove."

Attolia's executions had been limited to those actually guilty of a crime. Two of the barons suspended upside down above the gate had been among those whose rare loyalty was unquestioned, but she didn't choose to argue with Nahuseresh.

"I thank you for your concern on my behalf, Nahuseresh," the queen said, her voice pleasant.

"Of course," Nahuseresh replied.

Inside the courtyard Nahuseresh ordered grooms for their horses, a meal to be prepared, and an escort for the queen to her chambers, quite comfortably directing the queen's soldiers and servants. When they looked to their queen for confirmation of these orders, his face darkened.

"You don't object, I am sure," he said.

"Not at all," said the queen. "I rely on you."

He went on then with his orders, and the servants slid away without lifting their eyes again.

To one of his own guard he said, "The queen wishes to be undisturbed. You will see that no one enters her chambers," and excused himself to take care of what he called "other matters."

The queen walked with her escort to her chambers, leaving the Mede guard outside the door. Inside she found her attendants white faced and silent. Attolia pulled the cloak from her shoulders and held it out. An attendant stepped forward to take it.

"No doubt you will tell me later about the extra attendant that has been added to my retinue," Attolia said, watching them as they shook their heads in confusion. All of her attendants stood before her. There was none missing, and none who matched the Mede's description of his midnight visitor.

"Your Majesty," —one woman spoke for all—"we don't know whom the ambassador could mean."

"No matter," said Attolia. "I do. For now, tell me what has become of the captain of my guard."

As one, the ladies looked through the doorway behind her. Attolia turned to look over a shoulder and through the open doorway saw Teleus waiting in the inner chamber. Waiting with him were his lieutenants and several officers of the regular army.

The queen smiled. "Well done," she said. She glanced quickly at each man before her, as if calculating his trustworthiness. "Teleus," she said after a moment, "the Eddisian prisoners are being brought in, either to the atrium or into the megaron itself. The Thief of Eddis is among them, and if he has a choice, he will be dead by his own hand rather than face dying by inches. I don't want him to have a choice. Send one of your lieutenants to keep him safe."

Teleus nodded, and one of the lieutenants turned sideways to slip past the queen. "You are responsible for his continued well-being," she said as he passed. "Don't fail me."

"No, Your Majesty," he murmured.

The queen turned back to Teleus. "There are messages that need to be sent by the royal messengers."

"There are none, Your Majesty."

"None?"

"None of the messengers due have arrived. The two I sent out yesterday to Piloxides have not returned. The man I didn't send, the last messenger, was found dead this morning. He had a fever last night after eating something that disagreed with him," Teleus said meaningfully.

"I see. Then you will bear the messages yourselves," said the queen, giving her orders quickly. "The Mede outside the door has been ordered to let no one in. He seems to have let the lieutenant out without a squeak, but the rest of you will have to wait here until I leave, as I will do soon. I am going to bathe."

She turned to her attendants. "Is my bathwater hot?"

"No, Your Majesty."

"See to it then," she ordered.

In the warm bath she thought of Nahuseresh, so cultured and so confident, in every way prepared to be an excellent king for a minor addition to the Medean Empire. He thought well of her. She knew he appreciated her ruthlessness. He'd complimented her on her choice of military advisors as her land and sea war with Sounis had progressed. She'd been careful to take Nahuseresh's own advice, when she could, to reinforce his impression that she took advice from others. That had probably been to the cost of the barons whose bodies hung from Ephrata's walls. No doubt Nahuseresh had thought he was eliminating any advisors who might tempt her away from the role of queen to his king.

Her attendants waited with warmed robes as she stepped out of the bath. There was no chattering gossip. They all waited, no doubt, for her to ask about the missing attendant. She sat in a chair to have her hair combed. Aglaia tugged at the queen's ear and started to slide a wire through the lobe with a golden bee swinging from its lower loop.

"Not those," Attolia said sharply.

In the megaron Eugenides sat on the stone floor with his knees pulled up, leaning back against a red painted pillar. His eyes were closed. Like the other Eddisians, he was wet through, and from time to time a shudder shook him, as if a ghost had walked over his grave. The high collar of his uniform tunic hid any marks on his neck. Teleus, standing with the queen at the side entrance to the megaron, pointed him out as he explained to the queen, with Nahuseresh standing nearby, that the lieutenant, in passing, had noticed that the Thief was quietly being strangled in the chains of the prisoner just behind him. The prisoners had been chained in rows and then ordered to sit on the stone floor. The lieutenant, in haste to save the Thief for Her Majesty's pleasure, had kicked the other prisoner in the head.

"Very good." Attolia praised Teleus and his lieutenant. "I would have been sorry to lose him." She stepped across the painted floor of the megaron and stood in front of the Eddisians, tapping her foot impatiently. She wanted the Thief to open his eyes. He looked half dead and probably was.

Hissing in annoyance, she moved between the prisoners,

carefully stepping over their chains. Bending over Eugenides, she grabbed his head by the hair above his forehead and twisted. Eugenides's eyes opened, and his feet thrashed in panic. Looking up at her, with her face filling his field of vision, he stopped moving as if suddenly paralyzed.

"Goatfoot," she said, "do you understand what is going to happen to you?"

His mouth hung open, and he closed his eyes a moment, then opened them to go on staring at her. "Yes," he said at last, his voice breathy and hoarse.

"Good," said Attolia, and dropped him to walk away through the prisoners without a backward glance. "I want to send a message to the queen of Eddis," she said to Nahuseresh, walking across the room to seat herself on her throne. There was no seat for Nahuseresh. Attolia's servants never provided one except at Her Majesty's explicit command, but Nahuseresh didn't choose to impede the process of the queen's revenge by sending for one.

"Your messengers have been sent to the capital to order the palace secured against traitors," he explained.

"Nor would they know where to reach Eddis quickly," said Attolia. "We are only assuming that she is with her army. She may be elsewhere. It is better to use someone else. Teleus, you say your lieutenant kicked one of the prisoners in the head?"

"Yes, Your Majesty."

"Is he conscious?"

"I believe so, Your Majesty."

"Well, let's have that one, then."

The guards brought the Eddisian she'd chosen to stand before her. As she'd guessed, it was the gray-haired man who'd fought beside Eugenides on the mountain.

He moved a little stiffly and screwed up his eyes like a man with a headache. He was a little taller than average, but not noticeably so, a little heavier, but not stocky. His closely trimmed beard was gray, as was most of the hair on his head. Attolia gathered, when Nahuseresh made no comment, that he saw nothing exceptionable about her choice.

"You are a soldier?" There was no sign of rank on his tunic.

"I am, Your Majesty." His words were a little slurred. The kick had been a solid one.

"You don't seem to have risen far for your years."

"Maybe I'm not ambitious." The man shrugged.

"Maybe you should drink less," the queen suggested. The man narrowed his eyes at the insult but didn't contest the implication that he was a drunk.

"Will you carry a message for me?" the queen asked.

"I can hardly decline, Your Majesty," answered the prisoner.

Attolia wondered what Eugenides had said to him in the few minutes they'd had before the man had been dragged from the rest of the Eddisians to stand before the queen.

"Tell your queen that I will not return her Thief a second time." The prisoner just looked up at her dully. She couldn't know how much he understood. How hard had the lieutenant kicked him?

"What remains of his life, he spends with me, do you understand, messenger?"

"I believe so, Your Majesty."

"Eddis sent her Thief to steal me from my throne and bring me back as her puppet. I think Eddis does not understand my attachment to my allies the Medes." She carefully did not look at Nahuseresh. Her voice was hard. She leaned forward in her seat, the fabric of her long skirts bunched in her hands as if she were holding the prisoner's attention with them. "When he thought I was safely distant from any rescue, her Thief proposed life or death to me and let me choose my fate.

I am in my own megaron and have an answer to the Thief's proposal. Do you know what my answer is?"

"Yes," the prisoner said.

"Yes," the queen repeated after him, enunciating the word clearly. "You may tell the queen of Eddis."

She nodded to the guards, who took the man by the arms, pulling him backward toward the door of the megaron. She waited until they'd almost reached the door. "Tell Eddis," she said, and the soldiers stopped. "Tell Eddis that if she asks nicely, she might save her Thief some suffering. Tell her she can send a message back to me so long as she sends it with you. And tell her it must arrive by the seventh hour of tomorrow morning. No later . . . on pain of death." She smiled. She turned to her guard captain. "Teleus, see him escorted to the forward edge of our army at the pass."

Attolia flicked Nahuseresh a glance below her narrowed eyelids. "Now we wait," she said, not bothering to hide her smile of delighted anticipation as her guards conveyed the messenger out the door.

"Wait for what?" the Mede asked.

"Hmm?" Attolia focused herself on the present. "Good heavens, I don't know," she said. "Eddis produces such lovely threats when her Thief is concerned. I can hardly guess what she might come up with now."

"And the rest of your prisoners?" the Mede inquired.

"Your prisoners, Nahuseresh. What would you like to do with them?"

"Hand them all over to you."

"Then we will send them off to be locked up until we hear from their queen. Except the Thief," she added. "I don't believe I trust him enough to leave him with his fellows, and I would like him to be nearer to hand." She directed her guards to lock him in one of the upper rooms of the megaron, several of which had been altered for the purpose of securing the prisoners of a former baron of Ephrata.

For the rest of the day Attolia remained in her own chamber, pleading tiredness after her forced journey. She joined Nahuseresh for dinner. The main hall was the only one large enough to hold the queen, the Mede, and those barons still lingering in the megaron. She hadn't tried to order them back to their commands and supposed that Nahuseresh hadn't either. She didn't want them interfering with the soldiers, and Nahuseresh must have wanted to keep a close eye on them for reasons of his own. Her attendants, moving freely through the megaron, had brought her news of the Mede's messengers sent and returning, no doubt carrying orders for the Attolian army that the Mede expected to be followed in the absence of the barons.

Attolia knew that he found the presence of non-noble generals in her army ridiculous and repellent. He'd warned her that they would be loyal only to the money they made. At least they were loyal to something, Attolia thought. Her least favorite barons were those whose loyalties seemed to change directions the way a pennant blew in a shifting wind. Even a steadfast enemy was better than a waffler, and her new-model army and navy had never waffled. They would, she supposed, desert wholesale if she were dethroned or utterly bankrupt, but on the whole they waited very patiently for their pay. They earned it with their victories, and they seemed to trust her to deliver it. Their faith in their pay was often a comfort to the embattled queen. She tried not to test it unnecessarily.

She had altered the command structure frequently, promoting those who drew her favorable attention and redeploying them to keep their expectations from growing entrenched. The captain of her private guard she picked most carefully and changed from time to time before he could be corrupted by her enemies. If she was not happy to leave her fate entirely in Teleus's hands, she was at least content. She chatted with her barons and flirted a bit with Nahuseresh. He was smug, like a cat. She smiled and listened carefully as he explained how he had deployed his army in the best possible way to aid hers in case of an attack by Eddis.

chapter 18

*J*UST INSIDE THE pass the queen of Eddis sat on a rock surrounded by her council. She looked to her minister of war.
"What do you advise?" she asked.

"Attack," he said.

"Why?"

"Eugenides said to," he answered.

"While I have a great deal of faith in my Thief and in his
advice, I could wish, under the circumstances, that I had
more information than that on which to base my decision,"
Eddis said, and waited for her minister.

Calmly he shrugged. "We drive the Medes out now, or
never, Your Majesty."

Eddis sighed. He had stated the crux of the matter. He had
already told her everything he knew and had no more information to offer. The decision was hers.

She was silent while she considered. Eugenides waited in
the megaron at Ephrata. To fail to attack was to leave him and
the other prisoners to whatever mercy Attolia and the Mede
might show. Attolia would exact a hideous revenge either for
herself or to prove herself to her allies. On the other hand,
Eddis couldn't cast an entire army to destruction trying to save
one prisoner or the handful of prisoners Attolia held. But if it
cost the lives of every last man in her army to drive out the
Mede, she as queen must not hesitate.

"Very well," she said. "We attack at the seventh hour."

Attolia was awake in the dark waiting for dawn. Her rooms were at the back of the megaron, looking over the sea, and she watched the constellations move slowly, finally fading just as they set. The sun had risen over the mountains and the sky was changing from gray to blue. The armies would have begun to move on the plain at the base of the pass. How many times had she sat before a battle, wondering how it would end? She wished herself at the plain. She would have liked to be there to direct the army herself, though she knew her limitations and didn't pretend to be a soldier. She always remained at a safe distance with her personal guard to protect her. She envied Eddis, who could fight in her own battles if she chose. Not perhaps as dangerous as a soldier; still, she was trained and had been trained since she was a child.

"I have always envied Eddis," she said to herself as she stood up to pace. It was true. Eddis and she had both been the younger sisters of crown princes, but always it seemed to Attolia that Eddis was running wild in the mountains while she was carefully kept and groomed in the king's palace of Attolia. News had traveled with the merchants and the entertainers who came before both courts. Eddis was learning to ride a pony, Eddis was learning to use a sword with her male cousins, Eddis was hunting at the summer retreat, while Attolia was dressing in velvets that stifled even in the winter, learning to ape the costume and courtly manners of the continent, and learning to salute just so when entering the main temple. Eddis had gone on the winter hunts, and Attolia had been sitting, awkward and miserable, in the court of her future father-in-law, listening to his plans to rule her kingdom and hating the princess who would become the heir to Eddis when her older brothers died. Died of sickness, Attolia thought, not assassinated as her own brother had certainly been.

At Eddis's coronation Attolia had poured her advice like vitriol into the ear of the new queen, watching her face whiten, viciously satisfied to be the one to tell the girl what the world was like when you were a queen. And then none of that advice had been needed. Eddis had gone on as free in her mountains as Attolia had ever been enslaved. Eddis, with her loyal ministers, her counselors, her army, and her Thief to serve her.

"At any rate she won't have her Thief back," Attolia murmured, wrapping herself in her robe and sitting back down.

There was a knock at the chamber door, and a hesitant attendant stepped in. "Forgive me for disturbing you, Your Majesty, but the Mede ambassador has requested you to attend him."

"Me attend him?" Attolia raised her eyebrow. "Oh, he does grow bold. Tell him I will be with him shortly."

"He is in the outer chamber now, Your Majesty."

Attolia sat up. "How fortunate that I do not have to receive him in my nightdress. By all means show him in."

The Mede, when he entered, was fitted in the light armor for which the Medes were famous. He wore a curving sword at his belt. His beard was freshly oiled, and Attolia could smell the perfume from across the room even with the open window behind her.

"Your ad hoc messenger has not returned," he said.

"No."

"But my messengers report that Eddis is moving her army out onto the plain below the pass."

"My messengers have not yet told me so." She knew Nahuseresh was intercepting her messages.

"I thought to bring the news to you myself."

"She is a fool if she thinks she can defeat my army and yours combined," Attolia said, brushing invisible lint from her sleeve.

"I had thought her advisors were more sensible, but she is a woman and has no doubt overridden them in her desire to rescue her lover."

Attolia's smile was crooked with mischief. "Her beloved, certainly. Not her lover, I think."

Nahuseresh cocked his head. "I thought the information from Eddis said they were lovers."

"An exaggeration, I'm sure," said Attolia dispassionately. "He is too young. Much too young, I think, to interest a woman who is queen. A queen needs a man who is older, more experienced, more competent to rule. A man with a character that is mature and powerful enough to attract her."

She looked up at Nahuseresh, delighted to see him swallowing the implied flattery without a quiver. "As you say," he said, agreeing with her assessment. "I thought you might like to see the battle."

She hesitated, and he added, "My men can provide a safe place from which to observe. You needn't be afraid."

"Thank you, Nahuseresh," she said calmly. "I am not afraid."

In the courtyard Teleus was there to boost her onto her horse. There was no other member of her guard present. Excepting Teleus, she was surrounded by Nahuseresh's men. While Nahuseresh mounted his horse, her own captain looked up at his queen and quickly down again. "Where shall we watch from, Teleus?" she asked.

"The best spot is just the other side of the ridge, Your Majesty. Shall I show it to you?"

"Do, please," said Attolia, and Teleus mounted a horse to show them the way.

"You trust him near you?" Nahuseresh murmured to the queen when he'd pulled his horse next to hers.

"So long as you are near me as well, I want him close," said the queen.

Nahuseresh nodded. He could see the wisdom in that.

Teleus led them across the narrow stretch of fields to the woods, past the wooden cannon barrels the Eddisians had abandoned. As she saw them lying among the trees, Attolia's hands tightened. The narrow trail Teleus found led up the hills to a ridge above the Seperchia River. The ridge was steep, and the horses had to scramble at the last. From the ridge they could see across the Seperchia to the plain on the far side where the armies ordered for battle. Attolia could see the movement between the trees.

"Your Majesty."

It was Teleus. He'd dismounted and was standing by her boot. "There's a better place to observe if you will ride down the hill and take the trail on the right. There's a flat spot to picket the horses."

"Thank you, Teleus. Why don't you continue to lead?"

"My pleasure, Your Majesty." He took the queen's horse by the bridle and walked it down the narrow trail to a clearing. The clearing was long and narrow. At the back of it a granite cliff eight or ten feet high rose directly out of the turf, the highest point of the ridge of solid stone that turned the Seperchia River just before it reached the sea and forced it through the softer limestone in the Hephestial Mountains. On the opposite side of the clearing the land sloped steeply down to the river, so steeply that Attolia, sitting on her horse, was able to look over the tops of the trees growing on the slope below and have an uninterrupted view across the river to her army.

The night before, Nahuseresh had talked about "supporting" her soldiers. Attolia had surmised that he meant to keep his own men behind hers so that the Attolians might take the heaviest losses, exhausting the Eddisians' resources and leaving Attolia ever more dependent on the Mede for her defense. Before her, she could see the armies drawn up as she had expected, the Attolians spread thinly in an indefensible battle line, the Medes forming their phalanxes behind them.

Looking down at the field, Attolia thought again that she disliked excessively being out of touch with her generals.

"I'll go see about the pavilion for Your Majesty," said Teleus, backing up as the Mede's personal guard distributed themselves around the clearing.

"I wonder he isn't down on the plain," said Nahuseresh after he was gone.

"He's the captain of my personal guard. He's supposed to guard my person," Attolia said.

"Then I wonder he's gone off to fetch a pavilion like a steward."

"He knows how much I trust you," said the queen. "I wonder you yourself are not down on the plain."

"I am not needed there yet. I can send messages with one of my men, but otherwise I will wait out the morning with you, Your Majesty."

And later, when most of her army had been cut down, he would join his own army to direct the attack on the Eddisians.

Armies move more slowly than men. As Nahuseresh and Attolia sat patiently and watched, the army of Eddis maneuvered out from the defending walls of the pass. Horses dragged cannon, and men marched into place. Finally there was a shuddering along the ranks of Attolian and Mede, and Attolia thought it time to distract Nahuseresh's attention.

"The messenger I sent to Eddis, you didn't recognize him," Attolia said.

"Should I have?" the Mede asked, his eyes on the field below.

"He was Eddis's minister of war," Attolia said. "Eugenides's father."

The words took a moment to penetrate Nahuseresh's concentration. He turned slowly, like a defective clockwork, to look at the queen.

"You suborned my barons," she said calmly.

"What?" he said, shaking his head.

"You suborned my barons. They were to let the Eddisians through their battle lines to flank my army and destroy it. You, having landed your army at Rhea without my permission, would have been ready to rescue me gloriously. Eddis's Thief spoiled those plans, but you came about well, and here you are, once again ready to see my army decimated and your Medes heroes."

"You have heard some malcontent perpetrating slander. . . . Have I not been—"

"Undermining my throne for months? You have, Nahuseresh. You corrupted Stadicos before the First Battle of Thegmis. He changed my orders, and I lost the island to Sounis. I did not like that, Nahuseresh. It was not easy to get it back. You have bribed my barons and blackmailed them and riddled my country with your spies. Eddis distracted me for a day, and you hanged the three barons you couldn't suborn. One wanted more gold from you; two were actually loyal to me. I don't have so many loyal barons, Nahuseresh, that I can sit by while you execute them."

"Your Majesty—" The Mede began again, but the queen overrode him.

"To be honest, Nahuseresh, you are almost more trouble than Sounis. Your saving grace is that you have brought me a great deal of gold when I needed it badly."

"Gold that must be repaid, Your Majesty," said Nahuseresh, glad to have a straw to grasp at last.

"The gold was a gift; you said so yourself."

"You are a woman," Nahuseresh said very gently. "You do not understand the world of kings and emperors, you do not understand the nature of their gifts."

"Nahuseresh, if there is one thing a woman understands, it is the nature of *gifts*. They are bribes when threats will not avail. Your emperor cannot attack this coast unprovoked; the treaties with the greater nations of this Continent prevent him. All he can do is stir up an ugly three-way war and hope to be invited in as an ally, and I did not invite him." The queen shook her head. "The problem with bribes, Nahuseresh, is that after your money is gone, threats still do not avail."

Nahuseresh stared, seeing a queen he hadn't guessed existed.

Attolia looked back at him. "I inherited this country when I was almost a child, Nahuseresh. I have held it. I have fought down rebellious barons. I've fought Sounis to keep the land on this side of the mountains. I have killed men and watched them hang. I've seen them tortured to keep this country safe and *mine*. How did you think I did this if I was a fool with cow eyes for any handsome man with gold in his purse?"

Nahuseresh's eyes narrowed. "You cannot escape the bargain now, Your Majesty."

"I made no bargain with you, Mede," said Attolia flatly.

"One way or another the gold must be repaid."

"So I am to overlook your treachery?"

"Diplomacy—in my emperor's name. And yes, you will overlook it if you hope to remain queen when I am king."

"I have said before that the next king of Attolia will be my choice, no one else's."

"Then you have only to choose me, and we will both be made happy, will we not? And your barons as well. While you were 'distracted,' they seemed very agreeable to my rule."

"They are mice, Nahuseresh, hiding in their mouseholes, hoping that their own familiar cat will come home to drive you away. At least when I hang people from castle walls, it is because they are traitors, not because they drive hard bargains. You seem willing to hang anyone that displeases you. How kind of you to show my barons that if I am a hard ruler to cross, you are a worse one to serve. I must thank you for that as well as for your emperor's gold. They will be most mousy and well behaved for months."

"And Eddis? Does Eddis do you any favors?" Nahuseresh smiled like a shark as he reminded the queen of the armies below them.

"Look and see, Nahuseresh," answered Attolia.

The Mede turned back to the battlefield, where the Attolians were moving, the battle lines slowly splitting and separating.

Nahuseresh swore. "What are they doing?" he shouted. He lifted a hand to call a messenger to his side, but Attolia forestalled him.

"My generals are merely dividing their forces and regrouping to allow Eddis to attack your army unhindered. If necessary, they can then flank what's left of your forces to prevent a retreat."

Nahuseresh watched the men moving a moment more. The horse under him tensed as his rider drew the reins tight, but before horse or rider could move, Attolia raised her hand and directed his attention with a languid finger to where Teleus lay on his stomach in the long grass on the ridge behind them, the crossbow in his hands cranked and aimed toward the Mede.

"Treachery," said the Mede.

"Diplomacy," said Attolia, "in my own name," as the rest of her guard rose up from the grass behind their captain.

*　*　*

The Attolian army below completed its maneuver as the queen explained to the ambassador that a rout could yet be avoided by a more gracious retreat. Eddis and Attolia would allow the Mede soldiers to return to Rhea, reboard their ships, and leave Attolian waters unharmed. They had no cause to fight the Mede. They only invited him to leave.

Nahuseresh, faced with a battle he couldn't win, ungraciously conceded.

"Eddis will want some surety for what treaties you make today. What do you give her that secures her trust?"

Attolia didn't answer, only looked at him, her face expressionless.

Nahuseresh thought back to the message she had sent by way of Eddis's minister of war, and he paled with anger. "You will make that boy Thief king?" he said. "When you could have had me?"

Attolia allowed a slight smile.

"A fine revenge for the loss of a hand," said the Mede, close to snarling.

"I will have my sovereignty," said Attolia thinly.

"Oh, yes, a fine one-handed figurehead he will make," spat Nahuseresh. Then he remembered Attolia's flattery earlier that morning. "Or do I insult your *lover*?" he asked

"Not a lover," said Attolia. "Merely my choice for king, Nahuseresh."

chapter 19

*W*HEN THE MEDE army had regrouped itself for a retreat and the Attolians and Eddisians had moved their forces into a combined opposition, Attolia sent her Mede ambassador back to Ephrata under guard. He had quite recovered control of his temper and kissed her hand before he went. "You are clever," he condescended to say, "to have made a fool of me. How heartbreaking, to leave just as I begin to know you. My opinion of you climbs with each passing moment."

"It will have time to climb higher," Attolia said. "You won't go far until your emperor sends me a ransom to add to my treasury."

"You overstep yourself," Nahuseresh warned.

"You don't know your own value, Nahuseresh. Your emperor needs you safely home."

"You don't understand your weakness, if you think the greater nations will protect you. We will see how much longer you rule your backwater, Your Majesty. You will soon enough discover the limits of your resources."

"Will I? I think you underestimate me still, Nahuseresh. While we are being forthright with each other, I admit that I find it tedious."

Attolia parted company with him and rode down to the riverbank, where a boat waited to ferry her across the Seperchia. The absence of a bridge was another cause, or perhaps a result, of the relative unimportance of Ephrata. The boat carried her across the turbulent water to where she was met by several of her own officers and the officers, ministers, and queen of Eddis.

There was a landing stage but not a true dock. The water of the river being well below the stage, the queen was lifted, as decorously as possible, from the rocking boat onto the shore. There were two bright spots of color on her cheeks as she sorted the folds of her dress and then raised her eyes to Eddis. Eddis waited politely. She was dressed in trousers and low boots, her overtunic identical to her officers' but embroidered in gold. She wore no crown. She was short and too broad to be called petite. Her father had been broad shouldered, Attolia remembered, and not over-tall. Eddis had a serious expression, but as she waited for Attolia to speak, her eyes narrowed with what looked to Attolia like puzzlement.

Attolia gave her a haughty look back. "We are in accord, Your Majesty?" she asked.

"Remarkably so," said Eddis gravely. She was not so much reserving her judgment as trying to unmake it. She thought she knew the queen of Attolia and wondered what Eugenides could have seen in her. Except of course that she was beautiful, but there were beautiful women at the court in Eddis, and Gen had never seemed much moved by their loveliness.

Attolia looked at Eddis's minister of war. "How is your head, sir?" she asked politely.

"Gray," he answered cryptically.

"With worry? You don't like our harum-scarum plans, sir?"

"I am filled with admiration for them, Your Majesty." Eddis's minister inclined his head. Attolia returned a royal half curtsy.

Eddis looked at her minister, curious. "Your head?" she asked.

Attolia explained. "He had to be forcibly dissuaded from strangling his son."

"So have we all from time to time," Eddis said seriously.

One of Attolia's eyebrows rose in carefully conveyed surprise. Eddis took note of the expression, amused to have found at last, she was certain, the original of the look Eugenides had copied. She smiled.

Attolia hesitated, then smiled herself, very briefly. In her expression Eddis saw some hope for her Thief, and her heart lightened.

"You are fortunate in your vassals," Attolia said.

"The dividing maneuver of your army was perfectly done," Eddis countered. "You are as fortunate in your officers."

"They are contract soldiers," Attolia said dismissively.

"So much the better that you command their loyalty when they are free to hire their services elsewhere. Where else could my barons go and still be barons?" Eddis asked.

Attolia was silent while she considered this. "I have to thank you. I had not looked at it that way before," she said.

"Your Majesty, Your Majesties," said Eddis's minister of war, correcting himself. "The Medes' retreat will need to be supervised. We thought it best if Your Majesties rode together as there may be details you wish to discuss."

Once mounted, the queen of Eddis turned to the queen of Attolia. "You will forgive me if I speak frankly?"

"Of course."

"What treaties have you made with the Mede?"

"None."

"None? But I had thought—"

"That the emperor was financing my war? He was, but it was on his own speculation."

"And your ambassador?"

Attolia uncharacteristically said the first thing that came to mind. "He sharpens his beard into points like a fork," she said of her ambassador, "and uses cheap hair oil."

"Well, that certainly is frank on your part," said Eddis, laughing. "I had thought you were fond of him."

"So did he," said Attolia dryly.

By evening the army of the Mede had marched back to Rhea. Rhea was a large port surrounded by sufficient arable land to support a thriving town. Like Ephrata, it was hemmed in by the coastal hills, but unlike Ephrata, it had a wide pass that made it accessible to the hinterlands and justified the construction of the bridge across the Seperchia. Attolia and Eddis sat side by side on a hill overlooking the town and watched the Medes embark.

"I am not comfortable sending back the emperor his soldiers," Eddis admitted.

"It is a small army by his measure. The loss of it wouldn't have hurt him, only put him further out of temper with us."

"You think he will not mount another attack. Perhaps he will think we are too secure?" Eddis said hopefully.

"Nahuseresh has said a woman cannot rule alone," Attolia said blandly.

Eddis chuckled.

"The greater nations of the Continent don't want the Mede emperor's power extending to this coast," said Attolia. "No doubt he will harass our ships at sea, but we can expect the Continent to give us aid if he sends an army against us." Eddis took note of the comfortable presence of "us" in the queen's analysis.

"And that will stop him?"

"In the short term that will prevent him from an overt attack. In the long term I rely on his disease to curtail his empire building."

"His disease?"

"The emperor of the Medes has Tethys lesions," Attolia explained.

For a moment the only sound was the creak of saddle leather as one of the horses shifted its weight.

"You are certain of this?" Eddis asked.

"He was diagnosed two and a half years ago. He executed his palace physician and his assistants, but one of the assistants had sold the information to one of my spies in exchange for an annuity for his family."

"He knew he would be executed?"

"Oh, yes."

Eddis tried to imagine executing Galen.

"I don't know if you are aware that the Mede emperor passed over his own son in choosing a nephew as his heir?" Attolia asked.

"Yes, I knew," said Eddis. "It's remarkable that the signs of the disease have been concealed so far. Of course the nephew will have to consolidate his power more quickly than he anticipated. He'll keep his loyal generals near to hand . . ." Eddis mused aloud. "And your late ambassador is . . ."

"The heir's younger brother."

"Yes. Well, then, they will all be busy for several years, won't they?"

"I think so," said Attolia.

"You know—" Eddis hesitated, not sure how far to push the Attolian queen.

"Go on." Attolia inclined her head.

"I was going to say you look like a polecat when you smile like that."

"Do I?" Attolia still smiled. "You look a little vulpine yourself."

"Yes, I suppose so."

The two queens sat for a moment in happy agreement.

Eddis looked around as if recalling a question that had nagged at her for several hours. "Where's Eugenides?" she asked.

For a moment the Attolian queen was immobile, her smile

gone as if it had never been. The horse under her threw up its head as if the bit had twitched against its delicate mouth.

"Locked in a room," Attolia said flatly. "In Ephrata."

The smile faded from Eddis's face.

"I ordered the other prisoners released," Attolia explained. "I forgot that I had him locked up separately. I doubt my seneschal will have released him without my specific instruction to do so."

"You forgot?" Eddis asked.

"I forgot," Attolia said firmly, daring Eddis to contradict her.

"You will marry him?" Eddis asked, hesitant again.

"I said I would," snapped Attolia, and turned her horse away. Eddis followed. When they joined their officers, Attolia gave brisk orders and then rode on, heading back toward Ephrata without waiting for Eddis.

Attolia's liaison explained that the main part of her forces would return to the bridge across the Seperchia and to their camp. Attolia and a small guard would ride to Ephrata along the coast. The track was narrow, but the ride much shorter.

"Then we will do the same," Eddis said, and gave her orders to her own officers. Eugenides's father and her own private guard stayed by her side for the ride back to Ephrata.

"What do you think?" the minister of war asked his queen.

"I don't know what to think," she answered. "I suppose I must go on doing as I have done all along."

"Hmm?" her minister prompted.

"Trust in Eugenides," she said, shrugging.

In the courtyard at Ephrata, Attolia dropped from her horse and left it for someone else to lead away. She strode up the steps to the entrance to the atrium at the fore of the megaron. Her seneschal and her guard captain waited for her there.

"Your Majesty, the Mede ambassador—"

"Don't tell me about the Mede ambassador," said Attolia. "Is the Thief of Eddis still locked up?"

"Your Majesty gave no orders," the seneschal began hesitantly, "and I'm afraid that Ambassador Nahuseresh—"

"I said that I don't want to hear about Nahuseresh," interrupted Attolia. "Give me the keys to the Thief's cell," and the seneschal obediently hunted through the rings of keys attached to his belt and pulled one ring free. He picked one key out of the rest and handed it to the queen.

"This key, Your Majesty."

Careful not to let the key slip down among its similar fellows, Attolia took key and ring and strode away.

The guard looked at the seneschal, who looked back at him, raising his eyebrows and shaking his head.

Eddis, arriving in the courtyard, had seen the queen. She, too, had dropped from her horse and left the rest of her party milling behind her as she hurried up the steps to follow Attolia. She passed the seneschal, and the guard captain reached out a hand to hook her elbow.

"Now then, young man," he said, stopping her in her tracks. "Where were you going?"

Eddis turned. The captain needed only one more look to see that he'd made an error. He withdrew his hand, and Eddis, without speaking, followed Attolia.

When she was gone, the captain looked again at the seneschal and grimaced, shaking his hand as if he'd touched something hot and burned it.

"That look would have boiled lead," agreed the seneschal. "You're not going to follow them?"

"Not I," said the captain. "I will be very glad to be somewhere else if those two are crossing swords."

He stepped out into the courtyard to engage his services in

sorting out the growing chaos there as Eddisian and Attolian officers and soldiers arrived.

The key turned in a well-oiled lock, and the door opened easily. Inside the room Eugenides looked to be sitting on the floor, his legs curled beside him. His head and shoulders rested on the bed, one arm for a pillow. The hook on the other arm lay across his knees. His eyes were closed. He didn't move. As Attolia waited in the doorway watching him, he didn't stir or wake. On the floor beside the bed a tray held the remains of a meal. There was a wine cup. It had tipped over and broken, spilling the lees onto the floor.

Attolia stood, caught at the threshold like one who has trespassed on the mysteries and been turned to stone. She thought of Nahuseresh. How many poisons did he have at his command? How many allies did he have among her barons? How easy would it have been to arrange the death of a successful rival? She should have listened to what her seneschal wanted to tell her. He would have warned her of what she would find. Unadvised, the queen found it difficult to bear.

How cruel of the gods, she thought, to send her a boy she would love without realizing it. How appropriate that the bridegroom she would have chosen to marry be poisoned. Who could contest the justice meted out by the gods?

There were footsteps behind her. Eddis, Attolia thought, was not going to believe that anyone but Attolia was responsible for the boy's death. She remained in the doorway while her rival queen stepped past her. Eddis slid by without touching her, without so much as brushing the flowing sleeves of her robe.

In the time it took for the other queen to move through the doorway, Attolia looked into the future. Eddis would return to war. Sounis would continue his attacks, the Mede would aid anyone but Attolia. None of it mattered. Attolia was alone as she had always been, but she had never felt so desolate. She cursed herself for her stupidity. Who was the Thief that she would love him? A youth, just a boy with hardly a beard and no sense at all, she told herself. A liar, she thought, an enemy, a threat. He was brave, a voice inside her said, he was loyal. Not loyal to me, she answered. Not brave on my behalf. Brave and loyal, the voice repeated. A fool, she answered back. A fool and a dead one. She ached with emptiness.

Eddis, having passed Attolia, halted between her and the bed. She looked at Eugenides's body and turned back to the queen in the doorway. "He's asleep," she said.

Attolia took her eyes off the future to focus on Eddis.

"Just asleep," Eddis reassured her.

At the sound of her voice Eugenides's head turned slightly, but he didn't wake. Attolia, seeing the movement, breathed again and pressed a hand to her chest where it hurt.

Eddis leaned over the Thief and poked him in the shoulder. "Wake up," she said.

Struggling to do just that, Eugenides at first had no idea where he was. He'd slept very little since he and Xenophon's soldiers had made the last part of their voyage by raft to land near Ephrata. He'd sailed along the coast, climbed up a cliff's worth of stairs, ridden back down a mountainside, fought a useless skirmish, and walked back to Ephrata. After Attolia's guards had locked him in the tiny room, he'd paced to keep himself awake, painfully caught between fear and a terrible hope as the night slowly passed. His arm had ached fiercely, but he hadn't tried to remove the cuff. He'd been afraid he wouldn't be able to get it back on, and no matter what happened, he told himself, he didn't want to face his destiny tucking his stump into his sleeve and clutching the hook in his remaining hand like some sort of bizarre athletic trophy. Twice someone had brought him food, which he hadn't eaten, and once a guard had marched him down the hall to relieve himself. The guard had not been friendly, and Eugenides hadn't dared to ask for news.

Finally, in the afternoon, a day after he'd been locked up, he had seen from the narrow window an Eddisian soldier on the megaron's wall walking with an Attolian. It had seemed like a good sign. Later a young woman came with another meal and told him that the other Eddisian prisoners had been released and the Mede ambassador had been locked in his rooms. She hadn't known the results of the battle on the far side of the ridge, but for Eugenides these two things were news enough of success, and he had sat down on the floor next to the bed and eaten all the food she'd brought. There was no table and no chair. The serving girl had laughed, telling him he didn't have to eat in a hurry, she would come back for the tray. Then she'd gone, and he'd been so tired even the pain in his arm couldn't keep him awake. He'd rested his head for a moment, he thought, on the bed. He hadn't moved for hours, hadn't heard the key turn in the lock, hadn't woken at the sound of voices.

When Eddis prodded him, his first fumbling thought was that his entire body ached and he must be in the king's prison in Sounis. His next thought was that he'd left that prison and it must be Pol or Sounis's magus prodding him. He didn't want to talk to Pol. Pol would want him to go somewhere on the back of a horse.

"Go away," he said.

Eddis sighed. "Eugenides," she said, "wake up."

"I would have expected a light sleeper," Attolia commented.

"Usually he is," Eddis said, growing more concerned.

"He looks—" Attolia hunted for the word. "Defenseless" came to mind, but it wasn't the one she wanted, nor was "young," though he looked even younger when he was asleep. "Quite guileless," she said at last.

"Oh, yes," said Eddis. "I'm always willing to forgive him

anything—until he wakes up." She leaned down and poked him again.

Eugenides finally opened his eyes and lifted his head. He looked confused and started to lift his right arm, then froze when the hook bumped his leg. He carefully lifted the other hand to rub his face. He looked from Eddis to the window, where the visible sky was already dark. He looked back, his gaze a little sharper, and said, "You forgot me."

Eddis shoved her hands into the pockets of her trousers.

"Don't lie," Eugenides said, pressing her. "You charged off in a haze of glory to chase the vile Mede from our shore, and you never gave me a thought until they were gone."

He twisted to address Attolia. "You forgot me, too," he accused.

Attolia answered coolly, "You were fed."

Eugenides looked up at her, and Attolia felt transparent, as if her mask were gone, as if he could see her heart and know that a moment before it had been stopped by grief.

"That's true, a girl brought me dinner," Eugenides said thoughtfully. "She was very pretty." After a pause he added, "*And* very kind."

Eddis had heard of the conversation between the Thief and Attolia on the relative merits of beauty and kindness. She winced at the intended rebuke, but Attolia only pressed her lips together in a thin smile and said, "It's not too late for you to end up chained to a wall."

"Oh, someone would rescue me," Eugenides said, rolling his eyes innocently. "And while I was there, that lovely girl could bring my dinner. I think," he said, with his head propped by his arm, looking into the middle distance, "I think when I'm king"—he repeated himself slowly—"when I am king, she can be my first mistress."

Attolia snapped, "You have any mistresses and I'll cut your other hand off."

Beside her, Eddis stiffened. Attolia raised her chin to meet the look that her seneschal had said would melt lead. Eddis opened her mouth, but before she could put her thoughts into words, Eugenides laughed. Laughing, he dropped his head onto the bed; then he looked up to grin at Attolia.

She looked back at him, and her cheeks flushed. She said, with sincerity, "You are a poisonous little snake."

"Yes," said Eugenides. Stiff, he climbed up to sit on the bed, running his fingers through his hair and yawning. "Yes. And I want out of this room."

Attolia leaned over him to catch his chin under her hand. She felt the barest flinch before he lifted his eyes to meet hers. He had looked so young when he was asleep, and hardly older once he was awake. He needed a nursery, not a bride, Attolia thought bitterly, though she herself had been engaged and married even younger. "You need a bath," she said, "and someone to see to your arm. You can wait here a little longer until I send an attendant."

But she didn't let go of his chin. She held him, looking into his face. He reached up to touch very lightly the earring in her ear, a square-cut ruby on a gold backing that matched the design of the ruby-studded band across her forehead. She'd been wearing the earrings when she bent over him in his chains in the megaron.

"Do you like them?" he asked.

"Yes," said Attolia. She straightened and went to the door.

"Will you send that nice girl who brought my dinner?" Eugenides called.

Attolia lifted her eyebrow. "No," she said, and was gone.

Eddis turned back to Eugenides, who was rubbing his cheek where Attolia's hand had rested and looked suddenly bleak.

"I think," he said slowly. "I think I didn't think all this out."

"Marrying her, you mean?" Eddis sat down next to him, concerned.

"Nooo," he said, and he looked over at her. In his eyes Eddis saw a hint of something she couldn't remember having seen there before. Panic.

"I didn't think about being king," he said, his voice hoarse, either from worry or from the bruises around his neck.

Eddis stared. "Your capacity to land yourself in a mess because you didn't think first, Eugenides, will never cease to amaze me. What do you mean you didn't think about being king? Is Attolia going to marry you and move into my library?"

"No," said Eugenides, looking sullenly at his feet. "I knew that I had to be king. I just didn't *think* about it."

"All those clothes," Eddis remarked thoughtfully. "Ceremonies. Duties. Obligations."

"People staring at me," Eugenides said, "all the time."

Eddis eyed him quietly for a minute or two while he contemplated, perhaps for the first time, the responsibilities of a king. "Attolia had no treaties with the Mede," she said abruptly. "Nor did she want one. Eugenides . . ." She waited until he lifted his head. "We could make a treaty without a marriage."

"No," he said.

"You are sure?"

"Yes," he said.

chapter 20

THE SENESCHAL OF Ephrata, the captain of the guard, several barons both Eddisian and Attolian, and various members of both households waited where the corridor came to the main atrium. Attolia looked them over. The Eddisians were certainly a barbarous lot—no wonder the Mede underestimated them—but they looked quite comfortable waiting at the edge of the atrium. Her own seneschal and guard captain as well as her barons looked distinctly unsettled, as if the ceiling might fall at any moment.

They were twisting between two worries. Her seneschal and guard had done something they knew she wouldn't like, while the barons worried that she'd sold out to the Eddisians as they thought she had sold out to the Mede. Attolia looked thoughtfully at Teleus and then sighed.

"You let Nahuseresh escape," she said.

Teleus, used to her insight, just nodded.

"You weren't watching that slave of his, the secretary."

"We weren't," Teleus admitted. "The slave released him, and in the confusion they managed to reach the outer stairs to the harbor. They swam to a Mede ship moored in the harbor and escaped. I'm very sorry."

"Well, you should be," said the queen, but to Teleus's great relief she wasn't angry. "I wanted a ransom for him but will have to be satisfied without one. If they had to swim to their ship, they must have left many interesting papers behind. I'll want to see those."

Teleus coughed.

"You said, 'In the confusion they reached the stairs to the harbor,'" the queen prompted.

"They set fire to their rooms."

"Of course," said the queen, and Teleus dropped his eyes in embarrassment.

"Well," Attolia said, "I hope the damage wasn't too severe. Baron Ephrata won't be happy to have had us as guests." The baron Ephrata lived in another of his several megarons and barely noticed that Ephrata existed.

Attolia turned to the seneschal. "Find someone to escort Her Majesty of Eddis and her Thief to better quarters and see that they are attended. No doubt you will regret the suite of rooms my captain has just allowed to be burned to ash, but I'm sure you will manage for the night. Tomorrow Eddis and her personal attendants will accompany us to the capital."

"No, Your Majesty."

The voice was a firm but quiet one and it took a moment for Attolia to locate the speaker: Eugenides's father, of course. Eddis's minister of war. She stared at him. Rarely did anyone say no to her and never with such confidence.

"The queen of Eddis does not ride unescorted to your capital."

"She isn't bringing her army with her," retorted Attolia.

The minister of war crossed his arms and waited.

Her own household, including the captain of the guard, looked on in awe, which irritated Attolia but also amused her.

"We are evenly supported here in the megaron," she said at last. "Let us remain for the night with our armies on the field, and I'm sure tomorrow we can find an arrangement on which we will all agree. Sounis will need to be informed of whatever accords we reach."

The minister of war inclined his head in agreement.

Attolia turned to the seneschal. "See that the Eddisians are settled comfortably," she said, and went away to her own chambers, leaving the seneschal to figure out how that might be done in the limited space of Ephrata.

In the darkness off the coast the Mede fleet navigated carefully. At the rail Nahuseresh watched the dark outline of the Attolian coast disappear. Kamet longed to leave him but dared not.

"Kamet," Nahuseresh said, and the secretary reluctantly, but obediently, stepped closer.

"Master?"

"I would like very much to strangle someone. Why don't you go away until I decide it isn't you?"

Kamet ducked his head. "Yes, master," he whispered in a neutral voice, and thankfully withdrew.

In the morning the Attolian army moved upriver and camped on the opposite side of the Seperchia from the Eddisians. The bulk of the mountain country's army settled on the plain below the pass. In the afternoon, after preliminary negotiations between Eddis's minister of war and two of Attolia's three senior generals, the rest of the Eddisian army was divided, one part to return to Eddis to defend against any attacks by Sounis, the other to accompany their queen as she rode to Attolia's capital.

Attolia offered to convey the queen of Eddis to the capital by boat, but Eddis, on the insistence of her minister of war, declined. Attolia sailed with her attendants and guard and a few selected barons. The rest of her retinue traveled overland. It was not a comfortable journey, being very hot and very dusty, but no one who had heard the news of Attolia's proposed engagement was unhappy to be on the road while their queen traveled by sea.

Attolia spent the days at the ship's rail watching the coastline of her country slide past. She spoke very little to her attendants and not at all to her barons. When Teleus stepped forward to address her, one of the attendants warned him away with a look. Teleus ducked his head in understanding and withdrew. Attolia saw but didn't call him back. Warmed by the sun and cooled by the sea breeze, she was busy with her thoughts.

The queen's city of Attolia sat in the sunshine like a gem in a setting of olive trees, on a hillside above the shallow Tustis River. The palace was situated on a gentle rise. There was a steeper hill behind the city, topped by the temple to the new gods. The city and megaron had originally been crowded onto the tiny plateau, but in the peaceful reign of the invaders both had moved down the hill to the slope above the harbor. The harbor was protected by a headland and a breakwater and by the shadowy bulk of Thegmis offshore, stretching up and down the coast.

The megaron in Sounis's capital was built of unfaced yellow stones, and Eddis's palace was small and dark, but Attolia's palace was built of brick and faced with marble. It glowed in the sunshine, a beautiful building with graceful proportions and ranks of windows that reflected the afternoon light like jewels.

In the palace, with her retainers surrounding her, the events of Ephrata seemed to Attolia very distant and unreal. The familiar tensions returned as she immersed herself once again in the struggle to exert her will in a world conventionally run by men, where she had to be not stronger but more powerful than her opponents. Making war was easy by comparison. Rumors had already reached the capital when she informed her barons of Eugenides's marriage proposal, and she watched the reactions carefully. There remained among her barons some who had still considered themselves probable candidates for Attolia's hand and throne. They veered between outrage and amusement, and under all the shouting she could hear the snickering, sniping glee.

In the privacy of her rooms, she paced. Her attendants were meticulous as always in their care, but for the first time she was visibly impatient. Where she had always been brisk, she became short-tempered; where she had been even-tempered, she was waspish.

To her surprise, her attendants drew closer to support her. She looked for fear in their servility, or hate in their attention, but saw none. Their affection and their care seemed genuine even as she surged to her feet while her hair was being braided, suddenly sick of the pulling and tugging, and retreated to her bedchamber, slamming the door behind her as she hadn't slammed a door since she was a minor princess of the king's second wife. They surrounded her throughout the day, urging her to eat something when she didn't want to eat, watching to see that she wasn't disturbed when she was busy, making the arrangements for the arrival of the queen of Eddis so that there was little for her to do but affirm their decisions.

Eddis delayed in Ephrata, having summoned her aunt and her sister as well as her attendants to soften the military edge to her visit. Eddis's aunt, a grand duchess, had insisted that she was too old to travel in anything but comfort, and had ordered out the royal carriage. She had then ridden quite cheerfully over rough ground on horseback to Ephrata while the heavy coach was hauled down the mountain road, carried by hand most of the way. Once in Ephrata, the duchess and the queen's sister, who was also a duchess, and the attendants combined their efforts to be sure that Eddis represented their country and their court as she should. Eddis had had just this support in mind when she summoned them, and she submitted to their ministrations with equanimity.

She had invited the magus as well, but he had politely declined. He still hoped to be reconciled with his king and so preferred to maintain the formality of his captivity.

When Eddis arrived in the capital, Attolia greeted her with grace and ceremony. Never once looking at Eugenides, she welcomed them to her palace and expressed hopes that their visit would be a comfortable one. If Attolia acted as if he didn't exist, her attending women watched the Thief of Eddis carefully and not as if they were pleased with what they saw. Eddis noted the hostility of the attendants as well as the remoteness of the Attolian queen. She worried that her Thief's great capacity for mockery might resurface to disastrous consequences, but Eugenides only bowed politely when introduced, and his bland expression was as fixed as Attolia's, even as she looked right through him, returning a royal half curtsy to his bow.

That evening Eugenides joined Eddis in her rooms just before supper. Eddis's attendants wandered in and out, stopping to put earrings in her ears and then discuss among themselves whether another pair might be better. The two duchesses looked on, offering their own sharp-eyed criticisms from time to time.

Eddis bore it all patiently. Eugenides looked on, amused.

Xanthe, Eddis's senior attendant, nudged the queen's hand, and Eddis obediently lifted her arms so that Xanthe could fasten a belt around her waist.

"I don't think Attolia's attendants treat her like a prize calf, Xanthe," she observed as the older woman patted the gold-embroidered cloth into place.

"I am sure they don't need to," Xanthe replied. "She is probably quite capable of choosing her own clothes and doesn't walk like a soldier in them."

Eddis bowed to the rebuke with a smile.

"I've seen golden calves guarded less fiercely," Eugenides remarked.

"I did notice the number of armed guards in the palace. Is it because we are here?" Eddis asked, her arms still held out to either side.

"No," said Eugenides. "They are always around her." It was an informed opinion, Eddis supposed.

"There will be music from the Continent and dancing tonight," she warned her Thief. "Protocol says that as a suitor you are supposed to ask Attolia to lead the first set with you."

"I've been practicing," he responded, and after supper, when the tables had been removed and the music was beginning, he obediently stepped to the dais at the head of the room and offered his hand for the first dance. Attolia accepted without looking at him and moved through the dance without speaking. He returned her to the dais at the end of the dance feeling as if he were replacing a manikin on its pedestal. He bowed and returned to Eddis's side.

"Attolia's court does not seem to favor the match," said Eddis as he settled himself in the space between the queen and her master of protocol.

"I haven't seen so many foul looks directed at me since I stole those cabochon emeralds," Eugenides said.

"I can't think they dislike you that much," responded Eddis.

"You have seen her guards?"

"Oh, yes."

"And the minister of ceremonies, and the help right down to the last wine bearer? The queen's attendants, as you can plainly see, are all ten heavily opposed."

"And the queen?" asked the minister of protocol, seated on Eugenides's other side.

"The queen abstains," said Eugenides shortly.

"Nine against, one undecided," said Eddis. When Eugenides gave her a puzzled look, she explained. "Attolia's attendants. I think you have one undecided, still."

"Really, which one?" Eugenides asked with his eyebrow raised.

"Figure it out for yourself and in the process go be civil to them."

"And risk being torn limb from limb?"

"I think you are safe from physical attack," said Eddis wryly.

"That's what you think," Eugenides answered. "There was sand in my dinner."

Eddis looked at him. "I thought you just weren't hungry."

"Sand," said Eugenides. "In the soup, on the bread, sprinkled on the meat."

"She wouldn't—" Eddis began before Eugenides interrupted, waving his hand in the air as if brushing away spiderwebs.

"No, of course she wouldn't. I'd say the kitchen feels the same as the queen's attendants."

Sighing, Eddis looked around at the beautiful hall, the exquisite tiles on the floor, the mosaics on the walls, the hundreds of candles, and the golden candelabra. The uncomfortable thought came to mind that she would rather sell Eugenides into slavery than marry him into the court of Attolia.

The negotiations began the next day, as Attolia had supposed, with a military treaty. The queens were not present. Their ministers and counselors met on their behalf. When the queens met face to face, they discussed the weather or the evening's entertainment. Eugenides, for his part, gravely asked the queen to dance and was as gravely granted the privilege, but Attolia spoke to him only in the most formulaic phrases, and Eddis knew that he responded with the acerbic comments sotto voce for which he was famous. If Attolia returned from the dancing flushed from more than the exercise, no one took it as a positive sign. Her attendants watched the Thief with narrowed eyes, and, as Eugenides said, if they'd had tails, they would have lashed them. Attolia's guards watched him like hawks waiting for a signal to attack a lure, and even the servants seemed to look down their noses as they addressed him. Attolia's lords didn't present a unified front. They were all rigidly courteous, but their courtesy concealed various motivations. Some bitterly opposed any king from outside Attolia; some were amused to see their own queen brought so low. None, so far as Eddis could see, cared if he would be a competent ruler.

The peace talks did not progress. Attolia, surrounded by her fractious barons, continued to be formal and remote. Eddis, with the well-being of her country at stake, was cautious. Her minister of war, unwilling to forget that the queen of Attolia had maimed his son, was reserved to the point of outright hostility.

Meanwhile Eddis complimented Attolia on her palace and her gardens. Attolia responded with invitations to musicals and dancing and excursions into the countryside.

"What snakes and weasels fill your court, Your Majesty," Eugenides said one evening, in a voice only she could hear, as they turned on the dance floor. Eugenides led with his left side, and his right arm held the queen around the waist. She could feel the wood of the false hand he wore pressing against her back. "Where do you find them all? Do you grow them in the dark somewhere in your hinterlands and then bring them to the capital?"

Attolia knew every limitation of her feudal supporters. She

stared without answering over his shoulder. She was still taller than he.

"Baron Erondites, for example." Eugenides continued conversationally. "He slithers up and hisses at me from time to time. And Susa . . . Do you ever let him off his chain, or is he too dangerous? He told me how pleased he was to see you marrying at last. *Droll* was the word he used, I think." He felt Attolia stiffen and chose his next target carefully. "Erondites's son . . ." He trailed off as Attolia slowly turned her face toward him.

"You say another word and I will have you *flayed*," Attolia said.

Eugenides smiled. Erondites the younger supported the queen and had supported her for years against his own father. She wouldn't stand by and see him insulted, but Eugenides knew he had planted a seed of doubt. She would wonder whether Erondites the younger had also called her likely marriage to the Thief of Eddis *droll*.

He was too kind to leave the seed to grow. "I was only going to commend his loyalty," the Thief said, "or his lack of originality. He stares right through me when we talk, just the way you do."

For a moment Eugenides hoped Attolia might say something. Then she turned her head to look over his shoulder, and the Thief's hopes dwindled. They finished the dance, and he returned her to her throne and her attendants. He smiled at their glares and turned to go back to his queen.

"Eugenides." Attolia spoke, and he turned back to her. She lifted her hand and laid it on the side of his face. It was all she needed to do. Though his expression didn't change, she could feel the tremor that went through him at her touch. He was afraid of her. Some part of him would always be afraid of her. That fear was her weapon, and she would encourage it if she wanted to maintain her authority as queen.

"Good night," Attolia said politely.

"Good night, Your Majesty," Eugenides answered, and stepped back to bow before turning away.

Safely back in his seat, he wiped the sweat off his forehead. He thought that the gray-haired attendant had smiled. Was she encouraged because she thought that her queen was showing him favor? Or did she know that Attolia was only putting him, very thoroughly, in his place?

That evening Attolia dismissed Chloe from her attendants, ordering the girl sent home to her father for no more than a clumsy accident. She had dropped a perfume spoon onto a tiny amphora, and the amphora had shattered. Attolia had risen to her feet, her rage making her seem as tall as the immortal goddess she had taken as a model. Chloe had stuttered an apology, but the queen had dismissed her and then left the room, stalking to her bedchamber without a backward look.

When she was gone, Chloe had dissolved into tears.

"Why should she marry him?" Chloe cried. "Why should she marry him if he makes her so angry?"

"She would be as angry at any man," one of the other attendants said.

"If only he were a man," said another. "If only they didn't humiliate her by forcing her to marry a boy."

"Nahuseresh—" said Chloe.

"Nahuseresh was a fool," someone interrupted her.

"And what is Eugenides?" Chloe asked bitterly.

Only Phresine had no comment to make as she tacked the sleeve into a dress. Chloe returned to her father's house the next day. The remaining women glared ever more balefully at Eugenides, drawing their ranks around their besieged queen. Only Phresine dared to say to the silent Attolia as she slid flowers into her braided hair before an evening of music, "Least said, soonest mended, Your Majesty, isn't the advice for every occasion."

Attolia turned her head, dislodging a flower, to stare at Phresine, and Phresine carefully replaced the blossom.

It had been three weeks, and the two countries were no closer to a treaty. Eddis was beginning to worry that having come so far, Attolia might restart hostilities. Her face was so expressionless, her conversation so polite and difficult to read it was impossible to guess what she was thinking.

"She won't give up Ephrata," she told Eugenides as they walked in the afternoon on one of the palace terraces overlooking the garden. Within the palace she had dismissed her honor guard, and they were alone.

It was one of Eddis's demands that the small coastal village of Ephrata become part of her country to provide an access to the sea for her trade, which she had never had before. Ephrata was a poor port but better than none, and she was adamant about having it.

Attolia was as adamant about refusing to give it up. There were other points of contention, and little progress was being made except between the ministers of trade. Those two were in complete accord and happy to spend their days discussing the exchange of pig iron and wool for olives and wine.

"Your father isn't helping. I gather he sits at the table eyeing the Attolians—you know the way he does." Eddis pulled her face into a stony glare.

"You must have relayed Attolia's threat to cut my other hand off. I'm not sure he saw the humor in the situation."

"I am not sure I did," admitted Eddis. "I don't mean to sound like Hespira's mother, but I wish you would come home, Gen."

"No."

Eddis went on hesitantly. "Her barons are part of the problem. They are not pleased at the idea of an Eddisian king. If they had a king, and were getting an Eddisian queen, it would be the cement of a treaty and unobjectionable. As it is, they don't like being ruled to begin with, and they like less the idea of a foreigner."

"Are you saying it would be easier to reach an accord with Attolia if we didn't hold her to marriage?"

"It might be," said Eddis.

"And how would you secure the treaty?"

"I don't know," said Eddis. "I'm beginning to see that I don't know anything about Attolia, really. I hoped you would."

"She won't speak to me," said Eugenides. "Just formalities."

"You talk when you're dancing," said Eddis.

"More platitudes," Eugenides said.

"Last night?" Eddis asked. When the queen and Eugenides had returned from the dancing, the queen had been rigid with anger.

Eugenides stopped walking and leaned against the low wall dividing the terrace from the garden. He crossed his arms and looked at his feet. "She was telling me about the history of the palace. Quite a lecture, in fact. I told her my distant grandfather had been one of the architects."

"Really?" murmured Eddis.

"Oh, yes, that's why we know so much about the building. There were drawings in your library until the magus came and I moved them out. I told Attolia he'd designed parts of Sounis's megaron as well. The good parts, I said. She looked at me as if I'd turned into a snake."

"I thought I asked you to thank her for her kind efforts to entertain us."

"I did that next. She said there would be a hunting party leaving this morning; perhaps I'd like to join it."

"And?" Eddis asked, looking at his arm. He hadn't ridden well enough to hunt on horseback even before losing his hand.

"I told her I'd already been hunted in Attolia, thank you very much."

"Oh, Gen," sighed Eddis.

Attolia had returned to her rooms after the dancing and dismissed her attendants immediately. As they left, she had said acidly to Phresine that she thought "Least said, soonest mended" might have been exactly the advice for the situation. Once the women had gone, she had pulled the flowers from her braids herself and thrown them to the floor, muttering, "Damn him, damn him, damn him," as each blossom dropped.

But it wasn't the Thief she was angry at, or Phresine. What a fool she was to offer hunting to a man with one hand. What a fool to fall in love with someone after she had cut his hand off. Well, she might be fool enough to love him; she wasn't fool enough to believe he loved her. She'd seen the look in his father's eyes, and if she didn't see it in Eugenides's eyes, then he was better at hiding it, that was all.

Standing on the terrace, looking out at the garden, Eugenides admitted, "I thought this was going to end like a fireside story. The goddess of love waves her scepter, and we live happily ever after." He shook his head. "The only worthwhile members of this court despise me. The most despicable can't stop chuckling under their breaths, and if it were up to the queen's attendants, I would have been hanging upside down for weeks now."

"Every day I have more sympathy for Hespira's mother. I'd rather see you go live in a hole in the ground of the Sacred Mountain."

"It isn't rational, is it? Do you think the gods have afflicted me?"

Eddis raised her eyebrows.

"No," said Eugenides, shaking his head. "If it is an afflic-
tion, it is as you said: The gods know me so well they can pre-
dict my behavior. They don't control it. They could know I
would love her, but they don't make me. I've watched her for
years, you know. All those times when you didn't know where
I went, mostly it was to Attolia."

"Did your grandfather know?"

"He knew I was fascinated by her. She's like a prisoner inside stone walls, and every day the walls get a little thicker, the
doorway narrower."

"And?" Eddis prompted.

"Well," said Eugenides, "it's a challenge."

"And that's all?"

Eugenides looked at Eddis. "Why are you prying all of a
sudden?"

"I have an interest in your welfare," Eddis said dryly, "and
the welfare of two countries. One way or another this government must be stable if Eddis is to prosper."

Eugenides stared at nothing. "I can't leave her there all
alone, surrounded by stone walls." He looked at Eddis, hoping
she would understand. "She's too precious to give up," he said.

"But she won't talk to you."

"No," Eugenides said painfully. "And she won't listen to me
either. And if she won't listen to me, how can I tell her I love
her?"

"If she won't listen, how can you lie to her?" Eddis asked.

Eugenides had been looking up at the roofs of the palace.
He dropped his eyes suddenly to look at Eddis. "I wasn't thinking of lying to her," he said.

"How can she know?" asked Eddis. "She is not in the habit
of trusting people. Why should she suddenly believe anything
you say? You might unlock the door for her; you can't make
her walk through."

The faults in Eugenides's character were too well known for him to need to make any reply. "She'd believe you," he said after some consideration.

"She would not," said Eddis.

"She would."

"Eugenides," Eddis protested.

"She would," Eugenides insisted. "You said you could settle on a treaty with a wedding or without one. You have no reason to lie to her. She would believe you."

"Eugenides, I am the queen of Eddis, not a matchmaker." If she had been a matchmaker, he would have been home, properly married to Agape.

The Thief only leaned back against the stone railing behind him and crossed his arms. He waited until Eddis threw up her hands. "All right," she said. "I'll ask for a private interview. I'll tell her we can have a treaty without a wedding if she would prefer it, and we'll see what she says."

"So the slipper is on the other foot now?" Attolia asked Eddis in the privacy of her apartments when the two queens had met, alone for the first time since the hillside above Rhea. "First I am forced to accept him, and now you try to draw him back?"

"And you will keep him to spite me?" Eddis asked. Attolia realized that the mountain queen was well aware of her jealousy.

"Isn't he your most prized possession?" Attolia asked.

"He's not a possession," Eddis said, her voice hard.

"But you want to keep him for yourself?" Attolia suggested. "Don't you? "

"Make him king of Eddis? I think you mistake our friendship," Eddis answered.

"No, not king of Eddis," said Attolia. "But you would keep him safe, marry him to some member of your court, have him to dance attendance on you indefinitely, tied safely to leading strings?"

Eddis scowled. "No," she said.

"Why not?" Attolia asked.

"It would kill him," said Eddis. "He cannot draw back now."

"Then why are you here?" Attolia asked, her smile insincere.

"I don't know," said Eddis, stung, and she stood to leave.

"Wait," said Attolia. Eddis paused. "Please," said Attolia. Eddis sat again, but Attolia rose and went to the window and was quiet for a long time.

"I like you," said Attolia at last, speaking to the window. "I didn't think I would. Still, to have you here in my palace galls me every day. I see you surrounded, even here, by people you can trust with your life. You are safer than I am, and it is my home, not yours. Do you understand?" she asked.

"Yes." Eddis nodded and waited.

"And what part of your resources can I have for myself? Your Thief. I have so little of faith or trust or friendship, and I should let him steal it from me?"

"Eugenides doesn't want to steal anything from you." Eddis fumbled for words.

"How can you understand?" Attolia asked as she turned to face Eugenides's queen. "He hasn't lied to you."

Eddis looked at her, surprise showing in her face. "Of course he has," she said.

"He lies to you?" Attolia asked.

"Constantly," said Eddis. "He lies to himself. If Eugenides talked in his sleep, he'd lie then, too."

Attolia looked stunned. "And you can't tell?"

Eddis thought for a moment. "I sometimes believe his lies are the truth, but I have never mistaken his truth for a lie. If he needs me to believe him, he has his own way of showing his veracity."

"Which is?"

"When he is being honest with you, you'll know," said Eddis, and nodded reassuringly to Attolia.

Attolia shook her head. "Let us face the truth. He is too young, and I am too old, and there is the not inconsequential fact that I cut off his hand. Try to tell me that this is not his revenge."

Eddis stood up to face her and to look in her eyes. "He is not too young. You are not old. You only feel old because you have been unhappy for so long, and *this is not his revenge,*" she said.

"What kind of fool would I have to be to believe it was anything else?"

"I wouldn't have allowed it," Eddis told her.

"You wouldn't have allowed it? Isn't it your revenge, too?"

"Irene—"

"Don't call me that."

"You were the princess Irene the first time we met."

"It means 'peace,'" Attolia said. "What name could be more inappropriate?"

"That I be named Helen?" Eddis suggested.

The hard lines in Attolia's face eased, and she smiled. Eddis was a far cry from the woman whose beauty had started a war.

"Irene, I wouldn't let Eugenides throw his life away on revenge no matter how he had been maimed." Attolia looked away, but Eddis went on. "And if he says you are not a fiend from hell, I will accept his judgment." Attolia slowly paced across the room. Eddis spoke again. "Irene? What choice do you have but to believe in him?"

"I might have to marry him," Attolia said in a low voice. "I don't have to believe anything."

"Yes, you do," said Eddis. "If you are going to marry him, you have to believe him. He isn't a possession. He isn't mine to keep or to give away. He has free choice, and he has chosen you. You must choose now. Between the two of us we can reach a treaty without a wedding. You don't have to marry him, but if you choose to marry him, you have to believe him."

Attolia turned, and Eddis thought that behind her mask the queen might be afraid, and so she finished lightly. "You have to believe him, because he's going to have your entire palace up in arms and your court in chaos and every member of it from the barons to the boot cleaners coming to you for his blood, and you are going to have to deal with it."

Attolia smiled. "You make him sound like more trouble than he is worth."

"No," said Eddis thoughtfully. "Never more than he is worth."

Attolia ceded Ephrata. When she learned that the proceeds of the ten seized Attolian trade caravans had gone to Eugenides, she tabled her demands to have the monies restored to her treasury. Despite the basilisk stares of Eddis's minister of war, a military accord was reached in a matter of days. The arrangements for a wedding finally began. And then halted when the queen of Attolia balked at the matter of consecrating an altar to Hephestia for the ceremony.

When pressed on the point, she uncharacteristically fled. Dropping the pen she held, she said, "There will be no altar to Hephestia in Attolia," and stalked from the room. Eddis and Eugenides, the ministers and aides, both Eddisian and Attolian, were left looking at one another in surprise and consternation.

Eddis excused herself, and summoning Eugenides with a wave of her hand, she followed the Attolian queen. Once in the corridor Eddis stopped.

"The throne room," Eugenides suggested.

They found her there. The empty room echoed their footsteps as they crossed the smooth marble floors. Eddis couldn't help craning her head to look around as she did each time she saw the room. Attolia's throne room was blue and white and gold instead of the more somber red and black and gold of Eddis's. The mosaics on the floor, the high ceilings with windows at the tops of the walls to flood the room with light, made it a more beautiful room even than the newer throne room and banquet hall in Eddis. Attolia didn't need to eat in her throne room; she had other, even larger rooms for dining and dancing. Glancing at Eugenides, Eddis thought he walked through the room as if it were so familiar as to be unworthy of his attention. Perhaps it was. Attolia ignored them until they were standing in front of her.

"There will be no altar consecrated to Hephestia," she said.

Eugenides continued up the steps to the dais and took her hand. "It is a token to the gods I believe in, no more."

"No," said Attolia.

"Because you do not believe?"

"Oh, no," said Attolia bitterly. "Because I believe and I do not choose to worship. I will have no altar dedicated to her and no sacrifice made."

"I made a vow," Eugenides said, "promising this if I became king—"

"No," said Attolia.

"Why?" shouted Eugenides.

Pale with fury, Attolia pulled her hand away from Eugenides and clenched her fists. "How did I catch you when you hid in my palace? How did I know you moved through the tunnels for the hypocaust? How did I know how you entered the town and how you would escape? *How did I know?*" she shouted.

Eugenides had grown pale as well. "I made a mistake," he said.

"You made a mistake," Attolia agreed. "You trusted your

gods. That was your mistake. Moira," Attolia said, spitting out the name. "Moira, the messenger of your Great Goddess, came and told me where you would be and that if I would have my men nail boards between the trees above the curve in the river after dark that day, then I would catch you there. She came back later to warn me not to offend the gods. Moira," she said again, "in the guise of one of my attendants, told the Mede where to find you in the mountains. How *else* could he have found you there at the Pricas? I do not worship your gods, and I will not be married before that altar."

Eugenides stared at nothing, numb. If he felt anything, it was that he was falling through space, as all thieves fall when their god forsakes them. Without a word, and without meeting Attolia's eyes, he left. Walking quickly, he crossed the empty room without turning his head. Attolia stood and would have followed him, but Eddis stopped her with a hand on her arm.

Attolia looked at her. "You knew," she said.

"That he had been betrayed by the gods? I guessed," said Eddis.

chapter 21

_E_UGENIDES MOVED LIKE a sleepwalker down a hallway he didn't see, remembering the sound of hammers as he had hidden in bushes near the city walls. Remembering, he began to move faster, down the long hallway to the kitchens, through them without speaking to a soul, and out to the animal pens in one of the lower courtyards of the palace. There were pigs kept there, and goats. He demanded a kid from the puzzled stable hand and carried it, wriggling, back into the palace.

There were many empty rooms in the palace. Eugenides knew of one that had been a solarium until recent building had obstructed its sunlight and left it too cold and too dark to be useful. With no anterooms between it and the hallway outside, and with a row of load-bearing pillars dividing the room in two, it was awkwardly sized and located. It was rarely used and had made a good hiding place on his previous visits. There was a stone table that would do for an altar. Anyone could make an altar, anyone could consecrate it with a sacrifice. Not everyone received a response from the gods, but Eugenides never doubted his invocation would be answered.

Shifting the kid under his right arm, Eugenides took a candle from a sconce as he walked. He passed people as he climbed back up the staircase. No one spoke to him. People stepped away and watched quietly as he passed. He climbed faster and hurried down a hallway to the empty room and kicked its door closed behind him.

The table was to the right of the door, pushed against the wall. The window was opposite him, its length divided into unequal thirds and each third into many separate panes. Once it had looked out on the acropolis that rose behind the city. Now all that could be seen through it was the blank wall on the opposite side of an interior courtyard. The sun was still high, and a beam cleared the rooftops to light the sill of the window and the dust motes floating in the air.

The kid bleated as he squeezed it under one arm while he fumbled for matches to light the candle. He had a silver match case that he could open with one hand. When the candle was lit, he tilted it to let wax fall onto the table, and chanted an invocation to the Great Goddess, deliberately choosing the one he had sung over and over in the queen's prison cell. Once sufficient wax had pooled on the tabletop, he jammed the candle down into it until it was well stuck. Then he swung the kid out from under his arm and onto the table. It kicked, but he pinned it with his arm while he freed his knife. Deftly he slit its throat, and as the blood spilled across the table with no ceremonial bowl to catch it, he turned the knife and slid it into the body just below the cartilage at the top of the rib cage. Then he dropped to his knees. He rested his forehead against the bloody edge of the table and his forearms on the tabletop and waited.

The blood cooled and dried. He went on waiting, unmoving, growing stiff and cold.

"The door won't open, Your Majesty," said one of the servants.

The door had no lock, but Attolia wasn't surprised that it was fastened closed. She hadn't expected otherwise.

"Leave him," she said. "He is talking to his gods."

The servants bowed and dispersed, murmuring a little among themselves, and Attolia knew that the news of the mad Eugenides would percolate through the palace, like water through soil. Attolians did not invest much belief in their religion. They dutifully attended temple festivals and used their gods for cursing and little else.

Eugenides knelt against the altar, his body beginning to ache and his mind numb until the daylight faded and the room was dark except for the light of the candle. A hand rested for a moment on his shoulder. He looked up to see Moira beside him. "How did I fail the gods, that they betrayed me to Attolia?" he asked.

Moira shook her head. "Hephestia sends no message."

"And the God of Thieves? Have I failed him, that he did not defend me? Are my gifts at his altar insufficient, that I lost his favor?"

"I cannot say, Eugenides."

"Then I will wait here." He laid his head back against the edge of the table.

"Eugenides," said Moira, "you cannot demand the presence of the Great Goddess. The gods are not accountable to men."

"I can," said Eugenides without lifting his head. "I can demand. Whether my demands are met or not, I can demand. I can act as I choose and not as some god directs."

"Eugenides," Moira warned.

"You betrayed me," said Eugenides. "Betrayed me to Attolia. You are the gods of Eddis, and you betrayed me to Attolia and to the Mede." His hand fanned out for a moment in the sticky blood on the table before clenching again into a fist. "You betrayed me, and I can demand to know why if I choose."

"Eugenides, no," Moira warned for the third time.

"Yes!" screamed Eugenides, and the windows of the solarium shattered and the air was filled with broken glass.

"Rare the man whose gods answer him," the queen of Attolia said dryly when an agitated household reported shattered
windows throughout the palace.

As every pane of glass broke into a hundred pieces that
filled the air and dropped and shattered again on the stone
floor, Eugenides threw himself to the floor, covering his head
with his arms. Glass pattered down over him. He lay and listened as the glass slid across stone, the fragments rubbing
against each other in quiet music. The wind stopped, and the
sound of the moving glass faded, but the pressure in the room
grew. He could feel it against his eardrums. He was terrified.
Not frightened as he had been in the past, but panicked like
an animal caught in a trap or a man whose solid world shifts
under his feet in an earthquake. He'd been in earthquakes before, in the mountains. He took a deep breath.
    "You betrayed me," he shouted, his voice muffled by his
arms. He remembered the Mede who had appeared on the
mountainside without any explanation. "Twice," he wailed.
"You betrayed me *twice*. What are the Medes, that you support them? Am I not your supplicant? Have I not sacrificed at
your altars all my life?"
    "And believed in us all your life?" a voice asked, a voice that
was a variation in the pressure in his ears. Eugenides shuddered at the gentleness. No, he hadn't believed. Most of the
sacrifices had been for form's sake, a meaningless ritual to him
at the time.
    "Have I offended the gods?" he asked in despair before rage
burned the despair away. "And if I have offended the gods," he
yelled, almost unable to hear his own words, "then why didn't
I fall? It is the curse of thieves and their right to fall to their

deaths, not—not—" He folded his arms across his chest, tucking the crippled one under and curling over it, unable to go on.

"Who are you to speak of rights to the gods?" the voice asked, gentle still.

The room was dark around Eugenides, and the darkness pressed him until he couldn't breathe, until he was aware of nothing but the pressure. He was nothing, the smallest particle of dust surrounded by a myriad of other particles of dust, and put all together, they were . . . nothing but dust. Alone, separated from the others, in the eye of the gods he may have been, but he remained, still, dust. He struggled to inhale and whispered, "Have I offended the gods?"

"No," said the voice.

"Then why?" he sobbed, clutching his arm tighter, though the blisters under the cuff were individual pains as sharp as knives. "Why?"

In the darkness behind his closed eyelids, Eugenides saw red fire flicker. When it was gone, the darkness afterward was a vision of a night with stars in the sky and a black silhouette that was the Sacred Mountain in Eddis. There was a gray plume of smoke, lighter than the surrounding blackness. The plume of smoke lightened, and the stars faded as the day dawned. Then, without warning, the top of the mountain exploded and the fire returned, flashing on the undersides of a cloud of ash and smoke wider than the mountain, wider than all the valleys of Eddis. Eugenides watched as boiling rock swept down the remains of the mountain, filling the valleys with smoking ruin. He saw the houses of the city exploding one after another and the people running, a woman with a little child suddenly engulfed in flame. The ground shuddered under his feet. The red, heaving wall of melted rock bore down on him, and he couldn't move. His skin grew warm and then hot until it felt as dry as paper and as ready to burn. He could smell the hair of his eyebrows singeing, and he still couldn't move. He squeezed his eyes shut, but they were shut already, and the vision remained as clear. He threw himself backward and could feel the broken glass around him cutting into his skin. But he was still on his stomach and no farther from the intense heat. The magma rolled closer. He screamed and screamed again.

On her throne Attolia sat and waited. The room was empty, and the silence echoed. All night the clouds had gathered above the palace, and the thunder had rumbled. After many hours she rose and left the throne room, collecting the inevitable retinue of servants and courtiers as she left the palace and rode to the temple of the new gods. The priests must have been warned of her coming. They met her in the pronaos and stood silently by while she wandered through the temple to the altar. She lifted the heavy gold candlesticks and carefully replaced them. She tilted the ceremonial offering bowl and listened to the musical jingle of the gold and silver disks carved with praise and supplications as they slid across the metal bottom of the bowl. She walked again the length of the temple. It was cold and empty. Perhaps the invaders' gods had left with the invaders. She didn't know. She knew only that the room was empty, as empty as her throne room, to which she returned. She sent her court away and her servants to bed and settled herself on the throne. When everything was still, she bowed her head and spoke to the darkness.

"Give him back to me," she said, "and I will build your altar at the highest point of the city's acropolis and around it build a temple in which you will be honored so long as Attolia remains." There was no answer. She sat and waited.

"Eugenides." A voice as gentle as rain and as cool as water called his name, and he ceased his screaming to listen. "Noth-

ing mortals make lasts; nothing the gods make endures forever. Do you understand?"

"No," said Eugenides hoarsely. Slowly the vision of the Sacred Mountain faded. He was still on his stomach on the floor
of the solarium. He sensed the solid stone walls all around him.

"Do you know me?" the new voice asked.

"No," Eugenides whispered.

"You sacrificed once at my altar."

"Forgive me, goddess. I do not know you." Beyond his conviction that it was a goddess who spoke, he could make no
guess at her identity. He wasn't sure if she meant that he had
sacrificed to her years ago and stopped or that it was only once
that he had made a sacrifice in her honor. He could only wonder how many different gods he had sacrificed to just once. All
his life he had left sacrifices in passing at various tiny temples
and altars in his own country and in Sounis and Attolia as
well: a coin, or a piece of fruit, a handful of olives, a piece of
jewelry he'd previously stolen and didn't care to keep. Lately
he'd been more thoughtful in his sacrifices, but he still didn't
remember most of them, only that he was careful to offer at
whatever temples and altars of water immortals he encountered, hoping to make up for any lingering disfavor on the part
of Aracthus. He'd made a particularly nice sacrifice at the
altar of Aracthus before he'd stepped into the chasm of his watercourse, but that hadn't been his first sacrifice to the river,
and anyway, it was a goddess who spoke. A goddess to whom
he clearly should have paid greater attention.

"You are thinking as I stand between you and the Great
Goddess that perhaps you have dedicated your sacrifices all
these years in error?" Her voice was amused.

Eugenides said nothing.

"Do not offend one power to attain the favor of another.
The Thief is your god, but remember, no god is all-powerful,
not even the Great Goddess."

She was silent then, long enough for Eugenides to wonder if she was gone and if he dared raise his head and if what had happened was all that would happen. Finally she spoke again.

"Little Thief," she said, "what would you give to have your hand back?"

Eugenides almost lifted his head.

"Oh, no," said the goddess. "It is beyond my power and that of the Great Goddess as well. What's done is done, even with the gods. But if the hand could be restored, what would you give? Your eyesight?" The voice paused, and Eugenides remembered begging Galen, the physician, to let him die before he was blind. "Your freedom?" The goddess went on. "Your sanity? Think, Eugenides, before you question the gods. You have much still to lose."

Softly Eugenides asked, "Why did my gods betray me?"

"Have they?" asked the goddess as softly.

"To Attolia, to the Mede . . ." Eugenides stuttered.

"Would you have your hand back, Eugenides? And lose Attolia? And see Attolia lost to the Mede?"

Eugenides's eyes were open. In front of his face the floor was littered with tiny bits of glass that glittered in the candlelight.

"You have your answer, Little Thief." And she was gone.

Eugenides slept and woke again in the dark. He was on his back, he realized. He was in bed. There was no fire in the hearth, but it was a clear night, and there was enough light to see Eddis sitting in a chair nearby.

He cleared his throat. "The mountain," he said. "I saw the mountain explode."

"I know," said Eddis.

"You've seen it?" asked Eugenides.

"In my dreams since midwinter."

Eugenides moved his head back and forth on the pillow, as

if trying to shake the memories away. "Once was awful enough for me. When do you think?"

"Not soon," said Eddis, leaning toward him to rest a hand on his forehead. "Someday, but perhaps not in our lifetime. Hephestia has warned us, so there will be time to prepare." She reassured him, and he slept again.

When he next woke, it was day, and the room was filled with light. He turned to see if Eddis was still beside him and found Attolia, patiently waiting for him to open his eyes. She was sitting with her hands folded, staring into the distance, but she must have seen his movement because she shifted to meet his gaze.

"Do you love me?" Eugenides asked without preamble.

"Why do you ask?" she answered, and he grimaced in frustration.

"Because I need to know," he said.

"I am wearing your earrings," Attolia offered.

"Being willing to marry me is not the same as loving me."

"Would you believe me if I said I did love you?" Attolia asked. It seemed a genuine question, and Eugenides thought carefully about his answer.

"I don't think you'd lie."

"Does it matter?" Attolia asked.

"If you are truthful?"

"If I love you," she said.

"Yes. Do you love me?" he asked again.

She didn't answer. "When we opened the doors to the solarium three days ago—"

"Three days?" Eugenides queried.

"Three days," Attolia confirmed. "When we opened the doors, we saw that the entire room was scorched black and you were on the floor possibly dead, surrounded by broken glass. Window glass is expensive, you realize that?"

"Yes, Your Majesty," he said meekly.

"You might have been dead, but you weren't. Not cut to pieces, not burned to a cinder, and when you woke, your queen reported that you didn't seem to be insane. Are you insane?"

"No more than usual, I think."

"Insane to think of loving me," said Attolia, and the emotions that colored her usually emotionless voice were bitterness and self-mockery.

Eugenides reached to take her hand, but she was sitting at his right side and he had to reach across his body. He raised himself on his elbow, but she freed her hand and pushed him gently back into the bed. Then she pulled the covers back to expose the stump of his right arm. His cuff and hook, he saw, were laid on a table across the room. He resisted the temptation to pull the arm back under the covers.

"It is not so sore," she said.

"No." Eugenides ran his hand over his arm. The ridges of calluses and the blisters were gone. He was free of the ache in his bones and the pain in his phantom hand. He thought of the goddess who had interceded on his behalf and thought the pain might be gone forever.

Looking at his arm, Attolia said, "I cut off your hand."

"Yes."

"I have been living with your grief and your rage and your pain ever since. I don't think—I don't think I had felt anything for a long time before that, but those emotions at least were familiar to me. Love I am not familiar with. I didn't recognize that feeling until I thought I had lost you in Ephrata. And when I thought I was losing you a second time, I realized I would give up anything to keep you—my lip service to other gods, but my pride, too, and my rage at all gods, everything for you. Then I see you here, and see what I have done to you." Gently she stroked his maimed arm, and he shivered at the warmth of her touch and its intimacy.

"You have spied on me for years?" she asked.

"Yes," Eugenides admitted.

"Watched me deal with my barons and my servants, loyalists, traitors, and enemies?" She thought of the hardness and the coldness she had cultivated over those years and wondered if they were the mask she wore or if the mask had become her self. If the longing inside her for kindness, for warmth, for compassion, was the last seed of hope for her, she didn't know how to nurture it or if it could live.

Unable to guess the answer, she asked, "Who am I, that you should love me?"

"You are My Queen," said Eugenides. She sat perfectly still, looking at him without moving as his words dropped like water into dry earth.

"Do you believe me?" he asked.

"Yes," she answered.

"Do you love me?"

"Yes."

"I love you."

And she believed him.

Author's Note

The landscape of Attolia and Sounis and even Eddis is much like the landscape that surrounds the Mediterranean Sea. I have taken bits and pieces of the region and history and fitted them into my story, but the story is fiction. Nothing in it is historically accurate. The gods and the goddesses in my book are not those of the Greek or any other Pantheon. I made them up. The Mede Empire is also my own invention.

In the real world, many empires have risen and fallen while attempting to surround and control the Mediterranean Sea. The Phoenicians, the Egyptians, and the Myceneans were some of the earliest. The Persians, in the fifth century B.C., tried to extend their empire to the Greek Peninsula and failed twice. They were defeated at the battle of Marathon and then at the battle of Salamis. The Romans managed to hold the Mediterranean for five hundred years and in the process exported their gods and insisted they replace at least officially the gods native to different parts of their empire.

After the Romans came the Byzantine Empire and the Islamic states, the trade empires of Italian city-states, and the Ottoman Empire, which did not disappear until the twentieth century, when the powerful nations of the European continent contrived to defeat and divide it.